CW00622044

Final Score

Also by Frank Palmer

FINAL SCORE

Frank Palmer

Constable · London

First published in Great Britain 1998
by Constable & Company Ltd
3 The Lanchesters, 162 Fulham Palace Road
London W6 9ER
Copyright © 1998 Frank Palmer
The right of Frank Palmer to be identified as the author of
this work has been asserted by him in accordance with the
Copyright, Designs and Patents Act 1988
ISBN 0 09 4792607
Set in Palatino by Set Systems Ltd, Saffron Walden, Essex
Printed and bound in Great Britain by MPG Books Ltd,
Bodmin, Cornwall

A CIP catalogue record for this book is available from the
British Library

For Rob and his family

The East Midlands Combined Constabulary is fictional. So, too, are all the characters in their cases.

1

'Free my innocent son, says campaigning mum. And the trial of a security guard accused of mugging an ex-beauty queen starts today.'

Boring, I sigh to myself, about to switch over to Classic FM for a bit of Bach to go with breakfast.

'In sport,' the male newsreader continues, 'soccer star Rob Hill ends his Italian job and comes home. We talk exclusively to his legal representative handling negotiations for his return to the domestic game.'

Ah, now, that is news, real news, and I see him in the white number 4 shirt he used to wear. The midfielder with the five million pound legs, they call him; hope he rejoins us.

'Today's weather: dry and bright.'

'Tea, tea,' says Laura. She points from her high chair to the breakfast bar. On it is a red Postman Pat beaker. In it is fruit juice, but every drink is tea to Laura.

I hand it to her, watching her guzzle contentedly through the spout, only half listening as the first sentence of the local lead story is repeated almost word for word and a different voice, a woman's, begins to expand on it. 'A man who has spent half his life in jail for the murder of a police officer he says he didn't commit is seeking a review of his conviction.'

A police officer? Did I hear that right?

'Scott Packard...'

Rings a bell, not one of my old pinches, I think, gratefully.

'...was just sixteen when he was convicted of the murder of PC Joseph Craig...'

Him I do remember.

Never knew him, not my intake, and I wasn't on duty the night he died. But, sometimes, admittedly very rarely and only in a roundabout way, I think of him.

Last time was a couple of months back when Laura had all her tiny friends here for her birthday. They played in a paddling pool in the back garden, splashing, shrieking, actually shuddering with excitement.

And I sat in a patio chair, grinning and thinking: had that gunman got in a second shot I'd have been denied all of this – marriage, building a home, fatherhood, hearing her say 'Dadda' for the first time, seeing her first steps, being a part of her birthday celebrations; could have been dead like Joey Craig.

Behind my silly smile anger gripped my heart as it does now, listening to this know-all reporter going on about 'the riots that swept Britain's inner cities in the early eighties' in a voice too youthful to have experienced the blazing cars and looted shops, the petrol bombs and bricks raining down, the freezing fear of just being there.

And I'm angrier still when some sprog of a new MP comes on waffling mysteriously and self-importantly about 'vital new evidence in the Scott Packard case' that can't yet be disclosed.

Anxiety now, as I realise that one of the CID team who put Packard inside was the great mate who stopped that gunman getting in a second shot so I didn't wind up like Joey Craig.

Can't believe he'd bend the evidence, I decide firmly. Then, weakening, I have to accept that I'm prejudiced. You can never be sure what a detective might do when a colleague's been slain on the streets. In such circumstances I couldn't even be sure of myself.

My thoughts are as scrambled as the eggs I've just eaten and I miss the details of the mugger's trial, Rob Hill's lawyer talking about negotiations with various soccer clubs bidding to sign him, even Laura demanding the return of the Postman Pat beaker she's dropped on the tiled floor.

'See to her,' snaps Em from behind the *Daily Telegraph*.

'Drink up,' I tell Laura, retrieving Postman Pat. Then, to Em, 'I was listening to that.' I gesture to the radio, pointless, because her head has remained behind the paper. 'One of Jacko Jackson's cases.'

'What?'

'The Joey Craig murder.'

10

'Joey who?'

Christ, I think. Sixteen years ago PC Craig's death was front page news and his funeral brought the city to a standstill. Now even police wives have forgotten.

Could have happened to me, I realise. 'Phil who?' someone could be asking.

2

Trouble, I know it. Something's always gone wrong when I get summoned by the chief constable.

What this time? I ponder as I stroll from the spartan, single-storey outhouse in tree-dotted grounds where I work in the peaceful isolation of the Complaints Department.

Who have I offended now? I wonder as I take the back entrance into the rambling old manor house that's been inelegantly converted into the headquarters of the East Midlands Combined Constabulary.

Taking a set of stone stairs, a short-cut to the flight deck, I kid myself into a smile with the thought that maybe he's going to promote me, and not before time. And I am still smiling when I walk into an office that's about the size of the Cabinet Room at Number 10.

He is beaming at me from behind his huge glass-topped desk with three phones and two decks of trays. A bad sign, that, I realise, no longer smiling to myself; strange and sinister.

Nothing personal, these reservations about my boss, because he's personable – fiftyish, bluff, blokish. But he performs. For visiting VIPs, for regional police authority bigwigs, Whitehall, the media. He's not too interested in the truth, but people's perception of it which can be managed and marketed with a good performance. He's all things to all people.

'Ah, good,' he says when his secretary heaves the heavy door shut behind me. 'Chief Superintendent Todd,' he adds, as if I didn't know.

While I'm making a longish trek on a thick blue carpet, he gestures heartily to a waif of a young woman sitting opposite one corner of his desk. She looks much too frail for the power suit she is wearing. Big round black spectacles make her delicate face look tiny. 'Miss Spence,' he says.

She half rises, rather awkwardly, understandably so. On the carpet, around her patent black mid-heels, are two overflowing briefcases and, bizarrely, a brown cardboard box with 'Stork SB Margarine' printed in red. That, too, is crammed with files. 'Alice,' she says, not at all timidly.

She holds out a dainty hand that looks all the whiter because of the jet black suit. The style is severe, matching the cut of her black hair.

I take her hand briefly. It's icy cold. She seems so delicate that I don't squeeze it. She hasn't the physique to be a police officer, or even a lady jockey.

'Phil,' I say with a tight smile. I take a few paces in front of the desk. Before I can sit in an armchair at the opposite corner, the chief goes on, 'With the Criminal Cases Review Commission.'

Trouble. Knew it. She is trouble. Her Commission can call on us to assist with their investigations where they think further inquiries are necessary.

With my back to her, she won't see my grimace. The Commission is a new independent body which has recently taken over from the Home Office the task of deciding which disputed cases should go back to the appeal court for fresh hearings. I've yet to work with them and I don't want to. Alleged miscarriages of justice and flawed convictions aren't among my favourite jobs. I'm going to get a shitty assignment, I just know it.

I half turn, looking down at the chief. He nods to tell me to sit. 'I thought you were the man for the job.'

Before I can ask, 'What job?', Miss Spence says, 'The murder of PC Joseph Craig.'

Holding off a groan, I lower myself into the armchair, that sinking feeling.

She looks along the front edge of the desk towards me. 'Were you here in 1981?'

Seeing a get-out, I nod energetically, hoping that being on the same force at the same time will disqualify me from any new inquiry. 'A constable on the beat, five years' service.'

She purses her lips thoughtfully, working out my age, I guess. I'd have owned up to forty-two if she'd bothered to ask, estimating hers at around twenty-five, though she looks a sixth-former.

'I was an inspector then, up north,' the chief butts in, already distancing himself from any potential comebacks.

She ignores him, brown eyes still on me. Behind the black specs they look extremely tired for nine in the morning. She must have been up early and driven a long way. 'Were you on duty on the night PC Craig died?' she asks in the neutral accent acquired by most lawyers.

I long to say yes because such involvement would be certain to get me off the job. I look at the mass of documents around her feet and suspect from the exhaustion in her eyes that she's read every scrap of paper that still exists about the job down to the duty rosters. 'No,' I answer truthfully.

The riots were sporadic and unpredictable and lasted about a week, I explain. 'Saw some action some nights, not that particular night.'

'Many towns and cities were hit,' the chief breaks in. 'Copycat stuff, following on from Brixton and Toxteth.' Then, languidly: 'It was nothing like as serious here.'

Easy to say when you were sitting behind a desk and not standing beneath the balconies of council flats being bombarded by flaming missiles, I think acidly.

Again she ignores him. 'But you weren't on duty that night?'

I shake my head.

'Good,' she pronounces.

Bad, I decide. Please, I don't want this bloody job. I lean forward. 'I have to tell you I'm a pal of one of the CID boys who took some statements.' It's about the closest I dare go to telling her that, if her Commission wants to be seen as truly independent, she should be calling in someone from an outside force.

'Who's that?' asks the chief idly.

'James Jackson, Detective Inspector, retired.'

The chief frowns to himself. Thirty years on the force Jacko served with some fine results; all forgotten.

Alice nods to herself – confirmation that she has read all the papers, already knows who was where and when and did what. 'There's no question here of anything wrong with the paper-work.'

'Have you had it carbon-tested?' the chief queries, a reference to a modern technique that highlights any alterations and additions after statements have been signed as correct.

'There was no need,' Alice replies, airily.

'What is the allegation then?' asks the chief.

She bends forward, feeling in one of the briefcases at her feet. 'It isn't falsifying evidence or anything of that nature.'

Her head comes up. In one hand is a white form, just a few stapled A4 pages, like those exam papers at school and college.

She sits back, opening out the form. I can no longer see her face, only the front page. Across it is 'Criminal Cases Review Commission'. Beneath that, in larger black type, is 'APPLICA-TION'. The chief's desk is too long for me to read what's under that.

She lowers the form just enough for a view of her fringe, furrowed forehead, black specs and weary eyes. 'Do you remember the details of the case?'

I sigh. 'Everyone in the force remembers the death of one of their own.'

'He was the only serving officer we've ever lost in the line of duty,' the chief adds, reclaiming PC Craig as one of his own, now that he deems it safe to do so.

'But the specifics?' she persists.

'My memory was refreshed this morning.'

The form comes down to her chest. A full-face view now, eyebrows arched, like an exam invigilator checking up. 'Who by?'

'The radio.'

'How did they know about it?'

How the hell would I know? I think, irked. 'They interviewed his mum and a local MP.'

14

'What did they say?'

She's cross-examining me, cheeky little upstart. 'That there was startling new evidence and calling for the case to be re-opened.'

'They didn't say that we'd decided to grant this application...' She waves the form.'...for a review?'

I shake my head.

'It can't have come from us.' She goes silent for a second. 'Must have come from him.' Then: 'I was going to tell him at lunchtime.'

'Who?' I ask.

'Scott Packard and his MP, Giles Johnson.' She gives the form another little flip. 'Johnson helped fill out this.' An instant's pause for thought. 'He must have leaked it to the radio.' She sighs. 'Ah, well.'

Her face disappears again. 'You'll remember that two police officers were injured that night, PC Craig fatally and PC Benson so badly that he was subsequently invalided out.'

Now that you mention it, yes, I do recall Benson, but only vaguely, so I say nothing.

She puts the opened form face down on her knee and begins to address the chief, deciding, it seems, that he is more in need of a briefing than me.

Scott Packard, she begins, had always admitted he'd got drunk after playing in a football match and went with team mates to an inner-city block of flats. A riot was on the go when they arrived. His group was chased and separated. He was cornered by a man in civvies, wielding what he claimed was a cosh and shouting racist abuse.

That's right. More is coming back. Packard was – is – black. Craig and Benson were undercover.

Packard always conceded he lashed out with a tent clamp he'd looted from a sports shop, she continues, and felled his pursuer.

Packard was one of a score of youths arrested in overnight raids. He was charged with murder; half a dozen more with riotous assembly which centred on a simultaneous attack on PC Benson.

15

When the case came to crown court, the judge ruled there would be separate trials – the affray first. All six on that charge were cleared, largely because PC Benson had no reliable memory of events and could make no identifications.

At the murder trial, the crown decided not to put Benson through the ordeal again. He was, however, offered to Packard's defence team.

They decided against calling him. He'd made such a sad, shambling sight in the witness box in the affray trial that they reasoned he'd do more harm than good to their client's case. So PC Benson's evidence, which didn't amount to much anyway, was merely read out to the jury.

In essence, she continues, Packard's defence was self-defence. The jury didn't buy it. 'Reading the papers, I'd say he was a tad unlucky,' she goes on. 'Manslaughter was about right, I'd say.'

That's easy to say, I protest privately. It's always a mistake to make judgements on what you read about a court case.

All the public get in newspapers is edited highlights, the juicy bits. You have to be there, right through the case, to reach a balanced conclusion. Jurors are there throughout.

Even when you've read the full official transcript – and she clearly has – you still miss out on those unguarded moments, the pauses and the looks that can tell you so much.

If the jury found him guilty, that's good enough for me.

Being under eighteen, Alice continues, Packard was sentenced to be detained indefinitely. He appealed on the grounds of misdirection of the jury by the judge and lost.

All this she is recounting without looking at any documents, such is her command of the paperwork.

Packard, she continues, seemed to accept his lot. At a young offenders' prison, he concentrated on sport. 'He was a very talented footballer on schoolboy forms with Forest.'

A Derby County devotee, man and boy, I think: that doesn't make him very talented. I try not to smile.

On transfer to adult prison, he threw himself into education, she goes on, got several O levels, learned a trade as a barber. 'People inside gave him no trouble.'

Well, of course, they wouldn't, I mull bitterly. As a convicted cop killer they'd give him only respect and a wide berth.

'And he gave no one any trouble either,' she goes on, as if reading my thoughts. 'A model prisoner.'

For the last two years he'd been in open prison, outside working parties and finally a hostel. 'Earmarked for release on licence. He'd accepted responsibility for his action, faced up to it. To cap everything, while living in the hostel, he'd given the police valuable help in solving a vicious crime.'

Currying a favour which he's now calling in, I suspect cynically.

'Then, quite suddenly, he went into denial, started questioning his conviction, claiming after all those years he was not a murderer.'

'Why so?' asks the chief, engrossed.

Because, being branded a cop killer, he'll be unemployable in the outside world, I grumble inwardly. It's bullshit. Half the prison population convince themselves they shouldn't be banged up. Over time, the fiction of innocence transforms itself into fact. They actually come to believe it. Crap. All of this. A waste of time.

Alice lifts the form from her lap. Her face disappears behind it. 'Part Five,' she read out loud. 'New information about your case.'

She brings the form down again. Five months ago, she recounts, no longer reading, her memory refreshed, he attended the magistrates court to give evidence for the prosecution in committal proceedings against a mugger he helped to bring to book. 'While there, he claims to have seen the man he's supposed to have killed sixteen years earlier.'

Now that, even I am forced to concede, could be accurately described as startling new evidence.

'So?' says Alice with a questioning inflection that is aimed at putting us to the test.

The chief fails it, looking nonplussed.

'Was any other plainclothes policeman injured that night?' I ask.

She shakes her head. 'Only Benson.' She smiles, giving me a pass mark.

17

Right. I'm going to get this over with quickly. 'Can I use that?' I nod at one of the chief's phones. 'To phone Pensions.'

Catching on, he picks up the phone, asks for Pensions and introduces himself. 'Ex-PC Benson.' He looks urgently at Alice.

'Anthony,' she says.

'Anthony,' he repeats. 'Invalidity pensioner. Can I have his details, please.'

The wait is less than a minute before he begins to write on a pad. He says, 'Thank you,' puts down the phone, tears off the top sheet and slips it across his desk towards me. He looks at me, slyly, pleased with himself for having contributed. 'Should be simple enough.'

3

Humping two bulky briefcases down the back stairs and across the vast grounds was warm work on a sunny October day.

Only a thin scattering of leaves has dropped on to the paths and dewy lawns from the trees, no frosts yet to turn their colours, a lovely Indian summer lingering on so long that I'm still wearing my lightweight grey suit.

I dump the cases on the fawn carpet in my office, a cubbyhole compared with the chief's. Uninvited, Alice places the Stork SB Margarine box on my desk. Before either of us have sat down, she wants to be off again.

'Where to?' I ask, testily.

'I want to view the scene.'

'There's no point.' I tell her all she'd find is a big supermarket. The flats at the centre of the riots were pulled down in the mid-eighties; only twenty years old. All their dark covered walkways had ever been were havens for muggers, junkies and prostitutes; a costly sixties mistake.

She looks more annoyed than disappointed. She'd fixed to talk to Giles Johnson MP at the railway station at one o'clock, she informs me. Before that, she plans to nip into the crown court to see when Packard would be available for interview.

Everything she says and the way she says it comes out as a declaration of intent, no consultation, no explanation, no 'If that's OK with you.' She's beginning to treat me like her assistant and I'm beginning not to like it.

'The trial in which he's to give evidence is listed to start mid-morning,' she adds. 'I thought it would be more convenient to see him there than at the prison hostel.'

'Today's case has nothing to do with an attack on an ex-beauty queen, has it?' I ask.

'Yes.' Surprised, she wants to know, demands, really, how I know. I tell her what I'd heard about the mugger's trial being previewed on the radio news over breakfast.

'The prosecution service insist we talk to him only after he's completed his evidence, she adds.'

Makes sense, I privately concur. They want to avoid any defence suggestion that we've been coaching him into beefing up his testimony. Lawyers will try anything to get an acquittal.

With a fussy flourish, she peers at a small gold wrist-watch. 'An hour and a half to spare. Any suggestions?'

Matter of fact, a long sit down and a cup of coffee would be a splendid idea, but I judge that it wouldn't go down too well with this mighty atom. 'Ex-PC Tony Benson lives on the way in.'

'Your car or mine?' she says over her slender shoulder, already on the way out of the door.

Hers, she tells me when I catch up, is parked at the Fairways Hotel, the HQ local; a rambling old coach house unspoilt by modern extensions. She'd booked in last night after driving over from the Commission's offices in Birmingham.

She lives alone, I guess. That's not just because there's no ring on any finger. Nobody with someone sharing their life makes an overnight stay out of a trip that takes not much more than an hour. I happily get up long before dawn to travel two hundred miles if it gives me another night at home. 'Do you know the city?' I ask.

'No, I've never been here before.'

19

'Mine then,' I decide without further debate, determined to rein her in, to pull, if not rank, experience and local knowledge on her.

His long, thin face looks to have been wrung dry without being washed first. His eyes are only half open and filmed over, like the front windows and paintwork of this rundown terraced house. His cheeks are unshaven, his brow deeply creased.

'Mr Benson,' I say, already holding up my warrant card for inspection. He peers at it blearily while I give my name and rank and introduce Alice as a colleague. 'We'd like a word.'

'What about?' he mumbles.

'It's just routine.'

'About what?'

'An on-going inquiry.'

He blinks, trying to focus. 'Not about the car, is it?' Behind us, standing on a tiny square of black asphalt where a front garden should be, is a dirty white taxi.

'Could be,' I reply instinctively.

He asks for and is given the time. His shiny eyelids close for a second. Sighing heavily, he pulls back the door and leads us down a short gloomy hallway. He's a burly man, wearing an off-white singlet, no shirt; grey woollen socks, no shoes. His dark blue trousers are baggy and unbelted.

I know we have woken him up before we reach a back room that reeks of body odour. Faded green curtains are drawn. A tartan blanket is in a heap on the stained blue carpet in front of a patterned sofa. Two unmatched cushions are perched on one arm of the sofa.

Tony Benson turns, coming round. 'What about the car?'

It's a hunch that's opened the door for us, so I might as well stick with it. 'Where was it on...'

I turn to Alice who gives a date in May.

'After all this time...' Benson stops, bewildered. '...how the 'ell should I know?'

'How about your records?' My pleasant smile.

'I don't keep 'em here.' A local accent, flat, dull.

'Could your office help?'

'Why the bloody 'ell should they?'

'It is important,' says Alice with a pleading expression.

'What is?'

I don't want her saying any more yet. 'Let's check with your office, just to refresh your memory.'

'Go there then. Don't come here disturbing me. Christ...' An exasperated expression and tone. '...I didn't finish till gone seven. What's wrong? Tell me.'

It's a request I'm going to ignore. 'It might mean having to return here to trouble you again.' My turn to plead now. 'Please, Tony.'

'Better be good.' Grumbling to himself, he walks a few slow, unsteady steps to a table in front of the curtained window. On it, among a pile of papers and unopened junk mail, is a mustard-coloured phone. With his back to us he prods out a number. 'Luce,' he says, 'have you got my runs for...' He half turns to us.

Alice repeats the date and he passes it on.

Something is said in a female voice at the other end. 'Got the law here.'

A short silence. 'No. No. To do with elimination, I suppose.' It's an off-the-cuff answer that draws on police experience from years ago, I acknowledge, but it's close to the mark. He looks behind him again. 'What time?'

'Lunchtime,' says Alice and he passes it on again.

We walk up behind him, standing at each of his shoulders. I still can't hear what's being said at the other end, only Benson. 'Mmm. Ah. Yeah. Remember him, tight-fisted sod.'

A passenger who was a poor tipper, I guess.

He grunts his thanks, puts down the phone, walks between us and then turns back to face us. '1 p.m. pick-up, had to hang about half an hour. Trip to Mansfield.'

'Where was the pick-up?' I ask.

'Mags.'

The reply roots me to the worn carpet. It's what policemen have always called the magistrates court.

Not so simple after all.

21

'Now.' Benson straightens his rounded shoulders and pulls in a beer belly. 'What am I supposed to have done? Who's complaining?'

'Nobody,' I say. 'Let's all sit down.'

Benson backs to the sofa and flops down, wearily. We pull out dining-room chairs from beneath the table and sit.

Alice takes over. 'I'm from the Criminal Cases Review Commission.'

He looks at her blankly, far too long out of the law business for the name to mean anything to him.

'We're reviewing the case of Scott Packard.'

He scowls at a name that does mean something. 'Not letting him out, are you, surely?'

'It's not an issue of parole.'

'It is for me. He should rot in jail, black bastard.'

Alice forks a disapproving frown. 'He was also at the magistrates court that day. Giving evidence for the police, as a point of fact...'

'Oh, really.' A mocking lilt to his tone. 'Bucking for release, is he? Seeking a trade-off?'

It's a thought that's already occurred to me, so I know what's running through his muddled mind.

'He claims to have seen you waiting in the foyer,' says Alice patiently. 'Were you?'

A nod, automatic. 'Good job I didn't see him.'

'Would you have recognised him, if you had?'

No response this time, just a narrow look.

'He recognised you as the person he assaulted back in '81.'

'What?' He feels the back of a full head of greyish-black hair. 'Why should he admit that after all these years? Found God, has he? Wants it taken into consideration, does he?'

Wiping his slate clean, he means, to make a fresh start.

'Done a deal, have you, for a clear-up?'

I move my head into a 'No.'

Alice plods on. 'All the records indicate the attacks on you and your colleague happened at roughly the same time, but some distance apart.'

22

She's trying to point out that Scott Packard couldn't have been in two places at once, but Benson doesn't get it. 'Does it matter?'

'Well, yes, it does, if true,' I put in.

'Not to me, it doesn't. It's not going to bring back me career. End of marriage. End of rugger. Reduced to this.'

He looks helplessly around the room, frowning, finally catching on. 'You're not saying...' He can't get his mind or his tongue round it. 'Are you trying to say he attacked just me? Only me. Not Joey Craig, too. That someone else...'

'That's what he's saying,' says Alice, primly.

'What about Joey's folks, eh?' His face has twisted in anger. 'Thought about them, dragging all this up again? All this fucking fuss.'

A fair point and I wonder how they will react. Will they accept it stoically, the typical police family? Or will they do the rounds of TV chat shows and give exclusive and highly paid newspaper interviews, like so many relatives of murder victims, proclaiming: 'Life means life.'

'Do you keep in touch with them?' I ask idly.

His head drops to tell me: No.

So much for his concern, then, but let's not be too hard on him. 'Help us sort this out quickly and quietly then,' I say, taking out my pocketbook.

Maybe he's in shock from what he's just heard. Maybe the memories are too painful or hazy. Maybe he's still dozy from his disturbed sleep. But all we're getting in reply to Alice's questions are glum nods and surly Yers and Ners, annoying after a while.

Yer, he confirms, there'd been trouble at the flats for several nights running, always after ten thirty when the pubs shut.

Yer, he and PC Craig had been detailed to wear plainclothes and tour the local pubs, mingling, trying to identify potential troublemakers, monitoring and reporting on their positions. In one crowded bar, they came across a score or so of teenaged rowdies, several in red and green soccer shirts.

Then a veritable flow of phrases. 'Some stripped to the waist. Some had their shirts tied round their necks. Piss heads or dope heads or both.'

A grim smile. 'Giving it plenty.' He is working an elbow to raise a hand to his mouth to indicate they were drinking rapidly. 'Talking about heading for the flats to join the fun.'

He repeats very gloomily. 'Fun. Some fucking fun for Joey and me, eh?'

When they left the pub, Benson and Craig followed. 'Before our very eyes...' He widens his own. '...they smashed the window of a sports shop and looted it. We couldn't believe what we were seeing. Well, what could we do?'

'Radio it in,' I suggest, knowing from my own nights on duty then that the area had been flooded with police vans, some unmarked, all packed with officers in riot gear and with dogs.

'Which we did,' he replies huffily, 'but we didn't know how many other incidents were on the go at the same time or how long back-up would take. No self-respecting cop can witness a smash and grab and do nothing, can he?'

Alice inches him on. 'So you gave chase, drawing your batons?'

'Yer. They scattered in all directions, into side streets, alleys. I just wanted one, any one.'

Catch one and you can often sweat out of him the names of the rest, I accept privately.

'I targeted two in soccer shirts with numbers on their backs, ran fifty, sixty yards after them. One turned under an archway into the forecourt of the flats. I turned the corner and...'

He stops, looks down, muttering. 'Nothing. I can't say it was like running into an express train or anything like that. I felt nothing. Not until I woke up three days later in intensive care. I felt it then, mind.' His head comes up. He's pulling a pained face.

He confirms with a curt nod that he suffered a fracture at the back of the skull and bruising of the brain. Headshakes tell us he still can't remember the colour of the shirts of his targets or the numbers on their backs.

He reverts to monosyllables. Yer, he did give evidence at the affray trial but couldn't positively identify anyone he chased or his assailant. 'Little shits got off.'

Ner, he agrees, he wasn't called as a witness at the murder trial that followed.

'So you never actually saw who hit you?' asks Alice.

He shakes his head carefully, as if it's still aching.

'So, you see,' she points out slowly, 'it is just possible that Packard has genuinely believed all these years that he attacked PC Craig when, in fact, he hit you and only realised it when he finally saw you at the magistrates court five months ago.'

Benson doesn't say Yer or Ner, just closes his eyes and lowers his head, not wanting to see anything at all.

'There's something in it,' enthuses Alice as we drive out of the sunlit side street back on to the main road heading for Trent Bridge.

'Might be,' I say, more cautiously.

'Be positive. Packard didn't see Benson at his trial because he didn't go into the witness box. He can't have recognised him from there. He can only have seen him on the night of the riot.'

'Or he saw his picture in the papers immediately after the event and seeing him again gave him the idea of belatedly cobbling together this story.'

She looks crestfallen. She'd never thought of that.

On the way here, I'd gently probed her background – university in Birmingham, staying on after graduation with a big legal aid firm of solicitors, head-hunted six months ago by the Commission.

We're from different sides of the legal divide. The police job is to build a case. Until now, hers has been to knock it down, in the same way that my little Laura likes to topple over the bricks I've carefully put one on top of another; a game really.

'Look at the way he...' She flicks her head back towards Benson's home.'...jumped to the conclusion that Packard was negotiating his release by helping the police in this current case.'

I say nothing, troubled. I've missed something. Something recently said should have been followed up. My mind's gone blank, that distracted feeling of walking into your bedroom to get something and not being able to remember what the hell it is.

'He's still very embittered, isn't he?' she adds.

What do you bloody well expect? I want to shout. Of course he's embittered, you insensitive, inexperienced little squirt, but I say nothing, just brood all the way up London Road towards the city centre.

4

God, I'm bored rigid. What are we doing here, sitting in on a court case that's got nothing to do with the job in hand?

'Let's pop in to see when Packard will be available for interview,' Alice had insisted. That was almost an hour ago and we've yet to pop out.

I stifle a yawn and let my mind drift. Heaven knows why playwrights and scriptwriters are so besotted with legal drama. They are theatres of total tedium.

In real courts, there are no surprise last-minute witnesses, no gasps from the packed public gallery, no emptying of the press bench in a mad scramble for phones.

Each side knows for weeks in advance from the paperwork the witnesses to be called and what they are likely to say. Most cases are so time-consuming and un-newsy that they are largely ignored by the media who cover the start and the end, if at all.

The only last-minute hitch – and it never comes as a surprise – is that trials seldom start on time; always for unexplained reasons, usually admin cock-ups.

And when they do get going, there can be more interruptions than in *Kavanagh QC* for commercial breaks. Juries spend hours outside rather than inside the court while counsel squabble over obscure legal niceties.

Like, for instance, the case of Garry Matthews, who sits in the roomy, railed dock, wearing a dark, double-breasted suit over his stocky frame and a sullen expression.

His hard eyes have lit up only once – when he emerged from the entrance to the cells and spotted a small knot of scruffy people sitting together in the spacious public gallery to his left; family and friends, I presume.

Far from being a packed gallery, only three other cinema-style seats are occupied – one by a lanky, denimed man with his greasy hair in a pony tail, and Alice and I sitting in the front row behind the empty press bench.

The black-gowned defence barrister has been pressing the red-robed judge not to permit the crown to refer to the establishment where Matthews and the witness, Scott Packard, resided as a prison hostel. This, he'd argued, would reveal to the jury that his client had a criminal past.

Whenever he seemed to be drying up, he was passed notes and marked law books by a sharp-suited solicitor sitting immediately behind him and off he would go again, mainly repeating himself.

The prosecuting counsel, a plump and plummy woman, with an ancient wig at a jaunty angle, didn't appear to give a toss one way or the other, but she took ten minutes to say so.

I don't know either barrister, but I do know of the briefing solicitor for the defence. The Caribbean Carman, his successful clients dub him, after Britain's best-known – and reportedly best-paid – QC. Legal Aid Lennie, his less successful customers call him.

Tall, black, handsome and a total shit, Lawrence Gomaz is the main mouthpiece of the inner city. A high proportion of complaints against the police that land in my in-tray at HQ originate from his office, many of them concocted.

It is rare to see him defending a white man; there must be a catch in it somewhere, but it's not my case and I can't be bothered to work it out.

The only other person in court that I recognise is Inspector Mann, not the brightest or the best. Portly and balding, he sits in a brown suit behind the prosecutor. On the ledge between them

27

are numbered exhibits. Mann is fiddling absently with a bunch of labelled keys as if they are worry beads.

The judge has just granted the application and looked across to the press bench to make sure they have noted his ruling. It is still deserted.

Now the jurors in waiting, a score or so, are being ushered in, like a herd of sheep.

When their names are called, twelve go into the jury box. They have less room than anyone, even the solitary prisoner in the dock.

From double swing doors, a middle-aged woman reporter with a pleasant face glides soundlessly down the centre aisle between almost empty rows of public seats and slides into the press bench in front of us.

Matthews stands up in the dock while the charges of attempted robbery and grievous bodily harm on one Linda Dwyer are read out by the clerk. He pleads not guilty in a firm voice. Both he and the clerk sit again.

At long last, the prosecuting counsel opens the crown's case. Miss Dwyer, a single woman of thirty-five, was walking home on a cold evening, she begins, when she was the subject of an appalling attack in a dark street.

Bravely, Miss Dwyer fought back, scratching her assailant on his cheeks. She didn't get a good look at his face, but could describe him and a tattoo on his hand.

A man out with his dog came to her aid, the barrister goes on, and would tell the jury what he saw, including a detailed sighting of the fleeing assailant.

Inquiries took police the following day to what the prosecutor carefully described as 'a hostel for men of no fixed abode' where they arrested Matthews. He had scratches on both cheeks and a tattoo on one hand that matched the victim's account.

A fellow resident, Scott Packard, would say that the night before his arrest Matthews had returned to the hostel in a dishevelled state and asked him to feign a fight – 'to cover up his visible scratches, damning evidence, you might think.'

Matthews explained to him that he had been settling a score with a woman for a friend. 'Now,' says counsel, slowing down a

28

little, 'we only have Matthews' words as reported by Mr Pack-ard for this supposed motive for the attack as Matthews himself refuses to confirm or deny that he was acting for or on behalf of anyone. Upon arrest and since, he has refused to say anything at all. Whatever his motive – and we say it is not the real issue here – the evidence we are about to call is, we submit, clear cut.'

Reading between the lines, she's saying that the police suspect Matthews was hired to do someone else's dirty work, but they can't prove it, and it doesn't matter anyway.

With only the slightest pause for breath, she calls her first witness – Linda Dwyer.

At my side, Alice stirs. I suspect that all she's been doing is killing time until the meeting she has set up with Giles Johnson, the MP who helped Packard with his application to her Commission.

Leaning towards me, she whispers, 'Doubt we'll get Packard before the overnight adjournment.'

I'd worked that out an hour ago. I stir, too, but the sight of Linda Dwyer pins me back into my seat.

She may be more than fifteen years on from her beauty queen days and, at an educated guess, 40–30–38, instead of the standard 36–24–36 of her late teens, but she's still something to behold – long blonde hair down to the shoulders of a tight-fitting jacket, lime green; pleated skirt that reveals plenty of leg.

She takes the oath in a soft, sexy voice, confirms her name, former address, and gives her occupation as 'beauty consultant'.

'Now . . . ' begins the prosecutor.

Alice touches my elbow. 'We'll be late.'

I rise and she follows me down the centre aisle.

Outside the swing doors, she says with an irritating smirk, 'Sorry to drag you away.'

I say nothing.

She needles on. 'I could see you were getting a long eyeful of her.'

Now I must say something. 'Didn't they teach you at your law school that if you move while an oath is being taken, you run the risk of a bollocking from the judge?'

29

She laughs lightly but a touch scornfully, irking me all the more.

A brisk walk – too brisk for me – for two or three hundred yards beyond banks, hotels and snack bars to the Midland station, a superbly restored old building, its carved brickwork rose-tinted in the sun.

Alice, who only comes up to my shoulder, sets a pace that's hard on my gammy leg.

A clock in the high, echoing foyer tells us we are a couple of minutes late, but no one approaches us going down the wide steps and along platform 5.

In the refreshment bar, where the dominant colour is an off-putting green, we queue for sandwiches – cheese and tomato for her, sausage for me – served by a youth in a baseball cap that matches the sickly décor.

'Will you recognise him?' frets Alice, sitting on a bench seat with plastic plants on a ledge behind her.

'I hope so,' I reply doubtfully, setting down two coffees on our table. I sit in a wooden armchair opposite her.

I'm dubious about spotting Giles Johnson because I have little interest in politics. My grasp of the subject, my Em tells me, has never risen above Janet and John level.

A few months ago, during that long drawn-out election campaign, I was repeatedly being held up at temporary traffic lights while roads were dug up, if not by gasmen, then for electricity cables or water pipes or phone lines; sometimes by different gangs at almost the same spot on successive weeks.

Pre-privatisation, I used to grin and bear it, acknowledging that public services were for the general good. Sitting in one long queue, it dawned that I was being delayed for the financial gain of shareholders.

Right, I told Em when I got home, fuming. That's it. I'm voting Labour. But they have no plans to renationalise, she pointed out, and among the shareholders taking their profits at my inconvenience would be the police pension fund. I still voted Labour, though, but with a heavy heart.

30

I couldn't recognise a single new Labour MP to save my monopolies-boosted pension. I reckon I'll spot the type, though – middle-class, a journo or college lecturer; youngish, black attaché case, portable phone in one hand, the *Guardian* in the other. The wonder is that he's not a pushy young woman, a bit like Alice, I think, amusing myself.

I'm surprised when a bespectacled man in his mid-fifties, greying hair, grey-suited, shabby raincoat over an arm with the *Daily Mirror* stuffed in one pocket, appears at my shoulder. He is looking down on Alice. 'Miss Spence?'

Johnson introduces himself and sits down, declining refreshment and apologising for not seeing her at more leisure at his constituency office. 'Fully booked,' he explains.

He has to catch the 1.33 to St Pancras, he says, so Alice goes straight in. 'How did you get involved in Scott Packard's application?'

He came to a Saturday morning surgery along with his mother, a constituent, he explains in an accent that's a little way to the north of here, like my own Derbyshire. 'I remembered the case well.'

Back in 1981, he was the district official for his union, which sponsored a team in the Unemployed Football League. Lots of organisations and businesses helped out by footing the bills for playing strips for various sides which gave themselves fantasy names like Standard This, Inter That, AC the Other.

My boyhood sporting dream was to play in the white shirt of the Rams, so I smile my understanding. 'The riots were in July,' I observe. 'Wasn't it out-of-season for soccer?'

'There's no out-of-season for the unemployed,' he replies sadly. 'They played – and some still do – morning, noon and night, all weathers, nothing better to do.'

'Did Packard appear for your union-sponsored side?' asks Alice.

A headshake. 'For Racing Club of Radford.' He laughs briefly to himself.

She presses on. 'Who sponsored that?'

I think I already know. Frenchie Lebois who opened a string of betting shops called Racing Clubs on the proceeds of loan sharking and other shady activities; a hard man, not at all nice to know.

All Johnson says is, 'A bookmaker.' There were lots of good young players in the league, he continues with a hint of pride. 'Scott Packard was on Forest's books, his half-brother eventually turned pro and then, of course, there was Robbie Hill.'

I'd like to dwell awhile, misty-eyed, on Robbie Hill, but Alice moves things on. 'Did his half-brother play in the same team?'

'In that match, certainly,' he replies. 'Campbell Robins, he's called.' He thinks. 'Not sure which side he played for.'

Same mother, different fathers, I guess.

'Campbell was at university at the time,' Johnson continues.

Alice looks perplexed. 'I thought you said the league was for the unemployed?'

'You didn't have to produce your UB40,' he says, evenly.

'Didn't clubs have to register their players with the league?' I ask, knowledgeably.

'Yes, but they'd play a ringer if one side was a man short; it happened all the time.'

I smile again, recalling my league début for my village cricket team up the Peaks at thirteen. I turned up to score. We only had ten men and I was drafted in to play under the name of forty-something Stonewall Fletcher, so named, not because he was a limpet at the crease, but because stone walls were what he built. The opposition knew of the impersonation, but never reported me – largely, I suspect, because I dropped a catch and did not bat.

At the time, Johnson goes on, Campbell was on long vac from his college where he later got a good degree. 'He still opted for professional football, a nippy winger, with some London club. The money, I suppose.' He pulls a disapproving face.

I ask a question beloved of all sports fans. 'Where is he now?'
'Abroad.'

'And Robbie Hill played in your league, did he?'

'Long before Derby County spotted him.' He doesn't go on to mention Hill's successful stays on Merseyside and in Milan and his Ireland caps.

To Alice's barely disguised annoyance, we talk soccer for a while. Johnson is obviously a genuine fan from the terraces, not a trendy convert to an executive box. I am warming to him.

Annoyingly she butts in with a question that's already been answered. 'Did Campbell and Packard play in the same side?'

'I can't be sure,' he repeats. 'Robbie Hill was certainly in the Hyson Harps team.' He chuckles. 'Sponsored by a pub with a large Irish clientele.'

'You've a terrific memory,' says Alice, a shade darkly.

He smiles, unoffended. 'It was a cup final, after all. Several sponsors were there to give their support, though I didn't stop behind after the final whistle for the celebrations or see any of the subsequent trouble.'

His smile fades. 'In view of the dreadful events that followed...' A sad shrug. '...the riot...the policeman's death... it's a night that's etched on my memory.' He pauses. 'And, of course, I've had to go into some detail with Scott over his application form.'

Alice sits back, put in her place.

Johnson tells us what Scott Packard told him about spotting his supposed murder victim alive at the magistrates court five months ago. 'Like seeing a ghost,' he reports him as saying.

We don't tell him that we have already established that ex-PC Benson was in the same courthouse at the same time.

'Why did Packard come to you and not his solicitor?' asks Alice.

'He did originally consult his trial lawyer, in fact, but he couldn't take the case.'

I'm sure Alice knows the answer to this from her deep research on the case files, but I'm going to ask him anyway. 'Who's that?'

'L –' she begins, but Johnson beats her. 'Lennie Gomaz. Do you know him?'

She shakes her head. I manage to keep mine still, thinking: That shit.

'Good chap,' he goes on. Then, for emphasis: 'Excellent.'

I can feel myself going off Johnson as he recounts how Gomaz came to Nottingham to the university and stayed on as a new law graduate. He worked evenings as a volunteer at one of those alternative advice centres that sprang up in every inner city; a radical's rite of passage.

My Em did her left wing bit at some place down south called The Citizen's Centre. One night a man came in, demanding she report a leak in his lavatory to the council. She pointed at a phone book and phone and suggested he look up the number and call it himself. He complained she'd been unhelpful. She got a dressing down. She left soon afterwards, convinced that such centres merely promoted a dependence culture.

'Did a grand job, did Lennie,' he goes on. 'Still does.'

He clearly knows a lot about Gomaz, too much, in my view, so I'll try him with this, with a wintry smile into the bargain. 'But Scott Packard was found guilty.'

'Generally, I mean.' He seems put out at my bluntness. 'Over the years. In the community.' He recovers. 'Everybody else on the affray case was acquitted.'

No comfort to young Packard doing life, I think. 'Did Mr Gomaz defend them all?'

Johnson shakes his head. 'They were shared around various law offices. Scott's half-brother Campbell Robins . . .' He looks at me to make sure I'm following.

I nod.

' . . . Campbell was represented by a fellow volunteer at the law centre – Liam Harries. He's not practising any more. You'll know him, of course.'

Alice nods now, very briefly, but I've never heard of him, so I give Johnson my blank look.

'Agent to the stars, all those TV types and footballers.' He issues a friendly grin. 'Like your hero Robbie Hill.'

I wonder if Harries gave that interview on the radio this morning about Hill's impending transfer and wish I'd listened more closely.

'According to the case papers, Campbell wasn't charged with anything,' says Alice.

Johnson shakes his head into a 'No' and falls silent.

34

'So,' Alice continues thoughtfully, 'having had the 1981 jury find against him, Mr Gomaz didn't fancy taking up Scott's case again?'

'Wasn't that.' There's an edge to Johnson's tone. ' "Conflict of interest," he said.'

'With what?' Alice cross-examines.

'He didn't say.' He looks distinctly uneasy. 'I hope, if this review's successful, you're not going to dump this miscarriage on him publicly.'

We say nothing, forcing him on.

'Lennie's been terrific to me; all of us. And he's just been appointed to a Home Office committee on crime.'

They're close, very close, too close, I decide.

Abruptly, Alice changes the subject. 'Have you informed Scott or his mother that his application for a review has been granted?'

'No,' he replies, 'I was waiting to hear what you had to say first this lunchtime. I'll phone her with the good news from the Commons when I get there.'

The train is announced over the tannoy and I wait until the stops on the way have been listed. 'Did you tell local radio about Scott's application for a case review?'

A curt nod. 'With his and his mother's consent.' He gets up.

I rise and follow him to the door. 'How did that come about?'

A freelance radio reporter, a woman, often phones him after surgeries to see if he's launching any newsy campaigns or pursuing constituents' complaints of public interest, he says. MPs, especially virtually anonymous back-benchers, like their voters to know how busy they are, I realise.

We walk with him across the platform to a first-class coach with a reserved seat, a perk of the job.

He gives us contact numbers which I note down and he tells us he'll be in his constituency office on Saturday morning if we need to see him again. 'My home base,' he calls it, making it sound very humble.

Through the opened door I ask a final question: 'Were Mr Gomaz and his law centre colleague Mr Liam Harries at that cup final?'

35

'Liam played, Lennie was a linesman, as I recall.' He pulls the door shut but continues talking through the opened window, very urgently. 'Don't drop Lennie in it now.'

I wave him goodbye.

'Why's he so anxious to protect Gomaz's position?' asks a puzzled Alice, walking back along the platform.

So she noticed it too. Good. 'Because,' I suggest with a cynical smile, 'he rounded up all his old dependent law centre clients and delivered a big vote for him.'

Climbing the stairs, I ask, 'Was Packard badly defended?'

'Gomaz seems to have briefed counsel to run the case on the paperwork. Lots of witnesses, even an eyewitness, had their statements read instead of being called to test their evidence.'

'Why?'

'Their main plank was that Packard feared he was being chased by armed fascist thugs and struck out in a panic.'

Crossing the foyer, she discloses that she'd seen the name of Harries in the paperwork but couldn't remember coming across a statement from Campbell Robins, Packard's half-brother, in the documents she'd studied.

'Maybe,' I jest, 'he gave it in the ghost name he played under to escape the league's registration rules.'

Without consultation, she decides she wants to pop back to court to ask the crown's barrister if Packard is likely to be in and out of the witness box by late afternoon or whether we should return tomorrow.

Suits me. My Volvo is parked there anyway.

Rounding a corner by an old pub, a lithe black man, thirtyish, in denim jacket and grey flannels, runs towards us, stepping nimbly into the gutter to pass by. Rushing for a train, I expect, but oddly, I note, he carries no bag or even a paper to read. In my days on the beat, I'd have kept a suspicious eye on him. These days I don't even turn to see if he's gone into the station.

Further up the street, I tell Alice that Gomaz is the defence solicitor in the mugger's trial we heard being opened.

She ponders this in silence for several steps, then expresses doubt that Packard's involvement as a witness in the current case would be the conflict of interest Gomaz mentioned to Johnson.

She ponders on. 'You'd have thought, though, that Gomaz would have applied for ten hours' work on Packard's behalf under legal aid. It's almost automatic to grant it, just to suss things out, see if there are grounds for a new investigation.' She makes up our mind. 'We'll talk to him, too.'

Rounding a bank on another corner, she asks what I made of Giles Johnson.

I shrug. Privately I've gone off him. Trade unionists like him did not condemn the violence on the picket lines in the winter of discontent in the late seventies and the miners' strike of the mid-eighties and made excuses for the inner-city riots in between.

Extremists among them fermented some of the trouble against which we (it's always us) had to stand firm while under fire. I wonder if I was right to have trusted his party with my vote.

None of this I say, of course, having only reached the Janet and John stage of political development.

Anyway, I have to accept, the real reason is that I don't like the fact that Johnson likes Gomaz.

On the top step of the Floral Hall style entrance to the courthouse waits a frantic-looking Inspector Mann. 'The judge wants us both in his chambers.' He looks down on me. 'Now.'

'Why me?' I ask, unaccountably unnerved.

'You're senior officer in the court precincts. He wants you and me as officer in the case.'

'Why?'

'There's a panic on.'

I raise my voice. 'Why, for chrissake?'

'Scott Packard's escaped.'

I can feel a panic coming on, too, and a sausage sarnie revolves violently in my stomach.

5

'It's my fault.'

Everyone in the judge's crowded chambers, standing room only for Inspector Mann and me, focuses on a small, middle-aged usher in a black gown, who's just spoken.

Understandably so, because it is very rare in any public service for anyone to carry any can for any cock-up – ever.

That's also understandable. Anticipating that the media will be seeking a scapegoat and with the public baying for a head to roll, they shuffle off all responsibility, pass the buck, pull up the drawbridge.

For example, walking up the steps and through the court to get in here, a twitchy Inspector Mann had said, more than once, 'Don't blame me.'

Yes, the usher agrees with the judge's grave-faced clerk, sitting at a small desk next to his boss, she had been in charge of the witnesses' room where Scott Packard waited with four others to be called.

And, yes, Inspector Mann, she goes on with a flick of her head towards him, did instruct her to keep a special eye on Packard on leaving the room to consult with the crown prosecutor. Mann's face fills to overflowing with relief.

He didn't tell her that Packard was the convicted murderer of a policeman and he wasn't in prison uniform or handcuffs. Anxiety rises in Mann's face, then falls as she adds, 'But he did say he was a security risk.'

During the lunch break, she'd accompanied Packard to the cafeteria up a further flight of stairs for a snack. Then he asked to go to the ground-floor toilet.

'I couldn't very well accompany him in, so I waited outside.' After a few minutes with no sign of him, she asked a male usher to go in and check. The window to the car-park was opened.

They'd searched the building and the car-park; no sign. 'Sorry,' she concludes with a sorrowful face.

The judge, royal blue braces attached to black pin-striped trousers over a white collarless shirt, looks up at Mann. 'It's not as though he's any longer regarded as dangerous, would you say?'

So overawed is Mann that he doesn't know what to say.

'I mean...' The judge pats a bundle of papers on his desk. '...he's no longer in a closed prison, is he? He's been living in the community in this hostel without the slightest concern for almost twelve months now, hasn't he?'

Mann's reply is a dumb nod.

'Very well. We'll leave this in the hands of the police, shall we?' The judge looks at the two counsel and their instructing solicitors seated on high-backed chairs round a polished conference table in front of him.

It's an invitation to them to speak that surprisingly is not immediately taken up. I'm expecting the defence's young barrister to seek an immediate abandonment of the trial.

Instead, after an awkward pause, the crown prosecutor goes first. She had intended to call Packard after the victim, Miss Dwyer, she says, but could substitute the dog walker whose arrival had saved her from further attack.

Together, she anticipates, their evidence and cross-examination would more than fill the afternoon. Tomorrow she could call Inspector Mann and two scientific officers.

'Hmm,' purrs the judge. Without wig and robes, he looks a rather amiable old buffer – sixtyish, greying, alert eyes but with the weight problem of his sedentary job.

'I was thinking of adjourning reasonably early tomorrow anyway,' he goes on, languidly. 'In which event...' He smiles puckishly at her. '...you might still be able to produce Mr Packard first thing on Monday morning before you close your case.'

I'm becoming twitchy myself. We can't launch a hunt for Packard without revealing he's a convicted cop killer.

'But what about the search for him?' asks the prosecutor earnestly.

About time someone raised that, I think, gratefully, relaxing a little.

'You've ruled that there should be no hint of the defendant's criminal past,' she points out.

'Indeed.'

'Well, if and when Packard goes into the witness box and should the defence seek to discredit him because of his conviction for murder –'

Gomaz nudges his barrister seated next to him. He interrupts. 'That is not part of our strategy.'

'Then,' the prosecutor comes back, 'any publicity aimed at locating Packard should not refer to his past conviction, or there's a danger that the jury will put two and two together and work out that the hostel belongs to the prison.'

'Quite so.' The judge hums his agreement. 'Nor indeed that the absent Mr Packard resides at anything other than a hostel for homeless men, not until the end of the trial at the earliest.'

I am sitting on a window ledge with my back to a view of a canal and I know I must stand and speak up. 'But, sir, the media will not run police appeals for a thirty-two-year-old man missing from a hostel for the homeless. A convicted murderer on the run, yes, banner headlines, but not that.'

The prosecutor helps me. 'They won't even be able to make Packard's photo public as a missing prisoner because a member of the jury might recognise him from TV or the newspapers, when he does eventually appear in the witness box.'

The judge nods gravely.

He's got the message; terrific.

'If the prison background of everyone connected with this case is not going to be revealed to the jury, it would be most prejudicial to have it mentioned in any form in the media.'

He deliberates.

He's going to abandon the trial, I'm sure of it, to allow a full manhunt, photos, description, Packard's record, the lot. He'll start again later with a fresh jury when the public have helped us to catch Packard.

He tips his head towards me. 'Treat him for the time being as merely AWOL from his hostel, not as a jailbreaker, though I'm sure you'll leave no stone unturned. You've – what? – three and a half days to track him down. Let's see what Monday brings.'

My expression must be askance because he goes on. 'I know the lack of publicity is inconvenient, but use your initiative. You have my full support.'

Inconvenient? I want to splutter. Impossible, you mean, you doddery old fart. I can't catch an escapee in a city this size without the public's help. It's hopeless.

I've hijacked a windowless room on the ground floor. 'Judge's instructions,' I commiserated with the ousted court liaison sergeant.

The old bugger of a beak dropped me in this, but, at least, he did tell me to use my initiative and he'd back me, so, I've decided, I'm going to drop his name without shame.

I have asked the head of courthouse security to transfer the woman usher from the witness room to the courtroom itself. 'Judge's instructions,' I told him.

I asked her name. Carol, she replied. Then I explained her new role. 'Keep an eye open for any stranger who wanders in, shows the slightest interest in the case, and bell me on the internal.' I nodded at a cream phone on the wall outside.

Now I am back downstairs in the commandeered office and on the phone to the force's public relations chief, a sharp lady, at HQ. She confirms my view that the media wouldn't use a missing persons story on the information we're permitted to release. 'About as newsy as a bike without lights,' she declares dismissively. 'Forget it.'

Not quite. Radio Trent, I remind her, ran a piece at breakfast time naming Packard and reporting the campaign for a review of his conviction. They'd also previewed the mugger's trial, but wisely hadn't connected the two.

'Tell 'em, will you, not to repeat the piece? Don't mention the escape, just that Packard's a witness in an on-going trial which is subject to a contempt of court order.'

'I'll advise them,' she corrects me, leaving unsaid the fact that the media can't be told to do anything, more's the pity sometimes.

'In return for saving them from the judge's wrath, can you ask for the tape of their breakfast news?'

Something is itching at my brain and I need to listen again to the Rob Hill soccer story to find out if the man who'd done the

41

talking was Liam Harries, his agent, and Lennie Gomaz's side-kick in the inner-city law centre at the time of the riots.

'I doubt you'd get it,' she says. 'The media are loath to give up any tapes without a court order, awkward sods.'

I'll second that. My wife is a journalist, has a job share as a newscaster on breakfast TV. She can be very awkward, impossible on occasions.

The PR goes on, 'I know a freelance who records all bulletins. He'll deliver or he's off my mailing list.' She asks for my numbers to field any queries, then transfers me to Control.

I fill in the details for the duty inspector, including Packard's description – aged thirty-two, wearing blue denim jacket, grey flannels, black trainers.

Guilt engulfs me. I'm convinced he's the jogger who ran by on the way back from the railway station, and I didn't even second glance him. 'Try the Midland station first.'

'Why?'

I'm not going to admit that guilt to anyone. 'Because it's just round the bloody corner, isn't it?'

I tell him to issue every officer with a photo and the description marked, 'Not to be made public on judge's orders.' Special observations are requested on his mother's home and the hostel where he lives.

'Have any cars been reported missing from the court compound?' he asks.

'Not so far.'

'If he's without wheels, how about extending the watch to the bus terminus across the road from the court?' A logical suggestion I should have thought of. The admin done, I sit back, feeling besieged.

Through this flurry of phone calls, Alice has sat in silence across the desk from me. 'Do you think Packard's escaped to settle the score?' she asks in a deeply troubled tone.

'How could he have worked out who really did it?' A stupid question, I rebuke myself, because he's had sixteen years, most of it banged up in a cell, to think of nothing else.

'If Lennie Gomaz refused to reopen his case, he could have asked for all the old trial papers on file for a DIY defence and he'd have a legal right to them. He could have worked something out we haven't yet.'

'Check with the prison and the hostel,' I urge.

She picks up the green outside phone. I take the cream internal. 'Nothing yet,' blurts Carol, the usher, over-anxiously.

I ask her to tell Mr Gomaz that I'd like to see him when the court rises. 'Meantime,' I go on, 'fetch Inspector Mann from the witness room and put him on, please.'

After a longish wait, 'Yes, sir' comes into my left ear.

'Slip down to see me, will you?'

'What about my witnesses up here?' he protests.

'You've lost the only one that counts, so get down here. Now.' I slam down the phone.

Soon Alice comes off hers. Yes, she reports, the manager of the hostel confirms Packard has loads of legal files in his room. What's more, while living there, he's had a day job at a men's hairdresser's, plying his prison-trained trade; work experience. 'His wages are set against his upkeep.'

'But,' I say, 'a blind eye could be turned to tips.' I run a hand over the back of my blond hair, in dire need of a trim. 'I never take the change from a fiver for a £4.50 cut at my barber's.'

Over time such gratuities could mount into a nice little poke to have stashed away, enough to fund a getaway. Christ, it's going from bad to worse.

A knock on the door, but I don't answer. Instead I phone Control and add the hairdressing salon where Packard works to the places to be watched.

I'm switched to the chief. 'This job you reckoned would be simple enough,' I begin, then brief him and request him to authorise phone taps on Packard's mother's home and workplace.

He reacts cautiously. 'Don't know about that.'

He's dithering because the grapevine has it that the new government aren't as keen on phone taps as the old regime; civil rights and all that. I'll drop the judge's name. 'His Lordship has told us to use our initiative and he'll support us all the way.'

'Righty-oh then,' he says brightly, safe in the knowledge that a New Labour state will keep its hands off a chief constable acting

43

for a member of the judiciary wanting a convicted cop killer back.

After two more unanswered knocks, Inspector Mann walks in, uninvited, expression agitated. 'You wanted me?'

I return the receiver, don't ask him to sit. 'This unresolved business about the motive behind the attack on Linda Dwyer...' I lift my chin to indicate the upstairs courtroom. '...what's that all about?

'Why?' he asks petulantly.

I force myself to stay patient. 'Because Packard is a witness for the prosecution and it's just possible he may have done a runner rather than give evidence.'

'I doubt it.'

'It's got to be considered.' A firmer voice. 'What's it all about?'

The Dwyer woman, he says, still standing, is a sort of sex therapist as well as a beauty consultant. She'd apparently blabbed a bedroom secret of a client.

The unproven theory was that Matthews, her assailant, had been hired to beat her up, or worse. When Matthews returned to the hostel after the attack in the street, he'd said to Packard, 'I was settling a score for my patron.'

He pronounces it the English way – paytron – but I can feel juices working, acid beginning to coat my stomach, burning.

Matthews, Mann is explaining, was at the hostel because he was coming towards the end of a stretch for GBH on a gambler in heavy debt. 'Had him dispatched back to the closed prison as soon as I nicked him,' he adds, self-importantly. 'Been in solitary since.'

'He's been described as a security guard.'

'Yeah. Well.' Mann shrugs. 'More of a minder.'

'Whose?' I ask, already knowing the answer.

'The Frog's.'

Alice shoots me a puzzled look.

'Frenchie Lebois,' I say.

I haven't time to tell her this, but you don't call Lebois 'the Frog' to his face. Frenchie, perhaps, if you're close. Mostly it's 'Pat-ron' – French style. He likes that.

His family originally came over from the Channel Islands in the war and stayed on. He's about fifty now, married with two kids who probably don't know he started out as a henchman himself, collecting debts for a loan shark whose business he took over in a bloody coup.

He's always played on his French name. His Racing Club chain of betting shops got its after a once fashionable Continental soccer club that used to be known as the Arsenal of Paris because they, too, played in red.

He's wealthy enough for three big cars and two homes – a semi-stately one outside the city and a villa in Jersey. Recently it was reported he'd turned down a seven-figure offer from a nationwide firm of bookies for his business.

He's big, very big, in the underworld and very nasty.

I lean back and hold Mann in a steady gaze. 'Let me understand this. Matthews, the mugger, works for Lebois when he's not in jail. He told Packard that he did over the Dwyer woman for his...' I slow down to get the next word just right. '...patron. That will come out in public when Packard gives evidence, right?'

Mann nods unhappily.

'Well, that's a bloody reason for Packard to be scared off, isn't it?'

Mann says nothing.

'So what did you do about Lebois?'

'Sorry?' He's playing for time.

'To tie him in to the assault?'

He shuffles from one foot to the other. 'The Dwyer woman wouldn't confirm that she'd crossed Lebois. She's always passed it off as a random attack.'

'What was the bedroom secret she blabbed?'

'Christ.' A horrified look. 'She's too terrified to talk about it. The beating-up, yes; the motive, no. Everyone's terrified of him.'

Momentarily and darkly, I wonder if Mann is, too – or in the Frog's debt somehow. 'She's still at risk then, is she?'

'We've got her in a safe house. A hotel actually, cheaper than renting a place.'

'Where?'

'The Fairways.'

Alice sniffs, not pleased, I suspect, to be under the same roof as a sex therapist.

I give Mann a bleak look. 'So you did nothing to nail the Frog?'

'Matthews didn't exactly mention Lebois's name to Packard. He refused point blank to talk about it to me. And Crown Prosecution decided not to pursue the motive, satisfied with what I'd got.' A smug smile.

'How did you crack it?'

His smile vanishes. 'Packard. He read about the attack in the *Post* and phoned us to tell us what had been said at the hostel the night before.'

Without facing up to it, Mann is confirming that he did next to nothing. The attack on the Dwyer woman in the street was so appalling it had made the headlines. Mann had got his man, not because of any great detective work, but because of a telephone tip-off.

He'd taken the easy option, like so many second-rate detectives. To pursue it any further – to have proved that Lebois had hired someone to take his revenge and stick a conspiracy charge on him – would have meant time and effort and a bit of courage Mann doesn't possess.

He was overawed in front of the judge. He'd be overawed at the prospect of taking on a formidable foe like Lebois too. He's bottled it. If he's not corrupt, he's incompetent.

I give him a curt nod of dismissal, resolving to transfer him to the most boring of jobs when this case is over – court liaison, perhaps, operating from this cell of a room.

When we are on our own again, I reveal that Lebois was the bookmaker Giles Johnson MP had mentioned as shirt sponsor to the Racing Club of Radford side, Scott Packard's team.

'Intriguing, isn't it,' Alice responds, musingly, 'the way the names keep coming back to that soccer match in '81.'

Even more intriguing, I don't tell her, are these questions that now hang over me like a double-edged sword:

Has Packard escaped to settle the score with the cop killer he's done life for?

Or is he fleeing because he shopped Lebois's henchman and fears for his own life?'

In short, who's in danger – Packard or someone we haven't even begun to identify yet?

6

The door half opens after a timid tap and a bossy 'Come' from Alice.

Carol, the usher, cranes her head through the gap. 'Thought I'd best not let this one get away,' she whispers. She opens the door wider, pirouetting to hold it back.

A smaller, older woman passes in front of her, a lost look on a black, careworn face. She's dressed quaintly – cucumber-framed spectacles, dark brown felt hat that's almost a bonnet, thick fawn coat nearly down to the floor.

'Mrs Packard,' Carol announces formally. I half rise from behind my borrowed desk.

'Nothin' wrong, is there?' says Mrs Packard transferring a woeful gaze from Alice to me.

'No, no.' I throw out an arm towards a grey moulded chair, the usual courthouse issue. 'Sit down, please.'

She walks slowly and sits with feet in heavy, scuffed shoes wide apart. Her long coat is unbuttoned, revealing a gaudy woollen dress beneath. She rests a huge canvas bag on her broad lap, clasps both arms around it and hugs it.

She gazes around the room, an artificially lit bunker really. She won't see much – two desks, three ill-matched lockers, a small littered table with things for making drinks.

I study her while she takes everything in. She's between fifty and sixty; difficult to be more precise.

'I come 'ere to see me son,' she says in a richly honeyed accent. She inclines her head towards the now closed door. 'And that there lady brought me down 'ere.'

'Unfortunately, he isn't in the building right now,' I say, very honestly.

An irked look. 'Said he'd be 'ere.'

'He seems to have gone walkabout.'

She arches her eyebrows. 'Ain't allowed, huh?'

'Not really.' My shoulders work into a slight shrug, not wanting to alarm her. 'Not when he's due to give evidence.'

She sighs. 'Trouble then.' A flatter tone. 'Knew it.'

'Not if we can locate him in the next day or two.' I give her my comforting smile. 'Where do you think he might be?'

A frown ruts her forehead. 'Said he'd be 'ere.'

Scott, she discloses in answer to gentle questioning, often popped round for tea after finishing work at the hairdresser's. Curfew at the hostel wasn't until eight o'clock. He'd told her he'd been due to give evidence today and all about his part in the case. 'Came to keep him company, that's all.'

'Thus far, he's been very helpful to us in this current case.' My sincere smile now.

'Quite right,' she says, sternly. 'Beatin' up on a young lady like that, just walkin' through the street, mindin' her own business.'

'Which is why we can't understand why he's taken off so suddenly.'

She shakes her head deliberately. Me neither, she's saying.

Alice comes in. 'Have you spoken on the phone to your MP this afternoon?'

Another solemn headshake.

'We informed him this lunchtime that Scott's application for a preliminary review of his conviction in '81 has been granted. Mr Johnson said he'd call you.'

'Ain't yet.'

Alice gestures at me. 'We were hoping to see Scott this afternoon to talk about it.'

Mrs Packard blinks behind her spectacles, says nothing.

'So Scott doesn't know we are taking a fresh look at his conviction?' Alice probes on.

'Not if you've not told him.'

Lord, I think, if we'd been allowed to talk to him this morning, he might not have absconded.

Alice continues, 'We know from his application form and talking to Mr Johnson about his sighting at the court of the policeman he believed was dead –'

'Not 'ere,' Mrs Packard interrupts. 'Not in this building.'

Alice smiles sweetly. 'We know. The magistrates court. In May. Did you go that day? Did you see –'

'Weren't there, no. Not that time. I were at the doctor's for me back.' She straightens it slightly, then hunches over her bag again.

'Pity.' Alice pauses. 'What did he do immediately after the sighting?'

'Nothin'. Not immediate.' She pauses. 'Well, he brooded.'

When he came to tea, she says in answer to more questions, she could tell something was wrong. He said little, his mind far away. Eventually, he told her who he had seen. 'That cop they say I killed,' she quotes him as saying.

He wished he'd tackled him in the court foyer there and then, had it out with him, but he'd been so shocked he didn't think fast enough. 'Like seeing a ghost,' he'd said.

The same phrase he'd used with his MP, so there's consistency in what she's telling us.

He'd been back several times to the magistrates court during lunch breaks from the barber's shop, just hanging around outside, but hadn't spotted him again.

'What do you think about it?' asks Alice.

A bland expression. 'Didn't know what to make of it.'

'Had Scott ever questioned his conviction before – you know, protested his innocence?'

Over sixteen years, they'd hardly ever discussed PC Joey Craig's death, it seems, piecing together lots of nods, head-shakes, single-word and one-phrase replies delivered in a sleepy style with lots of pronouns dropped. She's friendly enough, but hard to interview, occasionally as monosyllabic as ex-PC Benson this morning.

I'm gaining the impression that Scott had more or less come to accept the verdict, wanted to keep his nose clean and come out as early as the parole board would allow.

We take her through his graduation to open prison, outside working parties, then home leaves and finally the hostel, Alice concluding, 'So everything was going well as far as it could in those circumstances?'

'Till May and seein' that there policeman.'

Alice beavers on. 'What did you do about that sighting?'

A brief but baleful look. 'Nothin'. I didn't want him rockin' no boats. Hoped he'd be out soon, home, on licence, a year, no more at the most.' A long-suffering sigh. 'He will...still...won't he?'

Alice offers some hope. 'One way or the other.' Then: 'We understand he saw his trial solicitor Mr Lennie Gomaz to report who he'd seen?'

'Took an hour off work, yes. Waste of time.'

'Why?'

'His lawyer thought exact same as me. Let sleepin' dogs lie, he told him. Just get the sentence over with, get out.'

'But Scott didn't want to let sleeping dogs lie?'

She squeezes her eyes shut. 'Didn't like the idea of being called a murderer if he weren't one.'

'Was it you who called in the MP?'

'Scott. Took a Saturday morning off work. I just went with him.'

'But –' I try to come in, but a ringing phone stops me.

The chief PR at HQ doesn't introduce herself when I pick up the receiver. 'Liam Harries,' she says. 'Yes, it was him talking on Radio Trent about this footballer Rob...er...'

I help her. 'Hill.'

'Want me to play over the recording?'

My turn to 'Er' as I look from Alice to Mrs Packard. Both are looking at me, waiting. 'Pop it in my pigeonhole. I'll pick it up later.'

'I've advised the news editor about the current state of play. Thanks very much, she said. They dropped the item. They'll be in touch to find out when it's legally OK to run it again.'

She asks a few chatty questions, seeking an update, and gets 'Yes's' and 'No's' in reply. She takes the hint. 'If you're busy, I'll let you go.'

'But...' I've forgotten what I was about to ask. No matter. Something else has jumped into my mind and it sort of stumbles out. '...in spite of your reservations, you know, about reopening the case and, er, therefore, the possible delay of his full and final release, you did speak in support of a review on the radio this morning.'

'Only natural,' she says simply. 'Any mother would.'

Alice had clearly used the break to think things through and takes her back to the beginning. 'Scott's your second and younger son.'

A nod.

'Campbell your first, three years older, now thirty-five.'

Another nod.

'Campbell Robins.' Alice waits for some clarification. None comes. 'From your first marriage,' she prompts.

'Not married,' Mrs Packard gives her an implacable look, just short of saying: Not that it's any of your business.

'Campbell was present that July night of the riot?'

'Home, yes, if that's what you mean, from college.'

'And he played in that football match earlier in the evening?'

A cautious nod.

'Did he go drinking afterwards?'

'Suppose so. Not much money, though. He were a student in them days.'

'But Scott did have money?'

'Guess you seen his record.'

I haven't, as a matter of fact. I've not studied a single document. I assume she means for petty juvenile crime.

Cammy – as she starts to call Campbell Robins – was home from a university on the east coast. Scott asked him to play in the cup final because his team was a man short. She didn't watch the game, stayed at home in the flats.

She went to bed early, heard all the commotion in the neighbourhood, didn't get up to look. 'Got used to it; always some racket goin' on.'

She heard someone come home, wasn't sure which son. Next she knew was the police raided their flat at dawn. They took Scott away. He was never to return to that flat. When the building was pulled down, she was moved to another block in a quieter part of the city. 'Much nicer.'

I have to get something clear. 'So Cammy wasn't taken in by the police?'

'Wasn't home. Slept at a friend's. They were always stoppin' out, one or other of them.'

'Where did Cammy stay?'

'Liam's, mostly.'

My pulses are stirring. 'Liam Harries, who worked at the local law centre in those days?'

She tilts her head down in a 'Yes.'

Alice and I look intently at each other, me recalling what she'd said only half an hour ago – intriguing, isn't it, the way the same names keep coming back?

And Harries is back in town on the day Packard escapes. Intriguing.

Mrs Packard sniffs. 'Went around together, Liam and Cammy. You know – students and stuff.'

I'm going to nail this down. 'Is this the same Liam Harries who was on the radio news after you this morning?'

'Same.'

'The soccer and showbiz agent.'

A nod.

'You see...' Alice leans forward, expression puzzled. 'We understood Mr Harries legally represented Cammy...'

'He did.'

'When?'

'When Cammy turned soccer pro after college.'

'Not on the day after the riots when lots of local youths were rounded up?'

'Told you.' She raises her voice, just slightly, but for the first time. 'Not Cammy. He was never involved in that trouble.'

52

Alice lapses back into silence and I return, 'Are they still pals – Liam and Cammy?'

'Cammy's been away a long time. Workin'.' She gives me a furtive look, knowing she's not answered the question.

'Where?'

'Turkey. Cyprus.'

'Are Scott and Cammy still close?'

Cammy, she replies, hadn't paid too many prison visits because of his work and his travels. 'They keep in touch. Last Christmas he sent him a bumper book of crosswords.'

Useful for a lifer, I think. 'Did Cammy give a statement to the police?'

'About what?'

'The riots, the policeman's death.'

'Told you.' She tosses her head, irritated. 'He wasn't there. He had a drink after the match, then went off. He was upset about it, wished, like everyone else, it had never happened. He didn't stay around too long afterwards; couldn't because of his studies.'

I can't help wondering if there's something about Cammy she doesn't want us to know. 'This was July. He was on vacation. It was the long summer holiday.'

'He had to go on a field trip. Jersey.'

Jersey? Makes no sense. 'What was he studying?'

'Marine biology. Got a first.' A glint of pride now in those sad brown eyes.

'But he still took up professional football, I understand.'

'For a while. It was better money. He was good. Very good. Both boys were.' She names two not-so-good teams Cammy played for down south, then one I'd never heard of. 'Istanbul,' she explains helpfully.

Turkey, where the has-beens and no-hopers often wind up, I muse. 'Is he still playing?'

'Only part-time. He's doing what he was trained for – working in a lab.'

I get to ask again, 'Where is he now?'

'Cyprus.'

Northern Cyprus with a Turkish career behind him, bound to be, I realise. 'So it's doubtful that Scott has taken off to see Cammy then?'

'Wouldn't have the money, now would he?' she replies, smiling bleakly.

A silly question, I chide myself, because he wouldn't have a passport either.

I slip a visiting card from my pen pocket and a pen from an inside pocket, copy the number from the green phone, add my portable's. Handing the card to her, I say, 'If he gets in touch, ask him to ring me, will you?'

If he gets in touch with her, I'll hear almost as soon as she does from Surveillance, but it looks less sneaky this way.

She studies the card, frowning, as if she's having difficulty focusing.

Focus? I ask myself with a start. Photos. That's right. Newspaper photos. And I find the question I was rummaging for in the bedroom of my mind on the way here.

'Back in '81, this case was all over the papers,' I begin.

'Not half,' she agrees with a sigh.

'Including photos of the dead policeman and one that was injured.'

A nod.

'So why didn't Scott say then, "Eh, this is the policeman I hit, not the dead one"?'

She gives it long thought and the answer comes slowly in bits and pieces. Taken together, her explanation is that there had been no remand facilities for juveniles locally then. He was held in a secure youth unit outside the county.

Yes, I point out patiently, but the case made all the nationals, not just the local papers.

More deep thought and finally it comes back. 'We didn't know straight off but they don't get papers free inside. You have to order 'em from the nearest newsagent to be delivered and pay for 'em. He'd been inside a couple of weeks or more before he asked me to fix it up.'

By which time the great wave of publicity would have been over, I have to accept. Then again. 'But both policemen's photos reappeared in the papers during the trial months later.'

'Yes, but I cancelled the order while the hearing was on.'

'Why?'

'His solicitor said so.'

'Mr Gomaz?'

A nod.

'Why?'

A puzzled headshake. 'You'd best ask him.'

We will, madam, I decide. We will.

7

A call on the cream phone: Carol, the usher, reporting that the judge has risen earlier than expected.

Climbing the stairs we pass the mugger's support group from the public gallery coming down. The man with the pony tail is taking the flight up to the cafeteria that's called Rumpole's Food Court.

Lawrence Gomaz is on a long seat outside court number 1. Next to him is his young barrister. Their heads are over bundles of papers on their knees.

Gomaz is doing nearly all the talking. Alice and I hang back, just out of earshot. He knows we want to see him because Carol has told him, but he talks on and on, flicking backwards and forwards in his file.

Nothing better to do, I test Alice's memory of the paperwork. Yes, she confirms immediately, Packard did have a record as a juvenile – shoplifting and snatching a handbag from the back seat of a moving car. She still frets about not being able to find the name of Cammy Robins anywhere in the documents.

I worry about how far I can push Gomaz. He lodges misconduct complaints against officers like a traffic warden scattering parking tickets. With the clock ticking on this job, I can't afford the time, the admin, the distraction of that sort of trouble.

The barrister gets up, clutching his dossier to his chest. Though it's only four fifteen, they exchange 'Goodnights' and he walks towards the stairs.

Gomaz beckons us, rather imperiously, then drops his head back over his papers. We approach, stop side by side and stand over him. He makes us wait a moment or two before looking up. 'You want to see me?'

He has a ruggedly handsome face, deeply dimpled chin and strong cheekbones, like roughly carved ebony.

Already I don't like his cocky attitude, so I won't say 'Please.' I give my rank and name, but only Alice's name. He pats the seat the barrister has just vacated. I sit next to him, she next to me.

'I saw you in chambers at lunchtime,' he says. 'I know Inspector Mann, of course, but . . .' His voice trails before he adds: 'Not you.' Then: 'Have you found him yet?'

I don't grant him a headshake, but go straight in. 'You know Packard, of course, having represented him at his trial for murder in '81.'

There's an instant's hesitation before he nods.

'And, in today's hearing, you're on opposite sides,' I continue.

Broad shoulders within a well-fitted silvery grey suit work upwards into a shrug. Happens in this business, he's telling me. He puts the pile of documents on the bench between us and stretches out long legs in sharply pressed trousers, laid back.

'He also came to see you four or five months ago, regarding reopening his '81 case,' I go on.

Still silent, he seems to be studying his buffed, black shoes, giving nothing away.

'We have spoken to his mother and his MP,' I reveal. I go silent, to force him to say something.

His head comes up and round. 'Well, since you already know, yes. He claimed to have seen the policeman he was accused of killing, wanted the conviction quashed and compensation, the usual, you know.'

'You advised against?'

An airy, dismissive little hand gesture. 'I urged the pragmatic view. You know the background?'

'A bit of it,' I reply.

56

'From the moment of his arrest, Packard always conceded...'
He pinches one thumb with the other thumb and index finger.
'...a, he was drunk; b, he looted a tent clamp from a shop; c, he was pursued from the scene; d, he struck out with said object when cornered and in panic...'

He pinches his little finger. '...e, the recipient of that blow died.'

He crosses one leg over the other at the ankle. 'Now, having accepted that for sixteen years, to suddenly disown responsibility for that act is, in my opinion, going to delay rather than accelerate release, and I told him so.'

In a melodious voice, easy on the ear, he launches into a little lecture on the policy of parole boards in dealing with lifers. They want proof that a prisoner has come to terms with his offence, learned his lesson before they will consider letting him go. 'Being in denial is a huge bar to release.'

Must make it hard on someone who's really innocent, I muse. The ultimate 'Catch 22'. You lie and say you did it when you didn't and you're out. You tell the truth and say you didn't do it when you didn't, and, tough, they keep you in. I'll not toss that in, not wanting a debate about the shortcomings of the penal system.

Instead, I go back a bit. 'You were present at the magistrates court defending your current client when Packard claims to have made the sighting of the murder victim, very much alive.'

He smiles and puts on a broad northern accent, not making a very good job of it. 'Hear all, say nowt section.'

It's a legal catch-phrase for old-fashioned committal proceedings. Magistrates normally rubber stamp the file for trial. 'Hear all' means a full dress rehearsal of the evidence of prosecution witnesses. Few defendants request it these days. Mostly they are prisoners who fancy a change of scene from their cells. 'Say nowt' means that the accused reserves his defence and the media can't report what they hear.

'Did you see the ex-policeman Packard reports spotting in the court foyer?' I ask.

'No, and there's another weakness. If he'd come to me straight away and said, "Look who I've just seen," it could have made the world of difference. But he didn't.'

He's speaking fluently, full of himself, and I'm going to have to dent his confidence a bit.

'A bit hard, that, don't you think?' I smile and pinch a thumb. 'A, he was in shock, thought he'd seen a ghost; b, you were representing his adversary in this current case; c, he'd think you'd changed sides.'

Gomaz gives me a hard, sidelong look, says nothing.

Alice chips in. 'My Commissioners –'

He breaks in, rather pompously. 'And who might they be?'

Alice tells him. 'We have granted him his review.'

He inches himself up and out of his languid pose. 'My advice was to get out first on licence and sort it out afterwards.'

He's uneasy now, shifting his ground and no wonder. Here's a potential miscarriage of justice case that most civil rights' solicitors would kill for. Packard had requested a rerun. Inside an hour Gomaz had sent him packing.

Using just a bit of guile, he could have tracked down ex-PC Tony Benson, like we did, and worked out that Packard might be on to something. He is not covering himself with legal glory here, and he knows it.

Alice leans a little way across me. 'The defence at his '81 trial was, as I understand it, self-defence.'

'With a degree of provocation thrown in,' he replies. 'He wasn't to know his pursuers were policemen and they were shouting racist abuse.'

He sets his jaw firmly, as if anticipating an objection, some closing of ranks. I raise none. Instead, 'He thought they were National Front, you mean.'

'They were stirring things,' he says icily, 'as you might recall.'

'According to my reading of the transcript,' says Alice pedantically, 'the possibility of mistaken identity between the dead and the surviving policemen wasn't raised.'

He works his mouth. 'Not by Packard, either. That was the way leading silk – and we had the very best QC – decided to play it in court.'

Now he's distancing himself from a flawed and losing tactic. 'How did you get the brief to defend Packard in the first place?' I ask.

'I'd represented him before in a few minor matters.'

'He came to you at the law centre about his shoplifting and handbag snatching, you mean?'

Gomaz looks down and away from me, picking up his papers, a signal that he wants to go. His cockiness gone, he's on the defensive. 'I don't quite see how this is helping you find him now.'

'It's just possible...in our view...' I cock a thumb at Alice. '...that he's taken your advice – sorting it out from the outside.' I pause. 'Unfortunately, without waiting for parole.'

Head down, he continues to collect his papers.

'We're going to have to go right back to that football match and the celebrations that preceded the riot.' Tersely, I add, 'No stone unturned. Judge's orders.'

He returns the dossier to the bench, getting the message that I'll report him to the judge if he doesn't co-operate.

Yes, he was at the match, he confirms, offhandedly. 'As a spectator,' he adds.

'Running the line, we've been told.'

He stops, either thinking or worried. 'I believe I was.' He makes up his mind. 'Yes, I was.'

I'll drop in another name now. 'With Mr Liam Harries on the other line?'

He shakes his head firmly. 'He was playing. That's why I went to watch in the first place. He was a chum of mine.' A flicker of enlightenment crosses his face. 'That's right, I got roped in to officiate.'

'Who did Mr Harries play for?'

'The Irish side, can't recall its name. His family comes from Dublin.'

He explains he and Harries were law students together at the university. I ask when and discover that their last year overlapped with my first, studying music with a conspicuous lack of success. I don't point it out, just work out they'll both be mid-forties.

'After coming down,' he goes on, 'we stayed on in the city and worked together in the law centre.'

'Mr Harries wasn't unemployed when he played in the Unemployed League cup final?' Alice checks.

59

Gomaz smiles nostalgically. 'He might as well have been on the money we were on.' He and Harries went separate ways when the law centre became redundant after the flats were pulled down and most of their customers moved out – 'those who weren't already in jail.' He laughs lightly. 'We lost touch, but I hear he's doing well.'

'As legal eagle to the stars, including Rob Hill,' I say.

He gives me a bemused look.

'Irish international. Played with Mr Harries in the same side in '81.'

A smiling little shake of his head. 'Always had an eye for talent.' He eyes me. 'Sporting talent.'

Gomaz says he doesn't follow football these days – what with the practice, his family and his work for the local council and Labour Party.

I was wondering when he'd hint at a direct line to the corridors of powder.

He hadn't heard Harries on the radio this morning, he adds, didn't realise he was back in town. 'I'm a Radio Four man.'

Again I steer him back to the night of the riots. He's adamant he didn't go to the celebrations that followed the cup final, but back to the law centre.

'Was Harries there?' I ask.

'He went to the party, I suppose.'

'With Cammy Robins?'

Another blank look.

'Scott Packard's half-brother,' I remind him. 'College boy and promising footballer in those days.'

'Liam was always a bit of a sporting groupie; too tubby to be much good himself. Yes, they might have been out and about together that night. They often were.'

The first he knew about the troubles in and around the flats was when he was called out from home to the police station in the middle of the night, he claims, when some of the rioters started demanding their right to legal representation.

'Total chaos. Drunks. Some with their shirts torn. Chaos. Lots were roped in. Only half a dozen or so were ever charged.'

'And everyone got off apart from Scott,' I put in.

He puts on an extremely sour face.

Two cleaners in green overalls who have been hovering over their Hoovers for some time decide to start work on the deep blue carpet at the other end of the long landing.

At this distance, the drone isn't conversation-drowning but Gomaz seizes his chance. 'We ought to get out of their way, I suppose.'

He retrieves his papers from beside him and stands. With the slightest of bows, not much more than a nod, towards Alice, he politely wishes us good luck and goodnight and turns on his highly polished heels.

We sit back for a moment or two watching him go, me cursing myself.

I should have marched him downstairs and continued the interview. There's lots more I need to know, not least why he ordered Scott's mother to cancel his newspaper for the duration of the trial.

I'd have liked to have bounced off him the alternative theory that Packard is on the run from his current client's confederates. I'd like to know, too, if Frenchie Lebois is a client.

We'd softened him up. Now I've let him off the hook because I can't get to grips with this case, don't know which way to turn, not because his reputation and his contacts scare me. That's what I tell myself, but I'm not sure I believe it.

I'd have liked to question him about his tactics in the on-going trial. Why hide the prison background of the accused? Nothing the mugger has done could be as bad as Packard's record.

If you want to discredit a witness, what better opening question than: 'Isn't it true that you are serving life for murdering a policeman?'

Imagine the effect of that on the jury, being asked to believe a cop killer. Imagine, too, Packard replying: 'Yes, but I didn't do it' – and naming in public the man who did. Imagine what the media would make of that.

Gomaz, I'm coming to believe, doesn't want the truth to come out.

61

Packard's attic room at the prison hostel is small and untidy with so many big padded bags on a chipped sideboard and a small cabinet beside a made-up single bed.

The manager was visibly shocked when we broke the news on the doorstep that he had a resident on the run. 'Not him, surely?' he'd said when he let us into what's two Victorian terraced houses knocked into one. 'Doing real well, he is, no trouble at all,' he'd said as he led us upstairs.

Now he is standing at the opened door watching Alice fingering through photostats in the overstuffed envelopes.

I ask questions while searching through drawers. 'When did you last see him?'

'Breakfast.'

If Packard had been warned off giving evidence at the crown court today, he tells me, he'd never reported it and no heavies had called at the hostel, making threats.

'Any visitors at all?' I ask.

'Some black guy with dreadlocks, don't know his name, but he's a pal.'

'When was he last here?'

'A couple of weeks ago.'

All I've found in the drawers are 'O' level certificates, hairdressing diplomas, a few photos, his mother's among them, but mainly of schoolboy soccer sides, reminders of his wasted chances in life, no bank book or letters from his half-brother in Northern Cyprus.

The manager is unsure whether Packard has taken a change of clothes, but there's a red Forest sports bag on the threadbare carpet.

Next to it is a black ghetto-blaster plugged into the only socket in the room. I pick it up and examine the dial. It's tuned to 96FM – Radio Trent.

So, I reason with mounting anxiety, after listening to his mum and MP on the breakfast news, Packard would have heard that Robbie Hill and Liam Harries are back in town.

On the way back to HQ, three impounded envelopes on her knees, Alice announces that her plan is to sort through his documents. She wants to compare them with her own files, discover what he's got that she hasn't. She pats the bags. 'The answer, I'm sure, is in here.'

So much has happened today, one thing after another, that we've not really talked since we drove here. I've had no time to size her up, hardly know anything about her, the way her mind works.

'We can't take it for granted,' I counter, 'that Packard has gone on the run to prove his innocence.'

'Of that I've no doubt,' she replies without a second's thought.

'What?' I'm so astonished that I snap it. 'That he's innocent or he's on the run to prove it?'

'Both,' she comes back immediately. 'He's bound to feel let down by the justice system.'

'Well.' I pause to rein back my temper. 'If he is innocent of PC Craig's murder, he's guilty of attacking Tony Benson and you saw the state that left him in.'

'I realise that,' she says, much quieter.

But not until it was pointed out, I realise. 'And if he is innocent, then someone else killed Joey Craig.'

'That's not the issue here.'

Now I do lose my temper. 'It bloody well is for me. Don't think for one moment I'm going to go to Craig's family and say, "Sorry, we're letting Packard out because he didn't kill your son, but we don't know who did." If he comes out, someone else is going in to take his place.'

We travel some miles in silence that's anything but companionable. Then I try again. 'There's still the possibility he's in hiding from Frenchie Lebois's heavies; nothing whatever to do with '81.'

I suggest dinner at the hotel with Linda Dwyer to find out what she knows.

'What can she possibly know?' Alice asks, that scornful expression again.

Christ, she hadn't been listening to Inspector Mann or even me talking to the manager at the hostel.

'She blabbed a bedroom secret about Lebois,' I remind her. 'He hired a hitman to get even. Packard shopped the hitman.

Maybe Lebois is out to settle with Packard and that's why he's on the run. We have to quiz her.'

'Oh, I don't know,' she says with a tired sigh.

'It's got to be checked out.'

She says nothing.

'OK, then,' I compromise, 'let's make it a foursome, and I'll invite the retired detective who took Packard's statement in 1981. That way we cover both angles.'

'All right,' she agrees, as I drop her off at the Fairways Hotel, wishing I'd never bothered – with trying to get to know her, with dinner, with this whole fucking case.

At my desk, alone at last – and very grateful for it – I listen to the sports interview that sneaked by me over breakfast, the recording of which the PR had left in my pigeonhole.

Liam Harries talks in an accent that owes little to his mother's native land, more transatlantic; phoney.

Rob Hill's a free agent, he's explaining, having completed his contract in Italy. 'He wants to return to the region where he learned the game, put something back.'

Only for mega money, I think, cynically.

Hill is having talks at Filbert Street, looking at the Leicester City set-up this afternoon. Tomorrow morning he has meetings with Forest executives and on Sunday he's going to watch his old club Derby County play at their new stadium.

There are, he adds, other lucrative options open to Hill and they're flying off to Spain on Monday to explore them.

A bit of financial arm-twisting, that, I detect, negotiations via the media.

Harries talks for a while about Hill's happy memories of the old Baseball Ground, now, sadly, no more.

'Is that where you first met?' asks the interviewer.

'Oh, no,' replies Harries. 'We go back even further – to local youth soccer in this city. I've handled all his moves since.'

They yarn a little about the places Hill has played, the honours and caps for Ireland he's won.

Harries undertakes to keep listeners in touch with developments and half promises to have Hill personally in the studios tomorrow lunchtime after his talks at Forest.

'He would have come this morning, but he's looking up old friends,' Harries concludes.

Not Scott Packard, I hope, or I'm going to look very silly, not having a tail on Hill, too.

I switch off, phone Witness Protection, ask them to date Linda Dywer on my behalf and book a quiet table for four at her hotel for eight thirty. Then I call the PR and request a quick check on Dwyer's press cuttings.

Finally I phone Jacko Jackson, buttering him up. 'I need to pick your brains.'

A real reversal of roles, this. Normally he picks mine. In retirement he's writing crime novels. His first series was roughly based on his own experiences in CID; his second on mine with names and locations changed and literary licence liberally applied. Risky, I suppose. If it ever came out, it would ruin my chance of making chief, but then Jacko did save my life.

'About what?' he asks, playing hard to get.

I'll tell him over drinks at eight, I promise, just the two of us. 'Then there's dinner in it for you.' Tantalisingly, I add, 'With a sex therapist.'

His books lack steamy sex scenes. That, I kid him, is because, at fifty-six, he belongs to a generation that kept the lights off and their string vests on. Being a Lincolnshire lad, he thinks a gobbler is a turkey.

'Done,' he says, the sucker.

Oiling the bare bottom of the great love of my life after a long bath together and a naked romp on a thick, warm towel, I'm annoyingly interrupted by the wife calling, 'Phone.'

I help Laura on with her bath robe – white with little black rams dotted about. It's far too big for her, but the shop at Derby didn't have her size. She'll grow into it.

Still naked, I pick her up, hand her to her mother and pad on across the landing to the bedroom and the phone. It's the PR with the Dwyer stuff, not much of it; doesn't take long.

My newly pressed fawn job, I decide, looking in the wardrobe, with cream shirt and old college tie.

I'm running a bit late and I still have a huge decision to make. Thomas the Tank Engine tonight? Or Postman Pat again?

Thomas, I think. Laura's getting a bit bored with him, but he's my favourite.

8

With a resounding clink, my second favourite author sets down an empty half-pint glass on the fake marble top of the cosy back bar at the Fairways Hotel.

Your round, Jacko Jackson is telling me as I walk up, apologising for being late.

He is wearing a thickish grey suit, his only suit, which has not visited the dry cleaners recently. He explains that his wife had dropped him off and returned home to supervise their teenage son's homework. 'English Lit; not so hot at that myself.'

'Hear, hear,' I second, and he laughs, never able to take his second career over-seriously.

He switches to a more expensive gin and tonic. He sees no point in going to the trouble of avoiding drink-driving if he's not going to drink and, if it's free, drink rapidly. I order a Perrier water to go on to the dinner bill.

He pulls a high, round stool into position and sits down, peering disapprovingly at my drink over the rim of steel-framed bifocals. 'On duty, eh?'

'The Joey Craig case,' I say, no need for further explanation about a job that every police officer in the service at the time will remember.

His face is unusually immobile, giving nothing away.

66

'The Criminal Cases Review Commission is taking a fresh look,' I continue.

He fishes for his cigarettes, takes one from a gold packet and lights up. It's not a signal that he's worried. He smokes forty a day.

'Nothing wrong with the paperwork,' I go on soothingly. 'No Bridgewater-type trouble' – a reference to a recent appeal court case with allegations of malpractices over statements.

No detective, past or present, likes an old inquiry being exhumed and trawled through. He covers up any feeling of relief by hissing through a cloud of smoke, 'I should hope not.'

It's a simple case of Scott Packard now claiming that he hit Tony Benson, not PC Craig, I go on, briefing him about the sighting at the magistrates court.

I'm half expecting some protestation on the lines of 'It was still an appalling injury that ended Benson's career' – the objection I raised with Alice in the car.

Should have known better, I chide myself, as his eyes glint behind his spectacles and he draws in on his cigarette.

'What is it – fifteen years . . .' He stops, does some mental maths. '. . . more, sixteen, for something he didn't do? What a yarn.'

Unfeeling sod, I grumble to myself. 'You're premature, as usual. No one can say that yet.'

'But,' he says slowly, 'if that's the way it works out . . .' He lets it hang there, short of saying, 'You know the deal.'

The deal is that I put the tale on tape and he works it into a book for his new series. 'First,' I tell him, 'you're going to have to sing for your supper.'

He hadn't been on duty that night, he begins, he was called in with scores of other detectives from outlying stations when the hospital certified PC Craig as dead in the early hours. A massive police operation began.

He was a constable himself then, hadn't even visited the scene, and had no wish to. He knew of Craig and Benson. They were spotters for the Snatch Squad, a tactic devised in the winter of discontent two and a half years earlier.

Undercover officers were detailed to mingle with demonstrators at peaceful rallies and join them in the pubs afterwards.

Trouble usually flared after boozy sessions and the task of the spotters was to get close enough to listen to the plots being hatched for strengthening, often illegally, the picket lines and to identify ringleaders.

These same tactics were used three years later in the miners' strike with spotters in NCB donkey jackets and wearing 'Support the Strike' badges.

They would relay the strikers' plans, descriptions and movements of potential troublemakers to the Snatch Squad, lying in wait, out of sight, equipped with headgear, shields, batons and sometimes dogs and horses.

On command, the squad would wade into the picket lines and snatch away targeted leaders, sometimes before any aggro had begun, thereby provoking it. In my view, they often caused more trouble than they prevented.

It was before the days of routine tape recordings and he took the notes when Scott Packard was interviewed by a long-retired superintendent – 'an honest cop'.

'Why was he arrested?' I ask.

Another team of detectives had worked through the night on a neighbourhood canvas. 'Someone reported seeing a white man in civvies being hit by a young black guy wearing a football jersey. Red, I think it was. Can't remember the number. But he...' He stops again in thought. '...maybe it was she.... anyway he or she gave us the number on the back of the shirt.'

He shrugs, easy-going. 'Just a question of getting hold of the team sheet from the match and working out who played for whom and in what numbered jersey.'

Packard was arrested and brought in. He was heavily hung over from the post-match party the night before and was given time to recover. He was questioned under caution in the presence of his probation officer and a young black solicitor.

'Packard denied he'd smashed the window of the shop between the pub and the flats,' Jacko recalls, 'but he admitted he took a tent clamp on display. Wasn't really able to explain why, except that he was pissed and everyone else seemed to be helping themselves.'

In claiming his spoils, he got separated from his gang and was chased by two men in civvies shouting threats and abuse.

'His defence was that he thought they were fascist thugs,' I remind him.

'You know what these things were like,' he replies evasively.

'Were Benson and Craig racist?'

'Other independent witnesses confirmed that some things they heard being shouted might well have been heard at a Ku Klux Klan meeting,' he answers, still obliquely.

I'm going to have to nail him down. 'So they were?'

'So they say,' he concedes unhappily.

In a written, signed statement made after the formal interview, Packard said one pursuer peeled off to chase someone else and one kept on his heels.

He tried to shake him off down a side street with a couple of alleys, then ran to the flats, stopping for breath at the end of a passageway into the courtyard. His pursuer came round the corner, brandishing what he thought was a cosh, so he lashed out with his souvenir, knocked him down and ran home.

'Where Forensics later found the tell-tale shirt?' I check.

'Haven't you read the bloody papers?' he bridles.

'No,' I bridle back. 'I only got the job less than twelve hours ago. And since then Packard's done a runner.' I tell him of my day.

'Jesus,' he says sympathetically. 'Well, yes. The shirt was the only real forensic evidence. Without the eyewitness and his statement there wasn't much of a case.'

'How did he react under questioning?'

'Pretty frank and honest, thick really, scared certainly. No violence in his record, as I recall. It was the old story – booze and blind panic, wrong time, wrong place for both of them.'

I tell him about well-read Alice and her view that Packard was unlucky not to get away with manslaughter.

Jacko doesn't offer an opinion. He didn't attend the trial because the statement he took down was not disputed, and he didn't see how Packard shaped up in the witness box.

I sense I've milked him dry. 'Let's join the ladies.'

69

Small wonder that Linda Dwyer has put on the inches since she reigned as a beauty queen.

She's polished off a big plate of whitebait and already downed two glasses of white wine, a hock she selected herself and which smells as sweet as her overpowering scent. Already there's no room to spare in a pale pink silk dress that seems to have been spun *in situ*.

Only Jacko is keeping pace with her. Being under witness protection hasn't affected her appetite, particularly for tongue-loosening booze, I'm happy to note.

Alice and I settled for Perriers and melon. She left hers half-eaten. The first-course chat was mainly about the hotel, Linda comparing it unfavourably with other places she'd stayed, most of them in London and abroad.

A highly exaggerated story from Jacko about a massage parlour he'd used while in a seedy hotel on an undercover job kept the conversation from lapsing into silence.

Linda laughed happily at it. Alice barely smiled. Given the choice, I already know who I'd rather have dinner for two with – not with sex in mind, thanks all the same, just fun.

The PR's digging revealed that Linda had been a village shopgirl. She entered her first contest for 'a lark' at the suggestion of her fiancé, a farm worker. One win led to another and soon she was on the national circuit. Somewhere along the line the fiancé dropped out of the news stories about her and, presumably, out of her life.

By twenty, she was being photographed dating long-forgotten showbiz stars ten to twenty years older and giving interviews about plans for a TV career.

Two years later, a swimsuit business in which she was involved went bankrupt and she dropped out of the news herself. I can only guess what's happened to her since – sugar daddies who became older and less generous and sunspots that became less exotic and lots of hard, lonely times in between. Sad, really, but she doesn't seem to have let it get her down.

From what I've gleaned from odd remarks dropped into conversations on our travels, Alice comes from a professional family in Cheshire – dad a solicitor, mum a doctor. She's not uttered a word about her social life and I haven't inquired, doubting that she has much of one.

When the plates have been cleared, Linda folds her hands on the starched white tablecloth. 'What about you then, luv?' she asks Alice, very chummily. 'Got a fella then?'

'Er.' Alice, in a Princess of Wales check jacket and a black skirt below the knees, stalls. 'No.'

'Keep 'em at arm's length, I say.' Linda chuckles warmly to herself.

Alice is not enjoying this, makes no attempt at banter. Instead she looks at me, a prissy look: Do something, she's ordering.

'Drink?' I ask Linda. She pushes a fresh glass towards me, telling me: Red. I fill it near to the top from an expensive bottle Jacko chose. He picks it up but is interrupted in the task of filling his new glass by the arrival of the main courses – roast duck for all but Alice who has selected cheese omelette; might have known she'd be a veggie.

I give Linda the line I gave Jacko. 'We'd like to pick your brains. About Scott Packard. Know him?'

Between mouthfuls, she tells me she'd never met him before he gave evidence when the case was committed for trial by the magistrates. She hadn't seen him again until today. Then, chin up: 'Why?'

'Because he did a runner at lunchtime.'

She chews on what must be news to her, because witnesses half-way through their evidence, as she was this morning, are kept apart from those due to follow. A worried expression adds a few more lines to a face that's attractive, but well lived-in. 'Will that affect the outcome?'

'Not if we can find him before Monday,' I reply breezily.

Alice stops nibbling. 'It's quite a strong case without him anyway.'

My turn for an urgent glance to tell her: Keep quiet. Turning back to Linda, I go on, 'When you were together this morning, waiting in the witness room, did he seem worried, nervous in any way?'

'We hardly spoke. Just nodded. He was reading a soccer mag. Why should he be worried?'

'Because it's possible someone doesn't want him to give his evidence and that's why he's gone AWOL.'

She eats more slowly, says nothing, digesting it.

'On the other hand...' Alice has not got my message. '...he could have gone on the run to prove his innocence.'

Jesus, this woman is a pain, I groan to myself. She knows the only aim tonight is to get Linda talking about Frenchie Lebois.

It's no surprise that Linda is looking baffled. 'Of what?'

'Killing a policeman in a riot years back,' Jacko puts in.

'Good God.' Linda grips her knife and fork. She knew he had been in prison for something, she says, because her assailant was in the same hostel, and she put two and two together. 'But not that. What happened?'

Alice eats with closed lips. Having introduced the topic she's now uncertain how much to tell.

Often, I've found, when you give something – share a secret on trust, for instance – you get much more back. Let's see if it works on her. 'In the strictest of confidences, OK?'

Linda nods, conspiratorially.

During the rest of the course, accompanied by two more red wines for Linda and Jacko, heavily doctored details are disclosed about the '81 case, no other names mentioned.

Jacko chips in by explaining how Packard was caught after the neighbour spotted a black youth in a red soccer strip felling an older white man.

Alice finally judges it safe to make a contribution. 'That witness was offered to the defence, but wasn't called.'

Fascinated, as most people are, with an inside story, Linda asks what she means.

Showing off her expertise, Alice explains that witnesses the police dig up in the course of their inquiries can be called by the prosecution and defence. If there's no dispute about their evidence, their statements can be read out to the jury, no questions asked. 'Her evidence wasn't challenged.'

Jacko comes back. 'Happened to me. There was no dispute about his confession so I didn't have to attend the trial.'

'So what's this Packard guy's beef now, then?' Linda asks, understandably.

I tell her briefly about the sighting at the magistrates court. Linda herself couldn't recall anyone resembling Tony Benson hanging around the foyer that lunchtime.

Soon, mercifully, Alice pushes back her chair, tosses her napkin on a plate that's only half empty and excuses herself with, 'More reading, I'm afraid.'

I nod, relieved, but don't rise, thinking: Now I can get down to the real reason for this incredibly expensive meal.

Immediately, the atmosphere relaxes, aided by the port Jacko and Linda are drinking with the cheese board.

'So, you see, we have to decide why Packard's disappeared – to prove his innocence or because of threats about your case. It would help to narrow down where to look for him.'

'Has he had any threats?' she asks in a warm, local accent that's growing thicker all the time.

'Dunno,' I reply, honestly. 'You have, I gather?'

'Not half.' A cloud passes over her face. 'That's why I'm holed up here.' She shakes her head heavily, wafting her blonde hair. 'Me and my big mouth.'

'It's possible that Frenchie Lebois doesn't want Packard repeating in the witness box what your attacker told him...' I pause to make sure she's following. '...you know, mentioning the word "Patron".'

She frowns. 'That came out in his evidence at the magistrates court months ago.'

'Yes, but...' In Alice's absence, I'll have to act as legal adviser, explaining that the defence had not asked for reporting restrictions at the committal proceedings to be lifted, so the media could only run the barest details.

'But, in the crown court,' I go on, 'they can report anything they like. It's open season. If that line about "for the Patron" gets in the papers, everyone will know it's a reference to Frenchie. He'll not like that.'

She nods, very gravely. 'Neither will his wife.'

'We'll treat anything you tell us in the same confidence I know you'll respect over Packard's case review and disappearance.'

Moodily, she swills what's left in her bulbous glass. 'It's down to this.' She sighs deeply. 'Booze.'

She'd got to know Lebois at a party after a racetrack charity meeting, she begins soberly.

For two years she'd been what she describes as 'catering for his needs'. Her blue eyes widen. 'I've met some weirdos in my time but...' She can't find the right words yet to express herself.

She coughs twice, tiny growls in the back of the throat to clear it, and explains how they 'did it' in a manager's flat above a Racing Club shop every Friday evening. 'When his wife was at the synagogue.'

He gave her a key and she'd let herself in. He was always there ahead of her. 'The same routine.'

She hurries through the routine...the handcuffs...the tight-fitting Latex mask...the slits for the eyes...the hole with a zip for the mouth fastened so tightly that only a narrow tube could be fitted in.

I've never come across a case personally, because they are rarely exposed. This sort of thing – perversions, sex games, call them what you like – can end up in tragedy. Men and, sadly, kids in puberty discover, God knows how, that restricting the oxygen to the brain can produce for them a sexual surge like electricity. Mistime it, too much restriction, and it's fatal.

Humanely, the media skate over most of the mind-boggling details that emerge at inquests, unless the victim is someone like an MP – and then it all comes out.

Linda holds nothing back...finger on the open end of the tube...reading his head movements to control the flow of air...grateful nods for 'More'...frantic shakes to tell her to take her finger away.

Without a trace of a smile, she goes on, 'When his manhood was really a-throbbing...'

A quaint Mills and Boon style phrase, that, for a woman of the world, I think, holding off a smile.

'...I'd get across him.'

With a look of total resignation, she shakes her head. Defeats me, she's saying.

I won't ask her how much she got paid. All I can assume is that her presence and participation stopped it from becoming solo auto-eroticism, a dangerous and elaborate form of masturbation; an attempt to normalise it, in Frenchie's view, anyway.

She finishes her port. 'My mistake was getting a bit drunk nightclubbing and telling a so-called friend. She shopped me to Frenchie, the cow. Now she's his regular.'

'What did Frenchie do about it?' I ask, quietly.

'Went ape, phoned up threatening all sorts. Took off with another girlfriend to Spain, I did, just to get out of it for a while. When I got back there were messages on the machine demanding his key back. Evidence of our arrangement, you see.'

She stops while coffee is poured. She sugars hers. 'I was on my way to post the key when I got ambushed. He grabbed for my shoulder bag. Stupid me, I hung on. If he'd said who he was, who he worked for, what he wanted, I'd have given it to him, and good riddance. Instead, he beat seven bells out of me and he enjoyed it. And, believe me, I know about these things.'

I believe her.

In hospital, her jaw wired, eyebrow stitched, arm in plaster, she gave Inspector Mann none of this background, terrified for her life.

When Packard later gave his account, including the attacker's quote, 'for the Patron', Mann went back to see her. Again she refused to implicate Lebois. Mann didn't push it.

'What's your feeling, then?' I ask. 'Could Lebois be after Packard?'

She considers the question carefully. 'Well, yes, maybe, if the poor little sod is going to drop that nickname out in public, then, maybe, yes, he's in trouble. Never thought of that.'

She drops her head and clasps her hands on the tablecloth. Sharing her story has drained her. She's clearly in deep, deep trouble with Lebois, a vicious villain, and fears for her future.

Jacko pats her hands, just the once. 'Don't worry.' He jerks his head at me. 'He'll sort it.'

His own hands go to his stomach. 'Good meal, that. Always feel a bit guilty, really, when I've eaten that well.'

I know what's coming – an oft-told boyhood tale, totally fabricated, of his mother dispatching him to the butcher's to get a sheep's head to boil that ends, 'And make sure the eyes are in so it'll see us through the week.'

She laughs through a stream of his ancient stories and is smiling when she leaves us at the lift with a chaste kiss for Jacko and a lingering handshake for me.

Waiting by reception for his taxi, charged to Witness Protection, I josh Jacko, 'Fancy a bit of that tomorrow night?'

'No,' he says, solemnly, shaken, I suspect, by what he's heard. 'Too rich for my tastes.'

Not mine though, I think, an idea forming, a dark, dreadful idea. Not if I can get the timing right.

9

'Beauty queen tells court of terror,' reports a woman newsreader. 'And rescuers aid Sammy, the stranded seal.'

'In sport,' a male voice takes over, 'soccer star Robbie Hill is down at the Forest ground today.'

'Today's weather,' the woman announcer comes back. 'More of the same.'

Sitting at the breakfast table munching cereals and toast, I concentrate, preparing to listen to the lot again in detail.

'Tea,' pleads Laura, jammy finger pointing. 'Tea. Tea.'

'Listen out for Sammy, the seal,' I tell her quite sharply.

'Don't talk to her like that,' snaps Em from behind the *Telegraph*.

Only a couple of minutes late but Alice is waiting, just short of tapping an impatient foot on the top step of the pillared entrance of the Fairways Hotel.

A few files have been added to the three overstuffed envelopes she brought from the prison hostel. All are being clutched, chest-high, to the front of a grey suit. The sheer weight of her load seems to propel her tiny frame down the steps.

I don't switch off the engine or get out to help, just turn in my seat, stretch behind to unfasten the child safety lock and push open a rear door while she approaches.

She bends to place her documents on the back seat. Instead of closing the door and walking round to the passenger side, she climbs in and sits next to them, making me feel like her chauffeur. She doesn't say 'Thanks' so I won't apologise for being late.

She slams the door shut. 'Guess what I found?' She doesn't wait for a guess. 'A pamphlet on colour blindness tucked away among his papers. Is he colour blind?' She partly answers her own question. 'There's nothing about it in his medical stuff on file.'

'It's easily checked,' I say, eyes on the narrow driveway flanked with shrubs heavy with bright red berries and fading pink and yellow flowers.

Among all the bumph, she gabbles on, she'd located a hand-written team sheet for the cup final and had compared all the players listed with statements obtained in the days that followed the riot and PC Craig's death.

'One name doesn't tally with the numbers,' she continues. 'Number 7 for Racing Club was listed on the team sheet as J. Robertson.'

I laugh briefly and out loud.

She goes silent for a puzzled moment. 'There's no statement under that name in either set of documents.'

There wouldn't be, I'd like to say, turning right on to the A46, Nottingham-bound.

'In the statements taken from both sides everybody says Cammy played on the right wing for Racing Club,' she continues.

Terrific, I think, acidly, running through the gears. Hours of reading, up half the night by the fragile look on her pale face, and she can now prove beyond reasonable doubt that Cammy played unregistered and under an assumed name sixteen years ago. That should earn him a two-match ban, at the very least.

77

I'll let her down lightly. 'Fits in with what the MP said yesterday about fielding a ringer – and he did describe Cammy as a nippy right-winger.'

I doubt that I've made myself understood. 'That's the number the right-winger wears – seven.'

'Oh.' Pause. 'Not my game.'

In that case, I won't explain why I sniggered at the name J. Robertson. It's obviously been pinched from the fine Forest winger John Robertson who finished his career playing at Derby and is currently assistant manager at Leicester: the East Midlands round of clubs now being trod by job-hunting Robbie Hill.

Half the players in the Unemployed League of the early eighties, I'll wager, used *noms de plume* to avoid maintenance orders, debt collectors and arrest warrants.

'There was a statement from Cammy, by the way,' she says slowly. 'Sorry about that.'

'What did he say?'

'Yes, he went to celebrations afterwards. Everybody from both sides did, it seems, and some officials and spectators, too; all very pally. In the pub there was some dispute with an irate onlooker.'

Happens all the time after Sunday morning games between pub sides, I concede.

'A minor fracas,' Alice recounts. 'He got his shirt torn beyond repair. Lots of witnesses supported his story.'

'And afterwards?'

'No, his statement said, he didn't go home to his mother's place in the flats and there were no witnesses to put him there. He went off with Liam Harries who played in the opposition side.'

'Did Harries verify that?'

'Confirms everything. The trouble in the pub, the fact that Cammy stayed the night at his place.'

I cross-check. 'So they were each other's only alibi for the time the death blow was delivered on PC Craig.'

'Correct,' she says, schoolmarmishly. Then, troubled, 'But there's nothing anywhere from Robertson.'

'What was Scott Packard?' I eye her through the rear view mirror.

'Sorry?'

'Where did he play?'

'Number 4 for Racing Club,' she replies without reference to any notes.

Wing-half, I think, eyes back to the ever busy road. 'And Robbie Hill?'

'Number 4 for Hyson Harps,' she answers, again off pat.

Same position in the opposition's midfield. 'What did Hill say?'

'Yes, he was at the party after the match. Yes, he saw – at least heard – the shop window going. No, he didn't take anything from the display, hot-footed it home to the flats. Yes, he saw a bit of the trouble there, bottles and bricks being lobbed off balconies, but, no, he took no part in it. There wasn't a shred of evidence that he was involved in anything. Released, no charge.'

She flops back. 'One thing I don't understand. Didn't you and the MP say yesterday that Hill went on to play for Ireland?'

'Indeed, he did,' I reply, with almost childlike pride.

'But he was born locally.'

'Oh, if your grandmother owns an Irish wolfhound you qualify.' I smile to myself at what's an original quip.

It gets a silent reception from the back; not her game. 'How about you?' she asks. 'Anything interesting?'

The mugger's case was briefly reported on Radio Trent, I reply. More accurately than their weather forecast, it occurs to me, looking at the grey, low cloud, no sign of the sun.

No mention of Scott Packard, his case review, his conviction or disappearance, I go on. Rob Hill and Liam Harries are still in negotiations hereabouts. The sports reporter promised one or other would be talking about progress on air at lunchtime, studio guest after the news bulletin.

'No. No.' Her irritated tone. 'Last night. After I left you. Did your...' She stretches out 'your'. '...Linda say anything interesting?'

I'm pretty sure that's not her game either, so, 'Not really.'

In the bunker, I phone Surveillance. Nothing of note on the tapes, they say. Next, the prison medical officer. Scott Packard has 20/20 vision with no defects.

At a loose end, I phone an old university chum, a music student a year older than me, a teacher at a suburban comprehensive school for twenty years now.

It's a long wait before he comes to the phone. 'Sorry about that,' he apologises. 'Just taking beginners' woodwind.'

'Just think,' I sigh. 'If I'd worked harder and got a decent degree, all that could have been mine.'

He guffaws.

I go straight in. 'Lennie Gomaz and Liam Harries. Do the names revive any memories?'

'The chap who looked like the African prince, Rigsby's lodger in *Rising Damp*, with the posh voice...'

I smile at a good description.

'...and stage Irishman. Both law students. You must remember them.'

'Can't say I do.'

'Gomaz is still around, high profile. Harries is a big agent, but he's back in town. Heard him on the radio yesterday. Why?'

I tell him their names have cropped up in a case I'm working on. 'They're only on the periphery. Why should I remember them?'

'Rabid left-winger was Gomaz. Weren't you one?'

Oh, happy days, I think. 'Only for a short while and only because I was lusting after Shirl Guevara at the time and she dragged me to a couple of rallies.'

Alice, ploughing through papers on the opposite side of the desk, doesn't look up.

'And Harries?' I prompt.

'Tweeds, huntin', fishin', shootin', but they were good pals, worked together in some radical law centre. Times have changed for Gomaz. He's New Labour these days, very influential.'

'Women?' I ask.

'Married. I teach one of his kids.'

'That's one Labour bigwig who sends his kid to a comp then,' I put in sarcastically.

'He's going to make a better clarinettist than you.'

'Not difficult,' I accept. 'And Harries?'

'Doubt it. That he's married, I mean.'

'Why?'

'Why do you want to know?' he asks cautiously.

'I need to understand relationships with old clients from the law centre. It's an age-old case. Just background, that's all. Don't want to put my foot in it.'

'I see.' He seems satisfied. 'A renowned Illy, wasn't he?'

Good Lord. That's the first time since my teens I've heard a gay described as an Illy. Only music students of our generation used it; a shortening of Ilyich, Tchaikovsky's middle name.

'Yet they were pals?' I cross-check.

'Strange, eh?'

Not really, I think acidly. Every leftie wanted a homo or a black chum in those days, a badge of honour. 'Yeah. But there was nothing going on between them, like?'

'Not like that, no. Gomaz was no ladies' man, very intense, too busy with his demos, but a straight. It was just a social thing for Liam, a chance to mix.'

I hunch over the phone. 'Was he...' I don't quite know how to put it.

'Promiscuous?' my pal suggests, helpfully.

I was thinking more on the lines of predatory, but it will do. 'Mmm.'

'Very. Toy boys, mainly. Lavished gifts on them. Took lots of chances. He was a butterfly. Everyone in our crowd used to avoid him. Neither's in trouble, are they?'

'No, no, no.' I'm trying too hard to assuage his concern. 'It was just that I couldn't work out some of the associations in the background.'

I'll push this no further and we chat for a minute or two, about old friends we never see, and promise to get together for a drink before Christmas down at a former haunt close to our old campus.

I put down the phone, tell Alice what I've discovered. 'Makes you wonder about the relationship between Cammy and Harries, doesn't it?'

81

And also with Scott Packard, come to think of it, I tell myself, and, indeed, Robbie Hill, but I'd rather not think of that.

She's unimpressed. 'How can your pal be so sure?'

He can be sure because he's an Illy himself, in a stable relationship for much longer than I've been with Em, but, again, I'll not tell her that.

The green phone rings. 'You'll never guess,' says the PR chief breezily. Not again, I groan to myself. Why do so many women open conversations like that?

She gets on with it. 'Your missing Mr Packard has broken surface.'

When I hear how and where, I groan out loud. I've had a phone tap put on almost everyone I could think of, but she never once crossed my mind.

The overworked receptionist at Radio Trent removes a headset with dinky mouthpiece, stands up behind her low counter, walks to a door, a ghastly purple, fingers a code into the security lock and pushes it open.

'That's Pauline.' She nods towards a ginger-haired woman who has her arms ramrod straight above her head, is wriggling her bottom into the cushion of a comfortable-looking chair and arching her back into a bow.

By way of explaining her callisthenics, she adds, 'Dawn patrol.' She's stretching away some of the stiffness that comes towards the end of a hectic early shift, she hasn't time to say before returning to her constantly ringing switchboard.

I lead the way through a small newsroom up to her desk. 'Miss Foster?'

A tiny, tired smile.

I give myself the full introduction, name, rank and warrant card, then cock a thumb at Alice. 'And a colleague, Miss Spence.'

Foster's grey-green eyes switch to curious.

'Our PR at HQ put us on to you,' I add. She's wide awake now. 'About Scott Packard.' No response, still appraising me. 'You interviewed his mother and his MP yesterday.'

'The day before,' she corrects me. 'It was recorded.' A guarded expression. 'Nothing wrong, is there?'

With both hands she scratches the back of her head, ruffling further already untidy hair. She's on the defensive. Reporters like asking questions, aren't so fond of being asked them, particularly if they think they could be in legal trouble.

She's thirtyish, almost a veteran in local radio terms these days; clearly knows the ropes. She has a pale face without make-up; wouldn't do for TV where all women look as though they have just had a full facial, my wife included.

'Not at all,' I say easily.

'Only the news ed...' She flicks her head towards a dark woman in a glassed-off cubicle. '...pulled the item. Judge's orders, she said.'

'That's right,' I confirm. Packard is due to give evidence in the beauty queen trial, I explain, and the judge has ruled there should be no reporting of the criminal records of anyone involved in the case.

'I never bloody well knew,' she grumbles. 'Not when we ran the story.'

My reassuring smile. 'No one is suggesting you should. The order wasn't in force when the item was broadcast. There are no legal difficulties here.'

She tries to mask understandable relief with aggressive features. 'What's the problem, then?'

She's allowed me to get to the point. 'I gather Scott Packard phoned you within the past hour.'

'Why shouldn't he?' she says, still bristling. 'He's out and about, in a hostel. It's not as if he's behind bars. Even inmates get phone cards these days.'

A tough cookie, I decide; no pushover. I'm going to have to give a little. 'The problem is that he is AWOL from the courthouse and the judge has ordered us to find him.'

'Oh.' She thinks, but only for a moment. 'Is there anything in it for us?'

If only the Inspector Manns of the police were as keen, I think with a touch of admiration. 'There may be, next week, when the judge lifts his reporting restrictions.'

She beams a 'That's all right then' and only now does she invite us to sit on the opposite side of a desk entirely covered with the tools of her trade – screen, keyboard, tape recorder in a brown leather case, phone, phone books, newspapers and more bits of paper than Alice has collected.

She looks at the tape machine. 'Shit.' She flops back in her swivel chair, exhausted. 'And I didn't record him.'

He opened up with, 'It's Scott Packard.' Dealing with dozens of names in a day, it didn't register at first, she confesses. 'You talked to my mum and the MP yesterday about my conviction. Heard it. Good. Thanks.'

She replied with something like 'My pleasure' or 'Any time.' The trouble with radio reporters, I've discovered from Em, is that, unlike print journalists, they don't take many notes. No need. They have most of it on tape. So I know that what I'm getting is best memory.

He wanted to know if she would be following the case up and was told: 'Certainly. When there are fresh developments.'

Then he said, 'There will be. They're out to get me, trying to shut me up. I want to get my side of the story in before they do.'

She asked what he was talking about. Best not to discuss it on the phone, he replied. He asked if he could come to see her and she said, 'Any time.' He requested the address.

'Isn't it in the phone book?' she responded, a question that would have delighted Em.

He explained he'd phoned Newsline, a number that's often broadcast to encourage listeners to call in with breaking stories.

He didn't say where he was calling from, asked for and was given directions from the Old Market Square, then: 'Is midday OK or will that clash with Rob Hill's interview?'

She told him to drop in soon afterwards as she was reading the noon headlines. Out of habit, she glances at a clock on a grey wall amid maps, assignment board and rosters. I follow her eyes: almost eleven thirty.

'Sure it won't clash with Rob Hill?' he'd repeated.

'He's talking live, the celebrity studio guest, after the bulletin at one.' Besides, she added, sport was not her department.

'See you later then.' Packard put down the phone.

Nothing of significance changes when I take her through it again. Now I'm taking her back to the start of her involvement.

She made a routine of phoning local MPs after their surgeries. 'Something I learned on my first weekly. Don't teach it at media college. They miss out on lots of good stuff.'

The MP had accidentally misinformed us, it soon transpires. She's a contract reporter, not technically staff nor freelance. But she had freelanced. 'And if you don't work, you don't eat.' She's a real pro and proud of it, I think, warming to her all the more.

Giles Johnson was a steady source of stories, she continues. He briefed her on Packard's application for a case review. When she heard that Packard was living in an outside hostel, and was, therefore, easily accessible to her, she was keen to interview him.

The MP was against it, arguing that, if it was made public that Packard, a convicted murderer of a policeman, was no longer behind bars, PC Craig's family might start sounding off, the way that the families of Moors victims are wheeled out every time there's even a hint of Myra Hindley being set free.

'He was also worried that giving an interview to the media without authority might result in his recall to Perry Road' – HM Prison Nottingham, she means.

Additionally, I muse, it might lead to a Tory MP who happened to be a paid consultant of the Police Federation questioning the government's pledge to be 'tough on crime' – and Giles Johnson's spin doctors might not thank him for that.

Johnson volunteered himself for a taped interview. In it, he talked of 'startling new evidence' which he declined to divulge 'at this stage'.

Foster expressed unhappiness. She wanted a second voice, she says, lapsing into the jargon of her trade, 'to change the pace. Johnson put up Packard's mother.'

'What do you mean, "put up"?' asks Alice, that prissy look again.

'He made all the arrangements for me to speak to her at her home. He organised her a bit too well for my liking – briefed her on what to say and she wasn't all that forthcoming.'

'Still...' Foster begins to look more pleased. '...she did come out with that line "Free my innocent son." Gave the whole package a lift.'

They ran the item yesterday morning and again at lunchtime when she went home at the end of her shift. Annoyingly, they didn't repeat it in the main evening bulletin to which she listened off duty.

She'd been very busy from 5.30 a.m. this morning and hadn't had time to find out why her piece had been dropped. Only after she had put down the phone on Packard did it occur to her to raise the question with her news editor.

She told her about the PR's advice yesterday on the contempt of court ruling. On her own initiative, she phoned force HQ to find out if the ban was still operational and told our PR that Packard had been in touch.

'What will you do when he turns up?' I ask.

'Get him on tape and worry about the legal ramifications afterwards,' she replies, smiling shrewdly. 'Unless you have any valid objections.'

I don't think I have. Foster can't broadcast it anyway – not unless she wants to spend a night or two banged up herself for contempt of court. 'That's OK.'

Radio stations, especially commercial, only use news in brief, so I ask to hear the unedited interviews.

'Have you got a court order?' Foster inquires, pointedly.

'No, but there's nothing contentious on them, is there?'

She lifts and wags her chin in thought. She slips her recorder towards her, seeks and finds a tape in a drawer, inserts it, flicks a button. We hear Johnson first, waffle mainly, then Mrs Packard, harder work than she was with us.

The only two significant sentences – 'vital new evidence' from him, 'They should free my innocent son' from her – have been lifted out and already used as news-bites.

'Thanks,' I say when she switches off. I nod at Alice. 'We'll wait.'

'Not here, you won't.' Foster is shaking her head determinedly. 'Don't want you nicking him here. He'll think I've shopped him.'

'We'll look after you.'

'It's not that. I can look after myself, thanks very much...'

I believe her.

'If he goes round saying I can't be trusted,' she complains, 'where will I get my crime stories from?'

'I understand,' I tell her, rising, thinking of an ideal stakeout.

'What will you do when he does turn up?' asks Alice as we stroll in newly appeared sunshine across a narrow red-Tarmacked street towards a pub with white plaster and black beams and a fine view along Castlegate.

I have already made a decision on that. 'March him back to court and let the judge worry about his security over the weekend.' In other words, I don't add, pass the buck.

Going into the Royal Children, she recalls Packard's remark to Pauline Foster: 'They're out to get me, trying to shut me up.' With a puzzled expression, she asks, 'Could he mean Lebois?'

At last, I sigh to myself, she's seen the point I was trying to make yesterday.

'This job,' she chafes, 'would be so much simpler if we knew which theory to work on.'

'All we have to do,' I say, confidently, 'is stick around and we'll ask him.'

I motion to a wooden table by a bay window with small, leaded panes and go to the L-shaped bar with her order for lime and lemonade, adding half a lager.

When I rejoin her with the drinks, before I've sat down, she asks pessimistically, 'What if he doesn't turn up?'

Questions, questions, I think, angrily. All she ever comes out with are questions.

I'm angry, I know, because I don't know the answer to that.

That seed of an idea that germinated after dinner last night, a sneaky idea, terrible really, is beginning to grow. I debate it with myself. It's risky and it's dreadfully cruel. Perhaps not.

On the other hand, it sounds a bit of fun and might produce a quick answer if Packard doesn't show. So perhaps. In which case, I'll be late home. In which case, I'd better eat while I can. 'Let's eat while we wait.'

'That's it then,' says Alice, forlornly watching Pauline Foster appearing between sandstone columns that complement the Trent building's Georgian elegance and walking away from us down Castlegate.

What she's suggesting is that if a ferret like Foster has given up on Packard, so should we.

'We may as well hang on,' I say, sitting in a polished wooden chair with carved arms. 'We've got to talk to Rob Hill and Liam Harries. Might as well be here.'

She's nibbled the last quarter of her salad sandwich some time ago and made her drink last an hour. I'd eaten two ham cobs with pickles, accompanied by a second lager.

'Another?' I offer, though it's not my turn to buy. She declines, eyes out of the window.

I get up, amble back across the stained floorboards to the bar, have to wait awhile in the lunchtime rush.

Suddenly I feel a little weak-kneed, like a gawky schoolboy on his first date. I know why and it's nothing to do with this gammy leg.

I'm about to meet a sporting hero, someone I've revered from the terraces.

Chief constables or special constables, cabinet ministers or cabinetmakers I treat as I find. If they are efficient and friendly, I'm at ease with them. If they are off hand, so am I.

Hill is ten years younger than me. Yet I look up to him, admire him, because he has played on my team, given me pleasure and memories.

88

Hope this turns out better than my encounter with a Test star I'd worshipped as a boy; my all-time cricketing favourite. In village games, I even wore my cap like him, pulled down over the left eye at a jaunty angle.

When he brought his county side to the Racecourse Ground one summer holiday, I plucked up the courage to approach him as he walked back from the middle after the pre-match wicket inspection and toss.

I swallowed, forced a silly smile and said as casually as I could manage, 'Who's batting then?'

He walked straight past me, didn't say a word, didn't even look at me, let alone smile. The worst moment of my young life, total rejection, and in that moment love turned to hate and I rejoiced every time he got a duck thereafter.

Walking back to the table with a fresh glass, I have a clear view through the windows of a yellow cab pulling up on double yellow lines in front of the sandstone columns.

Out of the back, as sleek as a cat, slides the unmistakable figure (to a Derby fan anyway) of Rob Hill, five million pound legs first.

10

'Let's go,' I almost gulp, putting down my full glass so quickly that lager spills on the table.

I lead the way out through the push door to the street, walking as fast as I can, don't hold it open, hope Alice will catch it.

My heart seems to stop at the sight of Hill standing in the middle of the pavement. He's half turned, watching expressionless as a white man climbs less than lithely out of the opened rear door. He is talking across his shoulder to the driver – Liam Harries, I guess.

I force that same silly smile, can't help it, and from some twenty yards away, call, 'Mr Hill.'

There's no time to add, 'A moment, please' because, simultaneously and from my left, comes a locally accented 'Aye.'

Walking forward diagonally and downhill across the street, I only have to turn my eyes just slightly to take in a black face, male, thirtyish. His tight smile goes when he sees me.

He is walking uphill and is some ten yards from the taxi and thirty from me. A hand is half raised – in greeting, must be, because he's too far away to be a threat.

In a blink, his face ties into a confused knot of fright and annoyance. The hand drops to his side and he seems to use it to swing himself into an about-turn.

His back to me, he walks, then jogs a few easy paces away, soundless in black trainers.

All this within – what? – five seconds, no more, and I note for the first time that he's wearing a denim jacket and grey flannels. The description I had circulated to every police officer yesterday flashes up and blinks at me.

Scott Packard, my brain screams. That's Scott Packard.

'Scott,' I call at his back. He doesn't slow, turn round or look back.

I break into a stiff trot, ignoring Hill and his companion, merely aware that they are standing beyond the taxi on the pavement, watching me.

'Scott,' I shout, forcing myself to run. 'Stop. I only want to help.'

Packard lengthens his stride, moving effortlessly, already off the red Tarmac and on the surface bricked over for pedestrian use only.

'Packard,' I holler, every other step laboured.

He's zig-zagging a path among walkers like George Best ghosting between a packed defence, a knife through butter.

I'm in the centre of the street, waving one-way traffic to my left out of my way, grinding my right heel into the asphalt, willing the leg to stretch further, go faster.

Oh, this bloody leg.

Breathing's no problem, never has been since my clarinet days. I know when to take air in and let it out and there's more than enough to yell, 'Police. Stop.'

Now I'm on the bricked bit of road. Heads right and left turn towards me, but not Packard's, well beyond the church now. No sound of footsteps follows in my wake.

He reaches the bottom of Castlegate and glides to his right and out of view. He has more than doubled the start he had on me and I throttle back to a dispirited, defeated jog until I reach Samuel's corner.

Right leg pounding, I just stand here, watching wave upon wave of shoppers and workers ebbing and flowing to and from the direction of the huge Broadmarsh shopping centre, and the courthouse and bus and railway stations beyond.

I don't really study them or seek out Packard among them; pointless, hopeless. Lost him. Failed. Twice now, if I count yesterday near the station. It was him; no doubt about it.

My eyes are wet, from anger, from frustation, not from looking like a fool in front of a sporting hero, not from exertion.

I'm barely out of breath, but, oh, this lousy leg. Christ, four and a half years ago I'd have kept pace, tackled him, brought him down, collared him.

Not any more. I'm a lame duck, a desk jockey now; a paper pusher.

Outside Marks and Spencer, a group of buskers, guitars, sandpipes and canned drums, are playing South American music. The beat is not nearly as heavy or fast as my heart.

I just stand here, boiling within, looking, but not seeing all the people about me on the street.

The street. Where real police work is. I don't belong here any more. A pen pusher is what I am. That's what I would have been doing if Packard hadn't gone on the run. Reading docos, pushing paper. That's why the chief gave me this job.

Me, the fastest runner in my intake, the quickest eye for trouble in punch-ups, who led Special Ops from the front.

Oh, this hopeless, useless, worthless leg.

Jacko Jackson should have let him finish me off. Into my mind come Em and Laura, smiling. What a dreadful thing even to think, I rebuke myself. All right then, I should have taken a medical discharge when it was on offer.

I shouldn't have come back, should have cut my losses and left, started afresh.

I can't hack it any more. I'm a passenger, a chair-bound passenger, riding on the backs of real policemen, the very sort I used to mock when I was on the streets.

I should quit, will quit. Quit, you cripple; quit.

Oh, this fucking leg.

I am trying hard not to weep.

'Are you all right?' Alice, face porcelain pale, is at my shoulder but I don't turn.

I nod ahead of me, say nothing.

'Only I heard you shout for help.'

I don't explain, just stare down the street towards the shopping centre.

'Was it him?'

'Yes.' Finally, I turn and start to walk slowly up Castlegate.

No taxi is parked ahead. Hill and his companion have gone inside, Alice reports. So will we, I decide.

If she heard me call for help, Hill must have heard me shout 'Police,' yet he never came to my aid. He could have succeeded where I failed and caught up with him and I could have 'cuffed him, a team job. Another let-down.

'I wonder what Packard wanted with Robbie Hill,' she says. Then, looking at her feet, 'I didn't realise he's black, too.'

Yeah, well, does it matter as long as he can play? I ask myself. Correction: could play. I hope he doesn't come back to County, don't want him in my team again, the has-been.

We walk some way in silence which she breaks. 'Sorry I didn't give chase. My brain must be slow or something. It just wouldn't accept that it could be him until it was too late.' A mournful face. 'Sorry.'

At least she tried, I acknowledge. More than that fallen idol Robbie Hill, the bastard.

No Latin lyricism dances over the airwaves. None has enhanced the speech rhythms of Robbie Hill from his Italian sojourn. In a flat, still local accent, he trots out the usual hackneyed soccer phrases that begin or end with 'at the end of the day'.

He thinks he has a good few years left in him at the top, is ambitious for more cups and caps, could still do a job for any of the three big East Midlands clubs chasing his signature, feels his European experience has added a new dimension to his game. 'My future is still in the talks situation.'

Grimacing at yet another cliché, I'm sitting on a couch with Alice in reception at Radio Trent, listening to the interview over a loudspeaker set high on a pink wall. After fulsome thanks from his questioner, Hill gives way to the Spice Girls.

Some Italian has rubbed off on his dress sense, I note, as he walks through the security door. His black suit is buttoned right up to the throat. Two inches of cuff reveal the brilliant white shirt beneath.

Behind comes his companion whose bulky figure doesn't look so sharp in an oatmeal-coloured suit. There's a dark brown trench coat slung casually over a shoulder. His hair is bleached almost white, his fair-skinned face reddened. A small, black mobile phone is in his right hand.

I get up and move forward, almost blocking their way. Holding up a warrant card, not quite as high as a referee with a yellow card, I get to say what Scott Packard prevented. 'A word, please.'

Hill smiles playfully. 'Catch him?'

'No.' I refrain from adding a sarcastic: But thanks for your public-spirited assistance.

Behind him, his companion grins. 'Not surprised.'

Hill looks at me mischievously, but speaks out of the corner of his mouth, towards the man behind. 'Gazza must be faster.' It's a cruel jibe about a brilliant, if wayward, player whose career has been plagued by injury.

A quick laugh comes over his shoulder and is then turned off just as quickly. 'Saw nothing. Can't help. Sorry.'

I detect more of a lilt in the voice than in Hill's; faint Irish. 'You Mr Liam Harries?'

A delighted nod.

'Do you know who he was?' I ask, yanking a thumb over my shoulder.

'I told you –' Harries says impatiently.

'Scott Packard,' I break in.

Harries doesn't try to finish his sentence.

'Do you remember him?'

An easy shrug from Hill and a cautious nod from Harries.

'Why do you think he wanted to speak to one or the other or both of you?'

Harries gives his head a dumb shake.

'Haven't a clue,' says Hill, airily. 'Is he out? What's he done this time?'

Getting no replies, he hurries on, 'Haven't seen or heard of him since...' The wind is leaving his sails.'...that night...you know...' His voice tails off.

He glances uneasily at the receptionist at her counter, not keen, I assume, for anyone employed in the media to overhear that he, an internationally famous star, once took part in a game that was followed by a riot and a police officer's death.

I couldn't care less. The station's news editor and her keenest newshound already know that the details can't be repeated while the judge's prohibition on publicity is in force.

Playing on that, I say quite loudly, 'We're going to have to talk about that night.'

'Not now,' Harries almost hisses.

'Now.' Louder still.

'We've got a taxi coming.' He turns sharply to the receptionist. 'Is it here?'

She gestures to the door. Outside, she's saying.

'Now,' I repeat.

Harries again, truculent. 'He's got interviews to do.'

'Quite right.' I gesture to Alice. 'With us. You, too.'

I lean forward, closer to Hill, taking in a scent that can't be aftershave because he has stubble that makes his face look much blacker than I remember from the terraces.

Very quietly, I speak over his shoulder at Harries, hoping both of them remember the local geography. 'Fuck me

94

about and you'll both be signing up for a long weekend in Perry Road.'

Harries comes back, bristling. 'Now look here –'

'Listen.' I raise a finger. 'Judge's orders. Do you want to come back to his courthouse and explain publicly why you're refusing co-operation?'

Neither attempt a reply, not used to being spoken to like this, I think gleefully, among their in-crowd of pampered players and fawning hangers-on.

I offer a getout. 'We'll talk there, here or Central nick. All the same to us. We don't give a toss.'

'Will our hotel do?' asks Hill, looking down, fiddling with his cuffs.

The taxi has to go round the bottleneck of Broadmarsh shopping centre, no choice in the one-way traffic system, passing the courthouse, then up a dual carriageway with the Royal Children on the right.

It would have been quicker to walk to their hotel and talk on the way, but that's not how sporting superstars get from A to B, I reflect moodily, sitting in the back.

Not a word is mentioned on the short journey about 'that night', presumbly because they don't want the amiable Asian driver to hear.

Harries doesn't mind talking behind the driver's back about the newspaper interview he's lining up. 'Reckon on another grand or two if we give the management a bit of stick – you played in wrong role etc.'

Hill nods and I suspect he's giving approval for an article criticising Ireland's team selections in qualifying games for the World Cup.

The truth, in my view from watching televised Italian soccer on Sunday afternoons, is that Hill has been dropped because he's not played well of late; lost a bit of pace. He doesn't appear to be over-troubled about the truth; not if there's an extra grand or two in it. If he's picked again, he'll simply say he was mis-quoted.

Makes you want to weep over what mega money is doing to the game, I seethe. Soccer is showbiz these days, the new Hollywood, a running soap. Papers can't get enough of it. Make it up, anything goes as long as they print your name – and pay up.

The taxi pulls off Maid Marian Way into a steep, narrow side street in front of a tall hotel that has changed its name since it was built in the sixties. Everyone still calls it the Albany.

The driver stops beneath a bridge that runs across the street to a multi-storey car-park. From it hangs a black clock with golden figures on 1.25.

He gets out and walks round the bonnet. He opens the front passenger door for Alice who'd travelled alongside him; ladies first.

Harries lets himself out, Hill follows, me last. Over the car roof Harries calls, 'This on the station?'

'Yes, sir,' says the driver.

Without a tip, even a thank you, Hill is already skipping up two or three mock marble steps and through automatic doors in a round capsule. Alice is trailing; ladies last now.

He heads across a low-ceilinged foyer with walls of Wedgwood blue to a pair of lifts with steel doors and fingers the 'Up' button. Harries peels off left to the reception counter. He is holding two keys when he rejoins us.

The journey up starts and ends with lurches. Not a word is said in between or on the walk down a long fourth-floor corridor.

As soon as we are inside a room at the end of the corridor, before anyone has sat down, Harries turns and says, sharply, 'What's this all about?'

'Scott Packard,' I say, just as sharp.

He cocks a thumb at Hill. 'We haven't seen him since.'

I smile thinly. 'Since that night, you mean.'

'Right.' A firm nod. 'I thought he got life.'

Him a law graduate and getting it wrong, I tut to myself. 'He was detained indefinitely,' I correct him, then, relenting, 'Same thing, I suppose.'

'What's he doing out then?' Harries demands.

'He's done sixteen years.'

There's a determined look on his reddish face and I sense his tactic is to get on top in this interview, dominate it, so I'll slip in an early tackle. 'And now he says he didn't kill our copper. Which, if he's right, means...' I look from one to the other.'... someone else did.'

'Christ,' mutters Hill.

Harries puts on an incredulous expression. 'Do you believe that?'

'Dunno,' I pause. 'Yet.'

'Which,' says Alice very slowly, 'is why we have to talk about that night. Do you remember it?'

As if all of a sudden weary, both sit down side by side on a double bed with a brightly patterned cover.

I lower myself into an easy chair in front of a window with closed net curtains. Alice sits on an armless chair in front of a desk-cum-dresser with a mirror above it on the cream wall. The surface is littered with badly refolded newspapers.

'Course,' Hill begins, looking somewhat shaken. 'You don't forget a night like that. Fucking tragedy all round.'

Harries nods gravely.

In tandem they confirm they both played for Hyson Harps, sponsored by an Irish pub. Hill was the regular number 4. Harries was number 2, a late call-up for the right back who'd had to drop out.

Hill was sixteen then, lived with his parents in the flats. They'd moved twice since, on the last occasion to the Wirral when he was playing on Merseyside. 'Nice place I bought 'em.'

Why do stars always make public private generosities like that? Lack of class, I decide, despite all the trimmings of it.

At the time, he goes on, he'd just left school and hadn't yet found a job in soccer or anywhere.

Harries was in his mid-twenties, a graduate working as a volunteer in the law centre close to the flats. He qualified to play in the Unemployed League because he wasn't paid for his services. 'Work experience.'

In the final they lost 3–1 to Racing Club of Radford. 'Scott Packard was their number 4,' Hill confirms.

'Did you know Packard in those days?' I ask.

'Everybody who played in the league did. He was their danger man.' Hill's expression saddens. 'Pity.' The way things turned out for him, he means.

'Did you know his half-brother Cammy?' I go on.

'Not as well. He was older than most of us kids, away at university or somewhere.'

I turn to Harries. 'Did you?'

He looks away. 'Yes, he was more my age group.'

And with a college background more his intellectual equal, I guess. 'He played on his brother's side for Racing Club?'

Harries nods. 'Last-minute replacement, I think he was.'

'Technically, under league regulations, Cammy wasn't qualified to play.'

Harries shrugs a 'Who cares?' or 'Don't recall.' Hill smiles fondly. 'It happened all the time. Ringers. Nobody minded.'

The bedside phone rings. Harries gets up to answer it, back to us. He begins to talk money and soccer (in that order) to someone called Harry.

Hill rises. He takes off his jet black jacket and walks towards the door to place it on a hanger on a trouser press. Inside the press are the pants from another dark suit.

In his white shirt with a collar stud, but no collar, he walks back, not returning to the bed. Instead, he slides, loose-limbed, beside my chair to the window, opening it slightly to air a room that's overwarm.

I turn and look out of the drawn-back curtains. There's no view from here of any local landmarks – the imposing council-house in the Old Market Square or the castle's old walls – only lots of towering square buildings, sixties mistakes that, unlike the flats, haven't been pulled down, more's the pity.

The noise of traffic floats up from Maid Marian Way distracting Harries who protests, 'Can't hear,' either to the caller or to Hill, difficult to say.

'Take it in your room then,' snaps Hill, looking down.

Harries promises to call back immediately and replaces the receiver. 'Will you be all right?' he asks Hill, anxiously.

Hill turns, looking pensive. 'Go easy. Say maybe they haven't seen too much of me in my new holding role. An out of sight, out of mind situation – that sort of thing.'

He appears to be getting cold feet about being over-critical of his adopted country's team selections, wants to keep open the option for a recall.

I resume as soon as Harries walks out and closes the door behind him. 'After the game, did you swap shirts? You know, like you see on telly.'

'No.' Hill sits down on the bed, shaking his head, grinning broadly. 'Outside of school soccer, they were the first proper strips any of us had. The real thing, they were.'

There was a presentation after the game to both winners and runners-up, he explains, at ease down memory lane. At the party that followed in the pub, someone took exception to Cammy keeping his winner's medal.

'The guy whose place he took, I think he was, 'cos he turned up too late to play. Can't remember his name. Afro-Carib. He'd played in all the previous rounds and reckoned he should have it.

'He threw a wobbly, went for Cammy and ripped his shirt. His number was hanging down, inside out, half off his back. The rest of their side waded in to break it up. Fucked up the whole set, see.'

'Did you join in the punch-up?'

A headshake. 'Nothing to do with us. None of the Harps got involved, stayed well out. We kept our shirts on.' He laughs at his own quip. 'Kept mine at home for years.'

I'll get back to this when Harries returns. Meantime, in his absence, a more pressing matter. I nod at the closed door. 'Is your agent gay?'

Alice tightens her small mouth in disapproval.

Hill shrugs, unconcerned. 'So they say. Does a good job for me, has done since I signed for Derby as a kid. Looks after me OK. Never tried anything on.' To underline his macho image, he adds, 'I've a wife and two kids back in Milan.'

And a love child in Liverpool, if the tabloids are to be believed, but I'll not go into that. 'Is Cammy gay?'

99

This time he asks, 'Why?'

'After the punch-up, he and Liam went off and spent the night together.'

He gives this genuine thought. 'Never married, has he?'

'Do you keep in touch with Cammy?'

'Liam does.' Finally, he partly accepts the proposition. 'He could be.'

He'd got to know Scott Packard and, to a lesser extent, Cammy, his half-brother, through Harries. 'He recommended all of us for trials with various clubs. Cammy turned pro after college, but didn't really make it...well...like big, you know. Scott, well, he was great, but...' Another sad headshake for the way it had turned out for Packard.

Harries returns, addressing Hill as he walks in. 'Toned down. Three grand on publication. OK?'

Hill brightens. 'Smashing.'

I look at Harries and gesture to Hill. 'He's been telling us about the fracas involving the Racing Club side after the game?'

Harries reclaims his place next to Hill, offers nothing.

'What's your memory of that?' I persist.

'Slight,' he grunts.

'You know...' Hill prompts him, recounting some of the details he's already given us. 'None of us in the Harps side mixed it.'

'Yeah, right,' Harries says, vaguely. He can't remember the name of Cammy's shirt-tearing adversary either.

Alice moves him on. 'You and Cammy left immediately afterwards?'

A doubtful 'Yes' then, more positive, 'Cammy was upset about the trouble, wanted away.'

'But not home to the flats?'

A nod.

'To your place?'

Another nod, no words.

'What happened to his torn shirt?' I ask.

An exasperated expression. 'It was binned, I suppose.'

Alice addresses Hill. 'Did you go home?'

'Yes,' he says straight away. He saw some of the riots at the flats, but didn't take part. He must be sticking closely to what he'd said in his signed statement at the time, because Alice queries none of it.

I look hard at Harries. 'Although on the opposite sides that night, you were close to Cammy?'

'We were pals, yes.'

'And Scott?'

'I knew him, too, naturally.'

'And in those days you were trying to promote their careers in soccer?'

'What do you mean "trying"?' Visibly stung, he flicks his head sideways towards Hill. 'I landed him trials at the Baseball Ground and got Cammy fixed up in London after he'd finished college. I did a lot for lots of lads.'

Words like promiscuous and predatory are springing into my mind, but, to be legally safe, I'll stick with a variation on a line Lennie Gomaz used yesterday. 'So you always had an eye for promising talent?'

'What's wrong with that?' His features are set aggressively, a nerve struck. 'I played a bit myself, combined colleges and all that, got a coaching badge. It was the only escape from inner cities for some kids, like boxers from the ghettos.'

He goes to some length to explain how he'd handled the youngsters' contracts and went on to build a career of it, making himself sound more of a social worker than an agent on the make. 'At that age, they can easily get screwed.'

'True,' I say and smile.

Silence, apart from the drone of traffic below.

'Yet,' I have to continue, 'though you were a volunteer in the law centre and knew Scott, he engaged Lennie Gomaz when he was arrested in raids that followed the PC's death. Why didn't he come to you?'

He gives this some thought. 'Because Lennie was more experienced in crime, had a day job with a big firm. I didn't, wasn't interested. All I did was advise local folk on HP contracts, money-lending agreements, things like that. Commerce was always going to be my line.'

101

'Do you still keep in touch with Mr Gomaz?'

He shakes his head. 'First visit, this, in ages.'

'And Cammy?'

'Why?'

'We're going to have to talk to everyone who played in that game,' Alice explains.

'Rather you than me after all these years. Some of 'em will be in jail.' A brittle laugh. 'Or dead from drugs.'

My eyes are still on him. 'Well?'

He looks away. 'Yes.'

Hill grins maliciously, about to embarrass him. 'Just back, aren't you?'

No response.

'From where?' I ask.

Hill answers for him. 'Cyprus.'

'So you're still pals?'

Harries picks his words carefully. 'We see each other occasionally, holidays and things. I've a place out there. He works there.'

'Could we have his address, please?' pipes Alice.

'Can't you ask his mother?' Harries grumbles.

I take out my notebook. 'We're asking you.' I eye him steadily. 'Judge's orders.'

He gives a street name in Kyrenia, confirming that Cammy works at a marine laboratory these days, plays only part-time for a club I've never heard of.

Alice waits till I stow my notebook. Then, surprising even me, she asks, 'Are either of you colour blind?'

Harries groans. 'What now?'

'Just answer it,' I snap.

He jerks his head towards Hill. 'He'd hardly be able to follow an orangy-red ball on grass, if he was, now would he?'

I look at Hill. 'That right?'

A smiling nod. 'Right.'

Back to Harries. 'Are you?'

Hill answers for him. 'An ace at snooker, him.' He can tell different colours, he means.

In a tone that's becoming increasingly hostile, Harries confirms, 'No, I'm not.' He sighs heavily. 'Bloody ridiculous, this.'

I return to an old question. 'Why do you think Scott Packard wanted to talk to one or other of you outside Radio Trent?'

Harries straightens. 'Been thinking about that. If he's out now...' He pauses. 'Is he?'

'In a pre-parole hostel,' says Alice.

He fixes me. 'If he's legally out and about, why wouldn't he stop and talk to you? That's what I'd like to know. Why run away?'

A good question that, I concede privately. 'He's AWOL from the hostel.'

'How would he know where to look for us anyway?'

'He heard your interview...' I look at Hill. '...being advertised on radio in advance.' I won't reveal that he cleverly double-checked the timing with Pauline Foster. 'All he'd have to do was wait.'

Harries follows up immediately. 'Why were you two there?'

This, I acknowledge, is becoming a skilled cross-examination, his legal training on display. 'We were tipped he was likely to be there.'

'How?'

Before I can tell him to mind his own business, Alice comes in. 'He had a tentative arrangement to chat to a news reporter about his case review.'

'Case review?' Harries' fair eyebrows arch, querulously. 'What do you mean?'

Alice explains Packard's application. Then she has to explain the work of her Commission, Harries claiming to be so out of touch that he'd never heard of it before.

He's quick to see the follow-up question. 'If his case is being reviewed, why did he run away from you?'

'He went AWOL before we could tell him his application had been granted,' Alice replies.

'Well...' He takes his time. '...it's just possible he happened to turn up at the studios at the same time as us. Maybe he recognised us, just wanted to chat.' He beams at Hill, spreads his hands, all but saying a very satisfied 'There, that explains it.' Hill nods sagely.

Harries gives the impression of the gofer, the key collector, the phone answerer, but he's the wheeler-dealer, the money man who knows how to keep his client happy. He's showing off, thinks he's finally on top. I'm going to have to put the boot in again. 'To chat about that night, you mean?'

'How should I know?' Not so self-satisfied now.

'You see,' I say, very slowly, 'if he's served sixteen years for something he didn't do, he's going to be pretty cross with who-ever did.'

They glance at each other, Harries rather anxious, Hill much less so, smiling. 'We have nowt to worry about,' he says. He looks at Harries. 'Have we?'

'Most certainly not,' he replies starchily.

Well, I decide, I wouldn't bank on either's innocence on Little-woods Pools, whatever the odds.

11

Strolling down and then under noisy Maid Marian Way, Alice ponders out loud whether the unaccounted-for J. Robertson was the Afro-Carib involved in the fracas with Cammy at the post-match celebrations.

Since Cammy played under that name as a ringer, he'd be fight-ing with himself then, I speculate, amusing myself. 'Dunno,' I say.

Passing Radio Trent in the much quieter Castlegate, she won-ders, 'Do you think that Scott just happened to bump into Hill and Harries outside here – a chance encounter?'

'No' is the honest answer to that. 'Dunno,' I repeat.

'You don't share your thoughts, do you?' she says waspishly. 'Holding something back, are you?'

Yes, as a matter of fact, but not on these questions; that dark and dangerous idea that won't go away. 'No point yet.'

She sighs, and more or less repeats what she said earlier in the Royal Children – that the job would be easier if we could isolate Scott's motive for escaping.

Walking through the bustling shopping centre, I make up my mind. 'Maybe I can.'

'How?' she demands.

'See a snout,' I lie, deliberately holding back. 'Tonight. Privately.' I look across my shoulder at her. 'OK?'

She says nothing, lips pressed together.

'I take it you're off home for the weekend?' I go on.

'Oh, no,' she says. A bright forced smile. 'But don't worry. I've plenty to do.'

Oh, God, I rail, trying not to squeeze my eyes shut in dismay, I'm going to be stuck with her all weekend.

Nothing, Surveillance report when we reach our ground-floor bunker in the courthouse. Not wanting a soccer star, albeit a fading one, to perish in a revenge attack (not on my patch anyway), a watch on Hill and Harries is added to their tasks.

The internal phone rings. As promised, the judge is knocking off early and is about to rise, Carol, the usher, tips me. Inspector Mann is just completing evidence of arrest. Scott Packard is the only prosecution witness left. 'Have him here on Monday,' she pleads. 'My job could depend on it.'

I won't tell her that if I'd been quicker on my feet I'd have had him here more than two hours ago, or, had I been more alert and street-wise, yesterday, before the judge even knew he'd gone. Instead, 'We're doing our best.'

Alice is already poring through her mountain of documents seeking the paper trail to the mythical J. Robertson.

I stand. 'I'm off to the barber's.'

She looks up and nods, catching on, no need for me to explain what's a routine inquiry.

I head for the stairs and up, not the door and out – another call to make first, far from routine, no need to tell her about it either.

The double doors to court number 1 swing open. Hardly a crowd rushes out. The jury always uses a separate entrance and not one press reporter has seen it through to the end of the second day of the hearing.

The mugger's groupies emerge together, the pony-tail man on his own, lawyers in pairs, Gomaz in conversation with his barrister. He passes within a yard of me without acknowledgement.

Inside the courtroom the raised bench is deserted, the judge and his clerk already in their chambers. Inspector Mann is standing where he sat yesterday, packing up the exhibits in a cardboard box.

I tell him what I want.

He pales. 'Can't.'

'Could be the key to the case.'

'It's an exhibit, property of the court.'

'But the court's finished with it.'

He jumps to the assumption that the prosecution will have to close their case without Packard. 'You haven't found him yet, then?'

I'm not going to answer that, since I hold him responsible for losing him in the first place, and I don't want a stand-up row. 'Packard wasn't a witness to the attack, was he?'

A headshake.

'Just a witness to what the mugger said afterwards.'

A nod.

'So...' I give him a confident smile. '...when he gives evidence on Monday he won't be asked to identify any exhibits, will he?' I pause. 'So the court's finished with them, right?'

He shakes his head again, less firmly. 'Even so...'

I nod at the closed door to the judge's chambers. 'You were in there yesterday lunchtime when he said: "No stone to be left unturned."'

'Yes, but...'

I motion towards the door. 'Let's go and get the old boy's permission, then.' To force the issue, I take a half-step towards the bench. 'I don't mind telling him it's a loose end that should have been tied up five months ago.' I don't add: 'By you, you idle sod.' I take half another step away from him. 'Now...'

Mann caves in. 'All right.' He rummages in the cardboard box for what I need. 'Make sure I get it back first thing Monday.'

I take it. 'I'll deliver it personally along with Packard.'

'Next for the bossman, please.' A cheery female voice calls from somewhere out of sight. Only the fish in a large tank that runs the length of one wall don't peer inquisitively as I stand and replace an ancient *Viz* on a low table.

According to a sign in the window beneath a red and white pole, a speciality here is 'Toupees discreetly fitted by the proprietor'. Everyone in the waiting-room, I assume, is straining to see the join of my blond wig.

I walk behind half a dozen chairs with sheeted-down customers under bright strip lights. Two of the crimpers are women. All the customers are men. Most are having short back and sides, back in a fashion that's never been out for me since college days.

The woman hairdresser at the chair nearest to the door who took my visiting card when I entered gestures with a comb to a curtained-off cubicle across the centre aisle.

With a swish, the heavy blue velvet parts. A tall, lean man in a short maroon coat appears like a magician making a stagey entrance. 'Sorry to have kept you, sir.'

He's fiftyish, bespectacled, dark hair receding to the extent that he may soon be in need of his own services.

'Sorry to bother you when you're busy.' I produce my warrant card and introduce myself; don't add my nickname of 'Sweeney'; inappropriate somehow at a barber's that's not in Fleet Street.

He doesn't invite me to sit in a tan-coloured leather chair with a footrest facing a mirror and a white basin sunk into a pine worktop. Nor does he sit himself.

'It's about Scott Packard,' I begin.

'Not on today,' he replies. He'd asked for yesterday off, he explains, and had forewarned him he might not turn in for duty today. 'He's had to go to court.' He hastens to add, 'As a witness.'

He eyes the inside pocket into which my warrant card has gone. 'No trouble, is there?'

'No. No. Er...' Packard, whether he was guilty or not, has done sixteen years. I don't want to harm his chances of future employment. 'He hasn't been called yet. You often get hold-ups in long trials.'

'When will we get him back, then?'

My confident smile. 'Tuesday, at the latest.' My smile slips a little. 'With any luck.'

He pulls a put-upon face.

'Er...' Difficult this, I realise. 'The judge in the case has asked me to make a few background inquiries before he gives evidence.' I clutch at the word in his window sign. 'Discreetly.'

He nods, very slow, to tell me: Understood.

I opt for a soft opener. 'How's he working out?'

'Excellent,' he replies without hesitation. Then, face clouding, 'You know where he's from?'

My turn for a slow nod.

He'd engaged Packard on the recommendation of the...whispered...probation service. 'First rate qualifications, not just City and Guilds, but Mastercraftsman.' He yanks his head to one of several certificates hanging on the cream wall above a cabinet with polystyrene heads, some bald, some bewigged.

He worked full time on...whispered...£150 a week which the boss paid to the 'appropriate agency'.

Since he's not mentioning prison or what Packard was inside for, neither will I. He assumes they make deductions for lodgings at the hostel and allow him pocket money. 'Then, of course, there are tips.'

'How much roughly?' I ask.

Now he does hesitate. 'Twenty-five, thirty quid a week.'

As tips should be declared to the taxman he may be underestimating. At a minimum, over almost a year, that's – what? – a grand, a grand-and-half, squirrelled away somewhere.

Should have got the judge to authorise a trawl of bank accounts, I chide myself.

'There's a permanent job here when he's available to take one,' he says.

I open up a bit more. 'Did you know that he is seeking a rehearing of his...er, the circumstances which got him into his current...er...' Robbie Hill's favourite word springs to my rescue. '...situation?'

He smiles, impressed, I'd like to think, with my discretion. 'He told me.'

'When?'

Soon after he had taken a day off to attend the magistrates court five months ago, he started asking for lunchtime duties to be switched, he replies.

He'd claimed, 'I saw a man there who could help me prove my case.' The boss goes on, 'He wanted to try to track him down, find out more about him. His colleagues willingly covered for him. He's very popular.'

'Did he explain his case?'

He glances at the curtain behind me, unsure if our voices are carrying, and continues to speak as if at confession. 'That he'd served too long.'

Not half, I privately agree. A sentence for the murder of PC Joey Craig instead of a non-fatal attack on ex-PC Benson. 'Is that all he said?'

'Well...' He thinks, then, still softly, '...and that, if he's right, he's served ten or a dozen years too many.'

That's about right, too, I concede to myself. 'So you knew he'd been doing life for murder.'

'Look.' The boss takes a quick step towards me, almost talking into my ear. 'Scott's not the first I've employed in these circumstances. They've all done well. One has a business of his own.'

He stops, thinks, trying to get it right. 'Some try to, well, minimise their, you know, involvement, salve their own consciences, I suppose.'

Precisely my thoughts yesterday morning when I was trying to wriggle off this job, I acknowledge. The bossman is a kind, wise bird, probably an experienced hand in rehab and prison after-care, worth listening to.

'You can't always accept things they say at face value,' he goes on expertly. 'Neither can you pry. They have to set the pace. Scott, as yet, has not revealed too many details.'

'What was the outcome of his lunchtime vigils?'

'All he said after a week or two was that he hadn't caught up with him again. He was very depressed, not himself.'

The boss advised him to share whatever was troubling him with his probation officer or a solicitor. 'Around a month back, he said he had been to see an MP and he was a lot brighter, his old self. Said it was being sorted.' He brightens himself. 'Is that why you're here – to reinvestigate?'

Not wanting to disappoint him, I nod. 'One thing the judge has to be sure about is that he's not giving evidence at this on-going trial merely to score brownie points and –'

'No such thing,' he breaks in. 'Most certainly not. It was my idea.'

One quietish day soon after he first came, late winter, Packard entered the cubicle carrying the *Evening Post*, required reading in the waiting-room. The front-page story reported the attack in the street on the beauty queen, with a police appeal for information.

Packard told his boss, 'A lodger in my hostel confessed to me last night he'd done this.'

The boss sat him down in his chair. 'This is a dreadful assault; terrible. Could happen again, next time to your mum or my wife. It's your duty to tell the police.'

He sighs. 'Took some persuading because, well, you know what they're like...'

They don't shop each other, a risky business, he means.

'But in the end...' He nods to a phone at the far corner of the pine worktop. '...he called you on that. Very brave of him. Didn't you know?'

The inspector in charge told me, I reply.

Without prompting, he adds, 'Caused him a bit of aggrava-tion, it did.'

'Such as?'

A few days after the preliminary hearing before the mag-istrates, a stranger walked in, went into the waiting-room, turned down a vacant chair and eventually sat in Packard's.

Afterwards, Scott came into his cubicle and relayed what the customer had said. 'Tone down your evidence or you'll wind up with both hands broken and your scissors up your arse.'

'What part of his evidence?'

He shakes his head into a 'Don't know' and continues, 'I told him he should report it. Interfering with a witness, very serious.'

'What was he like, this stranger?'

'In his twenties, thick-set, pony tail.'

Should have checked out that guy in denims in the public gallery, I rebuke myself; another cock-up. 'Dress?'

He shakes his head again, apologeticially this time. 'He was under a sheet. All I saw was the hair. He only had a trim; should have had a shampoo, too.'

No, he replies to the next question, a bribe wasn't offered. 'He didn't even leave a tip.' No, the threat didn't appear to frighten Scott into second thoughts about going to court.

'How could this stranger have known Scott worked here?' I ask, more or less to myself.

'Haven't a clue.'

I have. Lennie Gomaz would know from his statement in the mugger's court file. He could have leaked it to Frenchie Lebois.

Ah, well, I'll take him in by his pony tail on Monday and turn him over. I begin to wrap up, things to do – return Alice and her papers to her hotel, nip home to say goodnight to Laura and collect my camera. 'Well, thanks very much.'

'I hope some good comes of it.' He chatters on, as all barbers do, repeating himself, as most barbers do. 'There's a job here for as long as he wants it. He's an expert men's stylist...'

He wouldn't have had much practice on women where he's been, I think, amusing myself again, letting my mind drift as it often does in barbers' shops.

'...and he's got a nice way with customers. He's quite up to date with topics like sport and TV, despite...' He dries up to avoid saying 'where he's been.'

I try again to end the flow. 'Well, thanks.'

'He's building up a good clientele. Expert with dreadlocks, rasta and funky, so we're beginning to get Afro-Caribs. They're very particular, you know...'

No, I didn't, I think, a bit bored now.

'...but lots of professionals, too, estate agent, doctors, a couple of solicitors. They ask for him.'

I begin to concentrate again. 'He didn't, by any chance, pick their legal brains about his troubles while he was working on them, did he?'

111

He shakes his head. 'We're all trained not to.' He thinks. 'Only time I've ever heard him really questioning a regular about his work was on the subject of colour blindness.'

'Who was that?' I ask, pulling out my notebook.

Another waiting-room, more magazines to be flipped through, *Hello!* and *Cosmopolitan*, more upmarket, but the words begin to blur. Either the print size in *Viz* is bigger or my eyes are going.

Without thumbing through to the Problems Page, usually good value, I put down a *Cosmopolitan* on a rust-coloured chair beside me.

I look across to a poster advertising a recent National Eye Week, can see that all right. I gaze on to displays of spectacle frames in glass cabinets on two walls.

A pair will come soon enough, bound to with the amount of reading I have to do. Jacko's books apart (and they don't take long), little of it is for pleasure.

Reams and reams of paperwork drop into my in-tray back at HQ every morning. File after file flows across my screen, most of it close to gobbledegook.

Sometimes my eyes feel like Alice's have looked these past two mornings and I go home so bushed it's an effort to read *Thomas the Tank Engine* or *Postman Pat*. I wonder what sort of frames I'll pick – Calvin Klein or Giorgio Armani?

Still, no reading up on this job. Alice has done all that for me. It's a thought that should cheer me. Quite the reverse. Am I relying on her too much? Am I missing something?

'Mr Todd.' A woman receptionist who'd promised to fit me into the senior partner's tight schedule attracts my attention. 'First on the right.'

The first on the right is like a cell for a captive psycho with the highest possible security rating – small, one door, windowless and well lit.

I introduce myself to a middle-aged man in a crisp white smock who looks up from a tiny desk. His dark hair and beard are newly trimmed.

He swivels round on a typist-type stool and motions me to sit in a black leather armchair facing a chart in a mirror. At the top is A, but does the very bottom line start with an L or an E? Don't ask, I decide.

Instead, the usual opening. 'I'm making inquiries about Scott Packard.'

He frowns.

'Your hairdresser just down the road.'

Enlightenment on his face.

'He's giving evidence in a current trial at the crown court.'

An absent headshake to say he didn't know that.

'An issue in the case is colour blindness.'

'Deficiency,' he corrects me. 'Very few people are totally colour blind.'

'The subject is likely to crop up in evidence and the judge wants me to check a few facts.'

He nods.

'He raised the topic with you, I understand, when he last cut your hair on Wednesday.'

A look of slight alarm. 'Shouldn't we have discussed it with a case pending?'

'There's no problem like that.' God, this is difficult. 'But if he's questioned in evidence about it, he could be asked in cross-examination how he came by his knowledge.' Enough flam, I decide. 'Can you tell me what was said?'

'Can't you ask him?' he asks, understandably.

Mmm, but I'm only stumped for a second, on fine flannelling form this afternoon. 'Once they check into the witnesses-in-waiting room we're not allowed to talk to 'em. Could be interpreted as coaching.'

Satisfied, he asks, 'What's the trial about anyway?'

'It's been widely reported. The mugged beauty queen. He's a witness for the prosecution.' I'd better not add 'to something said rather than something seen' or we'll be back to square one.

'Well, yes. Scotty raised the subject,' he finally answers. 'He asked how the problem came about.' Inherited, the optician had replied, mainly in males.

113

Was red and green a particular problem? Packard wanted to know. Most certainly, in severe cases, against a brownish background or in poor lighting, he was told.

I nod, contentedly. I've played golf with a partner who can't find a red peg after he's driven his ball off the tee. 'Did he say why he was inquiring?'

'He said he had a mate who suffered from it, that's all,' he goes on.

'Did you give him a brochure on the subject?'

'No, but he'd read his mate's, he said.'

'Did he tell you about any problems his mate was having, reading traffic lights, things like that?'

'They learn to follow the sequence from top to bottom,' he says, trying to be helpful.

Not what I want to hear. 'Yes, but did he ask that?'

'No.'

'Any follow-up questions at all?'

A headshake. 'Just that.'

I can't think of any follow-up questions myself, certainly not, 'Is that an L or an E?' On second glance, it doesn't look like either.

12

Exhibit number GM3c is a precise, silent fit. No one behind the first-floor curtained window will have heard the lock turn. No one walks a street of mainly commercial buildings emptied for the weekend. Only an occasional car passes, headlights dipped in darkness that descended an hour ago.

Inside, I shut the dark red door carefully and quietly. Next to it is a shop-sized window of smoked glass with 'Racing Club – Lace Market' in red letters on a white fascia board above. Beyond that is the public entrance to the betting shop that was locked and tried by a youngish man who turned out all downstairs lights when he left.

Soundlessly, I mount a steep, well-lit flight of carpeted stairs, pausing often, listening, hearing only the sound of my own soft breathing.

On a landing, I stand with back pressed against a white wall, slide sideways, listen again. Nothing.

OK, then? I look around, then down and see something cream poking out of my pen pocket – the label from the exhibit that's marked: 'From contents of injured party's purse.' I poke it down out of sight.

A hand reaches across a maroon door to a round knob. All that's needed is a gun in my other hand pointing to the ceiling and the image of a cop on a solo bust would be complete, but I'm not armed, not equipped with radio, even a mobile phone. All I've got is my Canon Sure-Shot in its navy blue canvas case.

The knob is in a sweaty palm. Fingers tighten. Wrist hinges. The door clicks open an inch or so. I pull my hand back and rest against the wall. Listen. Nothing.

I lean a shoulder against the frame and with fingertips push the door further back.

Two shuffling steps give me a view of a long narrow room. The far end is softly lit by a standard lamp. This end is in semi-darkness. Enough subdued light reaches it to see a table with four chairs and a three-deck stereo on a low cabinet.

Eyes right, two windows, curtains drawn. Eyes left, three doors, the nearest half open.

Ears strain. All they pick up are faint sounds. Moaning; must be moaning, hope it's moaning.

The sound is followed across a thick carpet, a glance into a small kitchen through half-opened door, stop in front of the middle door.

Bending, ear not quite against the door, I hear muffled moaning. Not much to go on, I think, disconsolately. Then, louder, throaty groans; now, breathless gasps. Better, I think, cheering up.

I pull myself upright and survey the lit end of the room. In the far corner is a wide-screened television. Facing it is a sofa. Across the back has been tossed an off-white raincoat I have seen before. It was being worn by a woman with hair of roughly the same colour who'd arrived fifteen minutes ago.

On an arm of the sofa is women's clothing – white cardie, black dress, underskirt, tights, bra, pants; the order in which they'd been removed, I guess.

Ears take eyes back to the door. From the other side of it come the unmistakable sounds of an approaching and extremely noisy climax.

It'll do.

The camera in its case is taken from a side pocket. Crouching, I step forward, put my left hand on the handle, yank it down, shoulder open the door.

Arms extended, clutching the camera case in a two-handed grip, I drop to one knee and yell, 'Armed Police!'

The door hits something so hard that it rebounds and I have to back-hand it out of the line of vision. The resultant double-take makes it hard on the eyes to immediately sum up what they are seeing.

Take it slowly, I tell myself. OK, then.

What I am seeing is this: a man on a bed naked apart from a black face mask. He is on his back. His arms are above his hidden head. His wrists are handcuffed to a semicircular bed-head with black and gold spokes that look like half a huge wheel. In his mouth is something the size, but not the colour, of a large cigar. No smoke rises from it.

On the other side of the bed is a woman. She appears to be kneeling in what's not prayer. Only her face and shoulders are visible. The face is darkened with terror. The shoulders are quite chubby and bare.

I prise myself up and walk slowly in. The woman sinks further from view, only the top of her whitish-blonde hair visible.

I stuff the camera case back into my pocket. Even if there is a gun in a bedside drawer, the man is in no position to go for it, use it and claim self-defence afterwards.

Moving closer, I make out a flesh-coloured tube sticking out of his mouth, held vertically either by the grip of his teeth or by two zips drawn at the mouth of the mask from each side.

Bizarrely, a white ping-pong ball is resting at his hip on a floral bed cover.

'Sorry,' I say. I take out my warrant card from an inside pocket and hold it towards the man. Dark, moist eyes fix on it through two slits in the black shiny mask. Pink ears protrude from slits each side. I assume he's heard me, but just to make sure, 'Very sorry.'

The woman's head comes up slowly, like a soldier's from a trench at the end of a heavy bombardment. I show it to her, too. Her eyes try to focus, seem to fail.

The man's head begins to waggle violently from side to side. His arms pull at the bedhead making a metallic rattle. His body arches up, then flops back, up and down repeatedly. His Adam's apple works frantically into a sound like a seal at feeding time.

I smile down on him. 'Hello, Frenchie,' I say pleasantly.

The woman lifts her chin on to the edge of the bed, resting it there. Her shoulders are visible again, shaking uncontrollably. 'What the fuck?' she quakes.

I could ask her the same question, decide against. 'Sorry.'

Amid a stream of obscenities, I get the message that I'm about to be more than sorry. 'You scared the shit out of me.'

I hold up my hand. 'I was walking past, minding my own business –'

It doesn't stem her foul-mouthed flow.

'Hear me out,' I plead. '...heard noises that seemed like someone in distress, tried the door, found it open...'

This last claim is hotly disputed, understandably so.

'...and came up to check.' A feigned loss of temper now. 'What the hell was I supposed to do – walk on by?'

She indicates shrilly that she doesn't believe me.

'It's a betting shop with money about, for chrissake.' I pat my pocket. 'I faked having a gun in case the raiders were tooled up. It could have been an armed hold-up, someone gagged.'

Obligingly, Frenchie rocks the bed and makes a gagging sound.

117

'See.' I point down at him.

She doesn't want to see, just abuse me in a high-pitched quavering voice, and I know I am wasting time. I jerk a thumb over my shoulder. 'Go in the other room. Get dressed.'

Roughly translated, she says I can't order her about.

'Well, yes, I can, actually,' I say evenly.

Stripped of all colour her argument is that what takes place between adults in private is none of my business.

'Well, yes, it can be actually,' I respond.

Never having worked in Vice (mercifully, if this is what you have to do on a regular basis), I'm none too sure of the up-to-date law, but, in these situations, confidence counts for everything. 'If a masochist pleads "Hurt me," you're legally obliged to say no.'

I shrug, easygoing. 'Of course, you can smile sadistically while you're saying it.'

My mistake, I realise, because she doesn't see the funny side of it and I have to withstand another fusillade of fucks and threats.

At last I manage, 'What's happening here could, in the eyes of the law, constitute an offence. So go into the other room, get dressed, stay there and we'll sort it out.'

She presses down with her hands to push herself upright, exposing everything from the knees up. All I note is that her blonde hair isn't natural, then I look down again.

Far from a-throbbing, Frenchie's manhood is displaying the fact that he's in a mixed marriage.

I return to the bed after I've escorted the bottle blonde out and closed the door behind her. I pick up the ping-pong ball, study it, then sit on the bed and say, 'This how it works?'

I place the ball on top of the tube. He makes a noise like a walrus on heat. The ball shoots in the air as if on a jet of water in a funfair shooting gallery. I catch it deftly, replace it and hold it lightly down with my index finger.

He begins to struggle so violently that it is as if I'm operating on him without anaesthetic. I remove my finger. The ball shoots higher in the air and drops on the bed-cover the other side of him.

'Now, listen, Frenchie...' I lean closer to his nearest ear. '...since I happen to be passing, I'm going to ask some questions, and if I don't believe the answers I'm going to do that again – only longer.'

Carefully, I draw back the zip each side of his mouth. The tube bounces off his chin and falls on to his matted chest.

In language that's worse than the blonde's, he predicts that my career is about to drown under a welter of writs if I don't die slowly first.

Sighing dramatically, I rezip his mouth, stand, take the camera case out of my pocket and the camera out of the case. I move around the bedroom, flash off several shots from different angles. He is twitching and tossing and turning so desperately that most will be blurred, I fear.

I go back to the bed and sit again. 'Listen, Frenchie.' I run through my cover story again – the strange sounds at the street door, the suspicion that a robbery was in progress, having no communications to summon back-up, fearing they'd arrive too late anyway, going it alone.

I toy with the camera. 'Now I've pictorial evidence of a millionaire owner of a chain of betting shops in chains. Even a rookie on the beat is entitled to ask himself if he's being tortured to make him give the combination to the safe.'

I harden my tone. 'Sure you can complain, take me to a disciplinary hearing or to court and I'll produce this in my defence.' I grip the camera.

'Having nothing to hide, I'll make sure the press is present, including the *Sporting Life* and the *Racing Post*.'

I hold up the camera. 'I'll put the pick of these on the Internet. Is your wife on the Net, by the way?' Pause. 'What's it to be – complain or co-operate?'

'Scott Packard.' The standard opening is followed by, 'Are you after him?'

He shakes his head so fiercely that the wonder is that he doesn't crick his neck. Then he realises his mouth has been unzipped to allow him to speak, somewhat breathlessly. 'Why the fuck should I be?'

'Because you're after Linda Dwyer and he's giving evidence in the same case on her side.'

'I'm not, no. I'm not. Never.' He mumbles, as if he's just had a tooth out. 'Why? What's this all about?'

'Do you know Packard?'

'Of course.' He swallows hard. 'Of him, anyway.'

'What do you know of him?'

'Oh, for...' He takes in air. 'That he bumped off a cop.' His eyes blaze through their slits. I suspect he's fantasising about doing something similar. 'That he's coming to the end of his time. That he stitched up Garry Matthews good and proper. That's enough, isn't it?'

'Before all of that,' I say quietly. 'Back in '81.'

Rising up on the back of his head, arching his back, he pulls hard with his cuffs on the bedhead, making the whole bed rock. 'Undo me, for fuck's sake.'

'In a minute,' I promise, smiling down. 'Did you know of him then, back in '81?'

His chin drops, exhausted. 'He'd be a kid then.'

'A kid playing for Racing Club of Radford, a team you sponsored in the Unemployed League.'

He smacks his lips. 'Out of the goodness of my heart.' More abuse washes over me, water off a duck's back now.

I try again. 'How did that sponsorship come about?'

'The little bleeders had no jobs, did they? Nothing to do, except soccer. They approached lots of businesses for a bit of help. Now, after all this time... This is outrageous, criminal.'

'What was your contribution?'

'Provided them with shirts. Sent off to Paris for them. The genuine articles from Racing Club; a bit of a gimmick – that's all, good PR.'

'Red?' I check.

'Yes. Old strip, actually used, genuine numbering. Collector's items. Gave a ton or two. I forget how much exactly.

120

And what thanks did I get? They put the bloody bite on me again.'

'Why?'

'Because some of the shirts got buggered.'

'How were they buggered?'

'Buggered if I know.' He raises his voice. 'I told them to piss off, scrounging little sods.' He grips the black and gold spokes with both hands. 'Look. This is deliberate humiliation, there's no need for it. Unlock me.'

'Soon.' My soothing tone.

No, he insists amid more curses, he wasn't at the cup final at which his sponsored side made their last appearance in his colours or at the presentation afterwards or at the riots that followed in which the policeman was killed. 'What is this?' he asks plaintively. 'What are you trying to stick on me, you shit-head? What's the point of all of this after all these years?'

The point, I point out, is that the very same Scott Packard in the current mugging trial was convicted of killing the policeman.

'Well, I know that,' he whines. 'I've told you that already. What are you trying to prove?'

He didn't know Packard, only read about him at the trial, he insists. 'I'd forgotten all about him and the riots, the murder, everything, until ...' He gulps.

'Until what, Frenchie?'

He lowers his voice. 'Until this heap of shit.'

'Tell me about that.'

'Oh, for –'

'Please.'

It comes out in answers to questions, a headshake here, a nod there, never more than a single sentence.

He was having 'you know ... a thing' with Linda Dwyer. She talked about what they were getting up to in a nightclub. 'Out of order, that.'

He got to hear. He was 'cross, like'. Not cross enough to 'blow her away', just to 'bomb her out'.

Matthews came to see him after his transfer from closed prison to the hostel, seeking work. He'd previously been on the firm's payroll as a security guard. He'd done 'little jobs'

121

before, like debt collecting. He ordered him to track her down and get the key to this place back.

'Should have known better.' He loosens up a little. 'All that time in jail made him sex-starved. He roughed her up for fun, overdid it. That was never the idea, not part of the plan.' An urgent look through the eye-slits. 'Next day, he was arrested.'

Now I'm getting somewhere. 'And you fixed him up with a lawyer?'

'No.'

I coax him. 'Come on.'

'Honest. He's on legal aid, as far as I know.'

'He's being represented by Lennie Gomaz.'

'So?'

'So he's your solicitor.'

'No he's not. You've got that wrong. I never use him. Ever.' He names a big legal firm he does use.

Get out of this, I think. 'Then how did you know about Scott Packard coming forward as a witness for the prosecution against your boy?'

'Why shouldn't I?'

'It's never been in the papers, that's why. Who leaked it to you?' Now that Gomaz has gone from my mind into it jumps Inspector Mann. Is he bent as well as idle? They often go together. 'Come on. Who?'

'Nobody.'

'Then how did you know?'

'I had someone listening at the magistrates court.'

Oh, Christ, I think with a jolt. That could be true. Committal proceedings are not behind closed doors. Though magistrates can restrict publicity, they can't ban the public from sitting in and listening. I knew that, but ignored it, got caught up with conspiracy theories and leaks.

Hang on a minute, I calm myself. 'How did you know where to find Packard?'

'He's in the same hostel as Matthews, dummy.'

'Where he worked, I mean. The barber's shop.'

'My look-out followed him from court.'

Makes sense, too. That's how big-time crooks sometimes get to nobble jurors. They have them followed home, then they threaten or bribe. I've gone down a blind alley here. Oh, Christ.

Don't show him you're wrong-footed, I order myself. 'So when your look-out returned from court and told you that Packard had given evidence that your man Matthews –'

'He's no longer my man. He's a c –'

I break in. '... reported Matthews as saying "I did it for the Patron" – '

'I never told him to do anything other than collect the fucking key.'

'Whether that's true or false –'

He raises his voice. 'It's true.'

'Whichever, you sent another heavy round to warn off Packard –'

'Never did.'

'Interfering with a witness, that –'

'Not true.'

'What happened then?'

He takes a deep breath. 'Sod Matthews. He cocked it up and not for the first time. He can carry the can. What do I care? But, of course, I care about that "Patron" bit coming out in public; people making the connection between the nickname, me and Linda Dwyer.'

His wife especially, I have to accept. 'So?'

'So I sent a messenger to see Packard.'

'With what message?'

'Just to forget the "Patron" business, that's all, and I'd see him OK. The rest, whatever else Matthews admitted to him ... not my problem. He can give what other evidence he likes.'

'Your messenger actually told Packard he'd break his hands and stick his scissors up his arse.'

He groans wearily.

'Was that seeing him all right?' I go on.

'What a total tosser.' He shakes his head, rather sadly, as if saying: You can't get good labour these days. 'Then he was exceeding his orders.'

'This messenger of yours wears a pony tail. Right?'

He nods.

'And he's been sitting in the crown court for the last two days, right?'

Another nod.

'Doing what?'

'Keeping a watching brief for me.'

'To be seen by Packard when he goes into the box, you mean. So he gets the message that if he mentions "Patron" his number's up.'

'I'll take care of it,' he says, quietly.

'You've taken care of enough, Frenchie,' I say. 'So where's Scott Packard now?'

His eyes look glazed. 'How should I know? In the hostel or prison or somewhere. I don't know. Why? For God's sake, if you want him, he'll be in court on Monday. That's what my look-out said this afternoon. Why?'

'He's missing.'

He struggles and swears again. 'Why didn't you tell me that in the first place, instead of all this?'

I tell him nothing.

He settles again. 'Ahh.' He gulps in air, greedily. 'I get it. And you think I've got him or am after him, that I'm going to kill him or something to get Matthews off the hook. You're mad. He can rot in jail as far as I'm concerned, the pyscho. All I did was pick the wrong man for a routine job, that's all.'

'Two wrong men,' I say.

'I'll sort that.'

'No you won't.'

'Believe me.' A menacing tone.

Well, yes and no. I'm going to rule out the possibility that Scott Packard is on the run from him. The motive for his escape is to be found in that '81 cup final. Apart from providing one side with a playing strip, Frenchie Lebois had no part in it.

I'm certainly not going to accept that he merely instructed one heavy to collect the key from Linda Dwyer and the other to politely ask Packard to drop any reference to 'Patron' from his evidence.

But I can't prove conspiracy to commit GBH or interference with a witness. The manner in which these partial admissions have been obtained could land me in jail rather than him. The top priority here and now is to cover my back.

'OK, then, here's the deal. Call your dogs off Linda Dwyer and Scott Packard –'

'Aren't you listening? I haven't got any dogs on.'

'Fine.' I pocket the camera. 'The film will stay in my safe, undeveloped, and you'll get it back, all in good time.'

'That's blackmail.'

I can't argue with that, I concede privately, rising from the bed and walking out.

'Bastard,' he shouts at my back, rattling the bedhead again.

'Bastard,' echoes the now fully dressed blonde out of a cloud of cigarette smoke as I pass through the lounge.

Since I never knew my father, I can't really argue with that either.

13

No mention of the mugger's trial on the radio news, yesterday's evidence too routine, I presume, eating a full fry-up, the usual Saturday breakfast that normally fuels a shopping trip or a stint of gardening or decorating; not today, regrettably.

Not a word about Robbie Hill in the sports headlines which concentrate on team news from clubs playing this afternoon. The weather: unchanged.

I rise from the kitchen table, blowing kisses to the two ladies in my life.

No 'Good morning' from Alice, back in her black suit, when I walk into my office. With the courthouse closed for the week-end, we're operating from HQ.

She looks up from papers spread all over my desk and greets me with, 'Well?'

'We can rule out Frenchie Lebois,' I tell her, taking off the jacket of my brown suit and hanging it on the chair back.

'How can you be so sure?'

I'm not going to brief her on that, I decide, sitting down. 'My source is impeccable. Let's concentrate on the '81 game.'

She doesn't look convinced. 'Sure?'

'Positive.' I pick up the phone and dial Surveillance. Nothing from them, either. Odd, I think. Didn't her MP plan to call Mrs Packard?

'Now.' I lounge back. 'If Scott Packard didn't kill our policeman, who did?'

She hunts through the files on the desk. 'Maybe it's got something to do with the numbers on the shirts.'

'Or the colours,' I venture, thinking of the pamphlet she found at Scott's hostel.

The team sheet is shuffled to the top and she pores over it. 'Scott played in red number 4. Cammy played in red number 7 under the name of J. Robertson.'

My God, she's got it, I want to sing.

She shakes her head distractedly. 'Still no further trace of him in the documents.'

No she hasn't, I think, depressed.

She reads on, 'Hill played in green number 4. Harries in green number 2.' She looks across the desk at me, frowning. 'Could the eyewitness who saw the policeman being struck on the head with a blunt instrument by red number 4 be colour blind?'

Possible, I think, requesting a look at the pamphlet.

She delves into her files, extracts it and stands briefly to hand it to me over the desk.

It's just a slim folded brochure, the sort that advertises hotels and tourist attractions, which pulls out into six narrow pages.

On the front, beneath the headline 'Pick a number', is a circle of green dots. In the centre the figure 12 is clearly visible in rust-coloured dots. Below, it says: 'The standard test for colour blindness.'

I look at her over the top of it. 'Well, I've passed that.'

She smiles thinly. 'That's the test they use to detect fakes.'

Sighing, I skip on through 'Men more prone than women' to 'Most sufferers have difficulty with red and green' – confirmation of what the optician told me.

While I'm reading, she asks, 'If the optician didn't give it to Scott, who did, I wonder?'

'Search me.' Then, I ask her, 'Who is he, this eyewitness?'

'She,' Alice replies. She goes back in her files. 'Mrs Dorothy Evans,' she reads. 'Aged fifty at the time.' She adds an address in the now demolished flats.

She's bound to have moved, I realise, disheartened, if she's still alive, and the council housing offices will be closed.

Alice summarises her statement. That night she was watching telly in her first-floor flat when she heard shouting, couldn't make out what. She went out of her front door and leaned over the balcony. She saw a white man in a grey sweatshirt stagger from the alleyway to the street into the courtyard below, some fifty yards away.

Alice pats another dossier. 'Both the murdered policeman and ex-PC Benson were in grey sweatshirts with a college motif, by the way.'

They would be. Plainclothes troublespotters always dressed alike. In the heat of battle, officers in the Snatch Squad can't be expected to carry too many clothes descriptions in their heads. They'd simply be ordered: 'Don't nick anyone in a grey college sweatshirt. He's one of ours.'

I nod her on.

'A younger black man in a red shirt with number 4 on his back came up behind the white man and hit him with something on the back of his head. The man fell to the ground. The youth ran away.'

Now she quotes, 'It was over in a second. I had no time to shout a warning. I returned to my flat and dialled 999.' She couldn't describe the trousers or footwear of either victim or attacker.

Alice spreads her hands. 'None of this was challenged at the trial. It was accepted as fact by both sides and read out to the jury. Mrs Evans wasn't called into the witness box.'

She's repeating what she's already told me, not, I hope, because she mistrusts my memory, but because saying it again fixes it clearly in both our minds.

It's a technique I'm going to copy. 'And that was because his defence counsel, briefed by Lennie Gomaz, never disputed that

Scott struck the fatal blow on PC Craig, only that it was in self-defence.'

She mulls for a moment and continues in the same mode. 'But now Scott has seen the man he hit and it wasn't PC Craig but Benson – who is very much alive.'

I'm going to conclude this by returning to the question that started the debate. 'Therefore someone else killed Joey Craig. Who?'

She doesn't answer. Instead, 'You were at those flats on other nights during the troubles, weren't you?'

'Yes,' I confirm, 'and the concrete was badly weathered and the outside lighting often vandalised.'

I've made up my mind, pick up the telephone book. There's around a third of a column of D. Evanses and we don't know if she's under her husband's initial anyway. Hopeless.

I thumb on, then pick up the phone and dial. 'Emergency housing repairs,' says a male voice. 'What's the problem, please?'

I tell him.

'Don't know about that.'

'It's a police emergency,' I say patiently.

'Records are shut.'

'Then open 'em up.'

'Not my department.'

I give him the number of my mobile phone, then, very chummily, 'Listen, mate. I have the home number of the chairman of the housing committee here...' I make one up. '...and unless someone there comes up with an answer I'll be phoning him on the hour every hour right through the weekend, day and night.'

He asks me to repeat my number which I do, slowly. I put down the phone, pleased with myself, and look across at Alice.

She looks anything but pleased. 'I can fully understand why Scott, having seen the man he thought he'd killed, is seeking a review.'

A thoughtful pause. 'I can even understand why he's gone on the run. He thought we were dragging our feet. He wasn't to know we have a huge backlog of cases dumped on us from the Home Office.'

She sighs. 'What I don't follow is how and why he suddenly became interested in that.' She nods at the pamphlet on colour blindness.

'Because,' I speculate, 'he's gone back through all the statements and...' I can't immediately take it any further, stop and try again. 'Someone may have planted the idea in his head after all these years that Mrs Evans' evidence was open to doubt because of her eyesight.'

'Yes, but who?'

All I can think of, I tell her, is that his MP Giles Johnson may have done some research as well as filling in his form applying for a case review.

'Why don't we go and find out?' she suggests.

I nod, eyes back on the pamphlet, half reading, half musing. You know what it means if that eyewitness turns out to be colour blind, don't you? I tell myself.

Rob Hill, soccer star who wore green number 4 all those years ago, is a cop killer. It also means Scott hasn't gone on the run because of any delays in reinvestigating his case.

He'd heard on the radio at the hostel on Thursday that his MP was at least getting things moving. He'd also heard that Rob Hill was back in town for the first time in years and leaves again on Monday.

He knew where Hill would be yesterday lunchtime. That interview was trailed on air. He didn't turn up at Radio Trent to talk about his wrongful conviction to that reporter.

Scott Packard is out to settle a score.

My eyes halt at, 'In the worst red-deficient cases, sufferers see it as grey or black.'

Lennie Gomaz was press-ganged into being a linesman at the cup final. And what colour do linesmen wear?

I groan out loud which forces me to share my fears with Alice.

'But would a linesman have number 4 on his back?' she queries.

'No,' I concede, 'but American baseball gear was all the rage when we were both at college and they had all sorts of numbers on their back.'

She widens her eyes. 'What could be worse than having to accuse the legal darling of New Labour?'

Arresting a soccer idol, I think, picking up the phone with another job for Surveillance.

The home base of Giles Johnson MP isn't as humble as he'd made it sound when we parted at the Midland station.

To a backdrop of high, grey clouds, his constituency headquarters stands almost regally on a bend in a wide tree-lined avenue of what were once imposing turn-of-the-century houses, mainly flats and offices now and all a bit seedy in comparison.

It is big, square and solid, with none of the ornate Victorian fussiness of the fading buildings around, and is much better maintained.

A double door between two large bay windows and the stone-work at each corner are coated cream, very clean. The rest of the front is stucco, freshly painted a sage green; not a trace of traditional red anywhere.

'Looks more like the Green Party,' says Alice when it appears in view.

Or maybe the decorator was colour blind, I conjecture, pulling off the avenue into a concreted car-park that once must have been a spacious garden. A Mercedes provides a silvery-grey background to a collection of colourful cars.

Somewhere among them will be an unmarked vehicle from Surveillance Squad, probably the tattiest of the lot, but I won't bother to look.

Beyond the entrance is a cool, tiled hallway with an office to the right and a cosy lounge with a small, shuttered bar to the left, both empty. We take the stairs ahead of us.

In the first-floor corridor an elderly couple sit on a wall bench next to an ill-fitting door with a sign that says, 'Please knock and wait.'

From behind the door come voices, slightly raised. 'Why didn't you tell me earlier?' demands an educated voice. 'I saw no need, frankly,' comes a flat reply.

I knock and wait.

No 'Come in' comes from the other side, only: 'I had to hear it from that Commission girl first.'

'There was no secret about it. I released it to the radio.'

Normally I'd be starting to get impatient by now. I'm anything but, recognising both voices. I'm keen to hear more.

'Yes, but surely out of courtesy...' The tone of Lennie Gomaz doesn't sound so melodious today.

'Sorry. It just never occurred to me,' says Giles Johnson in the distinctive dialect of my neck of the woods that's never melodious. 'Just a tick.'

A chair moves and footsteps approach, both sounds cushioned by carpeting. The door opens. At the sight of us, Johnson's face drops, just an inch or two, then, being a politician, bounces up into a beam. 'Ah. Good to see you.'

He pulls back the door to present a view of Gomaz sitting in a pine-framed chair beside an ancient desk that's splintered on the front and littered with papers on the top.

He is wearing off-duty casuals – brown cords and lemon polo-necked sweater. Johnson is dressed down-to-business in shirt-sleeves, patterned tie in place. There's a rare sight of red in the colour of braces over a white shirt. The braces are clipped to dark blue trousers.

One hand on the inside handle, he motions to Gomaz with the other. 'We were just talking about it.'

I refrain from responding, 'So I gather.' Instead, 'We'd like to talk about it, too.' I crane my neck to look inside. 'To you, too, please.'

'How did you know I was here?' asks Gomaz, not attempting to get up. His expression tells me he's not so glad to see us.

'We didn't,' I lie. Surveillance started half an hour after that phone call from my office. His journey here was monitored all the way from his home in a fashionably expensive suburb. 'We were going to ring you.'

Johnson yanks his head sideways towards the waiting couple. 'I'll be a little while.' Constituents with a problem, I gather. He turns his head back at Gomaz. 'Perhaps you'll see 'em downstairs. It saves time.'

'In a few minutes,' says Gomaz with an imperious wave which Johnson takes to mean: Shut the door. 'See you soon,' he says as he does so.

Gomaz enters the lounge downstairs. He is pulling on a light brown suede jacket. He doesn't close the door to the hallway behind him, indicating that he doesn't intend to stay long.

He walks up to a low round table in a bay window where we are sitting, stops in front of us. 'Well?'

I open my mouth, but the pleasantries on the tip of my tongue don't have time to emerge as Alice looks up. 'On that night in July 1981 when you were running the line at the cup final, what were you wearing?'

If Johnson's face dropped an inch upstairs, Gomaz's drops a foot, flabbergasted. 'What the...What a question!'

Alice switches on a rare smile. 'We've lots more. Sit down, please.'

He glowers down instead.

Chin up, she continues, 'We are reviewing events that resulted in your former client, Scott Packard, being in jail, perhaps unjustly, for sixteen years.'

What a devastating opening, I think, surprised and delighted, as she motions to an empty chair between us. 'Sit down, please.'

He pulls his shoulders back. 'After all this time. Ridiculous.'

Alice fixes him with a hostile gaze. 'We are seeking your co-operation. If you wish to withhold it, fair enough. That's your right. But I shall report the fact to my Commissioners who will inform the Legal Aid Board.'

A sensational start, I recognise admiringly. Get binned by Legal Aid and bang goes the bulk of your business and your nice Merc outside, she's warning him.

Visibly taken aback, he blusters, 'The question, I mean. It's ridiculous after all this time.'

He turns with a sweep that makes his coat tails fly, goes back to and shuts the door rather loudly. On his return journey he complains bitterly that we should have made an appointment to see him on Monday.

'You know and we know that Monday will be too late,' says Alice sweetly, indicating again an empty chair.

'Now.' She waits for him to sit. 'Have we understood this correctly?'

Alice begins by taking him back through everything he told us when the court rose on Thursday, me taking notes on my knee, asking no questions, happy to sit back, accepting that I've totally underestimated her.

Gomaz nods curtly to everything – his post-university stint at the law centre, his friendship with Liam Harries that has not stood the test of time, going to the cup final to watch, being asked to stand in for an absent linesman.

'Were any group photos taken of the teams and the officials?' she asks.

A dismissive little wave of a hand. 'It was only a tinpot little tournament. I doubt it.'

'Well, you should know.'

'Why?' His face sets even more aggressively.

'I'd have thought such material would have come to light in the preparation of Packard's defence.'

She is questioning his legal competence at the '81 trial and he knows it. It's astonishing. She's dynamite, far, far braver than me on Thursday.

'No.' Then, to be on the safe side, he adds, 'At least, I never saw one.'

'Pity.'

'Why?' he repeats.

'Because it would have established who took part and what colour clothing they were in.'

'Why's that suddenly so important?'

Alice doesn't enlighten him. 'Were you wearing black...'

'Good Lord.' A noisy sigh. 'How do you expect me –'

She won't let him finish. 'Linesmen do, I'm informed.' She nods at me.

'I wasn't in uniform, little tunic and shorts, if that's what you mean.'

'But a black jacket, tracksuit top?'

He shakes his head uncertainly.

133

'Did you have one in those days?' she persists.

He gives me a hapless look and I have to help him out. 'There were lots about on campuses in your time. American baseball style, names and numbers on the back.'

'Yes, but...' He thinks for a moment. 'It was high summer. I doubt if I was wearing it.'

'But you had one?' Alice double-checks.

He sits back. 'I think I deserve some explanation.'

He gets none as Alice prompts, 'Or were you in grey, a sweatshirt perhaps, like PC Craig and his colleague were wearing?'

He looks down. Almost contritely, like a liar cornered in the witness box, he says, 'I honestly can't remember.'

I'm totally thrilled by her wonderful cross-examination. She's beaten him at his own game, I'm thankful that she hasn't gone home for the weekend. Head down over my notebook, I have to fight off a grin.

Remorselessly, she takes him on to the post-match celebrations which he still insists he did not attend. Nor was he a witness to the riot, he reasserts.

She moves him on to the call-out to the police station to represent Packard after his arrest, his client's admission that he hit a man in a grey sweatshirt with a stolen tent clamp and his excuse for doing it, his trial at which the eyewitness, Mrs Evans, wasn't called. Nothing changes in his story.

She brings him to his last meeting with Packard at his office when he told him of the court foyer sighting of the man he always assumed he'd killed and the advice he gave that reopening the case would merely delay his eventual release.

He remains adamant that his view had nothing whatever to do with representing the mugger, against whom Packard was a witness. Nothing new.

She breaks fresh ground. 'During that final consultation, did Scott raise any questions with you on the subject of colour blindness?'

'Absolutely not.' An immediate reply, very firm.

'Sure?'

'Certain.' An urgent nod. 'Why?'

134

Alice finally looks at me, wondering how far we should go.

The whole hog, I decide, putting my notebook on the table. 'Apart from claiming to have seen the policeman he's supposed to have killed, Packard appears to be pursuing a second line of defence.'

'Which is?' He's recovered his composure.

Alice resumes. 'That Mrs Evans may have got it wrong, confused the colours of the shirts, got mixed up between red and green.'

'Or,' I come back, very slowly, 'in the worse case of colour blindness, black or grey.'

'I see.' He doesn't like what he's seeing. Suppressed fury fills his face. 'You're surely not suggesting...'

'We're...' Alice tries.

'...that I, me...I can't believe this...' He looks as if he can't. '...killed that constable, then represented Packard...'

Alice is shaking her head. 'We're suggesting that Packard believes, perhaps with good reason, that the real killer has let him remain in jail for sixteen years. We think he's either gone on the run to prove it or to seek revenge.'

'Accordingly,' I say, quite formally, 'we're keeping a protective eye on a player who wore green, same number as Packard's red shirt, and, since you can't be sure if you wore black or grey or what, we're doing the same for you.'

He swallows. 'You can't believe that I deliberately mishandled Packard's defence to keep myself out of jail.'

'It's what Scott Packard believes that's important here,' I say, quite quietly. 'We're not asking your permission. We're doing it, like it or not, and I'll be happy to explain why to the Home Office, if needs be.'

'So...' A small smile for some recognition of his importance in Whitehall. 'You're not here by chance.'

I smile back. 'We have to see Mr Johnson anyway.' I pause. 'You were arguing.'

His eyes go to the ceiling. 'Just a slight difference of opinion between friends.' He hadn't heard Giles Johnson talking on the radio about his backing for Packard's case review, he expands. The first he knew was when we broke the news to him at the

135

courthouse on Thursday. 'I thought he might have informed me, that's all.'

'Why should he have told you?' asks Alice bluntly.

'I was, as you keep pointing out, originally involved.'

She leans forward. 'Yes, and you had two chances – first at his trial, then when he came to see you in May.'

He leans towards her, almost face to face. 'May I remind you that at his trial, he was accepting responsibility for the fatal blow. With regard to the review application, Packard raised no question about the reliability of the eyesight of any eyewitness. That's new to me.' A second's silence, then: 'Is she?'

'Is she what?'

'This Mrs Evans. Is she colour blind?'

I was wondering when he was going to ask and I'm glad it's not me who has to answer.

'Shouldn't that have been checked out before the trial?' says Alice, a perfect reply. 'Shouldn't she have been called into the witness box and put to the test?'

He sags back in his chair in a sulk.

I come in. 'Tell us, why did you ask Scott's mother to stop his daily paper during the trial?'

He pulls his head back, querulously.

I repeat what Mrs Packard told us about the daily delivery to Scott's remand cell being cancelled on Gomaz's instructions while the trial was running.

'It's my normal practice.' He tries to brush it aside with another little flick of his hand. 'I don't want clients tailoring their evidence to media accounts. Judges tell juries not to read press reports. Why shouldn't I tell my clients the same?'

It's not a bad answer, but Alice won't accept it. 'You see, if Scott had seen or ...' An evil smile. '... been shown by you the photos of the dead and injured policemen at the time, all this could have been sorted out sixteen years ago.'

'Oh, I see all right.' He pitches forward. 'You're out to damage me, aren't you? That's what it could do if this comes out.'

'Oh, it will come out,' she says, smiling sweetly.

Now he does parade his political clout, rising, glaring down. 'We'll see.'

I could kiss her, but when the door's been slammed shut, compliment her instead. 'Wonderful.'

She blushes.

Giles Johnson's friendly face appears in a widening gap in the lounge door. 'Lennie gone?'

I nod, not adding: In a huge huff.

The door opens fully. Johnson has put on a jacket that matches his trousers for the trip downstairs. He walks up to our table and sits in the seat Gomaz has just vacated. It must feel quite hot, I think.

I open with an apology. 'Sorry we didn't inform you immediately Scott disappeared...'

'That's all right.'

'...as you can imagine, we had lots to do.'

He nods his understanding. He spends a few moments lamenting Scott's stupidity. 'Can't understand it.'

Alice, whose mood has completely changed, regrets she didn't inform Packard earlier of the decision to have a fresh look at his conviction.

She asks, 'When you saw him here to fill out his application form, did he raise the subject of colour blindness with you?'

A shake of the head. The sole reason for the application, he says, was Scott Packard's sighting of the surviving policeman in the foyer of the magistrates court.

'He said he'd never forgotten the face of the man he hit, saw it most nights on his bunk in his cell, and he was certain that was the face he saw. He convinced me.'

Without being asked, Alice explains the pamphlet found in Packard's papers and I tell him of the questions he asked his optician customer at the barber's shop.

Alice reveals her suspicion that Packard might have received information that questioned the accuracy of a statement given at the time by an eyewitness. 'Mrs Dorothy Evans. Does the name ring a bell?'

He purses his lips. They keep voters' registers in the office, he says, but since the flats had been pulled down, there was no

137

point in checking them without a new address. He volunteers to look at his membership rolls, gets up and walks out.

In his absence Alice says, 'Scott's interest in colour blindness seems to have developed since he saw him.' She inclines her head towards the door that Johnson has just closed.

'And since he consulted Gomaz even earlier than that,' I point out, 'Lennie was telling us the truth.'

'About that, anyway,' she agrees, reluctantly.

She wonders again how and why Packard first cottoned on to the lead.

He's been in the hostel and about the streets for almost a year, I reply. Since May, he could have told anyone, any old friend or neighbour, someone in the hostel, at the barber's shop, 'I've seen the man I'm supposed to have killed.'

'That reminds me,' could have come the reply. 'That neighbour who gave such damning eyewitness evidence against you is as colour blind as a rainbow bat.'

Pointless to speculate, I decide, taking my mobile phone out of a jacket pocket, tapping in numbers I've noted in my book, and reintroducing myself.

'I was just about to phone you with the bad news,' says the man at Housing Repairs, a touch too gleefully for my liking. 'Mrs Dorothy Evans wasn't rehoused by us when the flats came down.'

'Which means?'

'She went into a private dwelling or moved away.'

Or she's dead, I think, gloomily, thanking and disconnecting him.

I toy with the idea of phoning the National Insurance people. At her age, she's bound to be on a state pension. But, without an NI number or address, what hope is there? How many Dorothy Evanses will they have on their books?

Johnson returns with more bad news. No Dorothy Evans appears in the membership lists. 'Sorry,' he adds, not sitting down again.

I straighten in my chair, about to get up, 'And I'm sorry you had to hear so late in the day about this unfortunate development.'

'Sorry?' he repeats, frowning.

'We should have phoned you at the Commons on Thursday, not waited until today for you to hear it second-hand from Mr Gomaz. Sorry.'

He smiles. 'But I was told on Thursday.'

If not by us or Gomaz, then by whom? I want to ask. Something troubles me and holds the question back.

'I phoned Scott's mother to tell her the news you gave me at the railway station,' he goes on after a moment's silence. 'She told me.'

But, I remind myself, no such phone call was recorded and reported by Surveillance who have have been plugged into her line since late afternoon on the first day.

Be careful, I order myself. You don't want an MP knowing about intercepted calls. Government back-benches are packed with civil righters. 'I tried her on and off most of that evening; no reply.'

'She's got a part-time job in a pub.' He names it. 'Didn't you know?'

No, I didn't, I think, glumly. I've gone to the incredible expense of having two men at risk tailed and I've got taps on half a dozen phones. And I failed to spot that gap; just never occurred to me.

Nobody to blame but yourself, I accept ruefully, rising.

14

'Some news?' asks a weary-looking Mrs Packard, showing us into an over-furnished sixth-floor lounge, its colourful cosiness a relief from the bleak concrete exterior of a regimented high-rise block that should have been pulled down with the flats.

'There was a positive sighting of him yesterday lunchtime in the city centre,' I say, truthfully, 'so we think he's still about here somewhere.'

She doesn't seem pleased or surprised, no discernible emotion at all. Where's her maternal instincts? Is she indifferent or merely laid back? I can't work out this woman at all.

I nod towards a mushroom-coloured phone amid a pile of catalogues on a cabinet top. 'Has he made contact?'

'Tried to give him your number,' she says, closing the door and plodding up behind us.

I'll take that as a 'Yes'. 'That's good.' Good? Brilliant, more like, but I'm not going to rush this.

'Not sure him listening,' she goes on.

'That's a shame,' I say with a sympathetic smile.

'He in a hurry, see,' she explains in a spare style that wastes so few words that it omits some.

I indicate a smart sofa with a hand. 'Mind if we sit down?'

'Sure.' She bursts into flustered activity, approaching at a trot to beat us to the couch. She removes some ironing, none of it men's clothing, from one of the arms. She carries it to a walnut sideboard.

On it is a staggered line of framed photos. The largest is of a serious-looking young man in a cap and gown with a blue lapel, clutching a beribboned scroll. Must be Cammy on graduation day.

He appears again – the only black face – in anorak and wellington boots in a smiling quartet shouldering fishing rods with a rowing boat behind them. I haven't seen many black fishermen on the lakes I've used, not their sport, I suppose, but then again, Cammy's a marine biologist with college and field sports friends such as Liam Harries.

There's a group photo of a football team, can't make out from here if it includes Scott or Cammy or both. They are not wearing red shirts so I won't find an excuse for a closer look.

Certainly her younger boy isn't prominently featured on the sideboard, but the only photos he'll have posed for in recent times are mug shots. I'll not read favouritism into it.

Ungallantly, I sit ahead of Alice. With a son who has spent half his life behind bars for allegedly murdering one of us, I assume Mrs Packard will be more anti than pro-police. As every door-to-door salesman knows, once you're seated, it's harder for someone to order you out.

140

I look up at her as she returns, decide on a slow build-up. 'Did Scott, on visits here for tea from the hostel, ever raise the subject of colour blindness with you?'

Her totally unreadable face forces me to go on. 'You see...' I turn my head slightly towards Alice who is settling beside me. '...she found a leaflet about it in his room at the hostel.'

That blank look still.

'And,' Alice adds, 'Scott was asking an optician at the barber's shop about the problem.'

Mrs Packard looks at Alice who has to continue, rather lamely, 'We're just wondering why.'

'No,' she finally says with a heavy headshake. She flops into a well-used armchair facing us.

Alice ends a longish silence with, 'We're wondering if he's querying the accuracy of an ex-neighbour who witnessed some of the events at the old flats on the night of the troubles.'

Mrs Packard isn't merely in the habit of not wasting words. Sometimes she uses none at all, just sits there.

Alice tries again. 'Did he mention that to you?'

A deep sigh. 'All he ever said was he couldn't have killed someone who's still alive.'

'No one in your family is colour blind, by any chance?' I ask.

'Not that I knows to.'

I wonder momentarily if it's possible to be colour blind and not know it. Surely, your folks would pick up on it when they were reading books to you? But what if the parents have the same problem – or didn't read books to you? 'Cammy's eyesight OK?'

'Should hope so in his job.'

I should hope so, too. I'm not altogether sure what marine biologists do precisely. In warm climes off Cyprus, I suppose they'd spend a lot of time identifying sea life. A teacher at his school would have spotted any problem in painting classes, surely; a university tutor on microscope work, certainly. I dismiss it from my mind.

'Have you told Cammy that Scott's gone missing?'

A throaty 'Hm-hm' – which I'll take as a 'No.'

'He's not phoned home recently then?'

'Hm-hm.'

'Does he know he's applied for a case review?'

'Ya.'

Christ, she's hard work. I'd better stop asking questions with simple ya/hm-hm answers or we'll be here all day. 'What does he think about that?'

'Same as me. No point this long into his sentence. Waste more time than it'll save. Delays gettin' him out for good.'

Alice comes in. 'Do you remember Mrs Dorothy Evans?'

She is presenting her with the opportunity of another one-word reply; a bit annoying, that.

Before Alice can add the number where Mrs Evans used to live in the flats, Mrs Packard says, 'Number 12B.'

Astonishing, I think.

'Do you know where she lives now?' asks Alice, a trace of excitement on her face at what amounts to a massive break-through in this conversation.

A headshake. 'Split up, us residents, years back, all of us.'

Gamely, Alice comes back. 'Was there anything wrong with her eyesight?'

She waggles her own spectacles making a loose nose-rest rattle. 'Wore these.'

We're getting nowhere. Time to push on, I decide, but carefully. 'So how is Scott?'

'Stupid boy.' She sounds like Captain Mainwaring rebuking Private Pike in *Dad's Army*.

I grin. 'Gave him a piece of your mind, did you?'

'Certainly did.'

'When did he phone?'

'Last night.'

'Where from?'

'Didn't say.'

To prevent her from guessing she's being tapped, I'm going to use the same ploy I pulled on her MP. 'I tried to get you last night myself.'

She doesn't bite.

'To tell you of the sighting. To put your mind at rest. He'll be back in a day or two.'

She nods her thanks. 'At work,' she says, barely stifling a yawn. She even volunteers the name of the pub, the Green, where she works three evenings a week, five-to-seven, tidying up between the busier times at lunch and in the evening.

'What did he say?' I ask.

By her standards, she becomes chatty and it takes some time to establish that the pub's landlord didn't mind her receiving the occasional call in slack periods, provided she didn't make any, a trust she never abused.

She'd given her MP the pub's number as an alternative to her home phone and he'd called on Thursday from London to report what we'd said that lunchtime at the railway station. She'd told him what we'd said that afternoon in the courthouse about Scott being missing.

Scott had phoned her last night. He opened with, 'It's only me.' She responded with questions like, 'Where you been? What you doing?' She told him the police were after him and tried to pass on my number.

Scott broke in. 'On 10p's and running short. Need to speak to Jay. He about the bar?'

I can feel Alice tense at my side, can't work out why.

'No, he ain't,' said Mrs Packard.

'Promised he would be,' her son insisted.

'He's back in Perry Road.'

Mrs Packard tried again to give him my number. Again she was cut short. 'Don't worry. I'll work it out. See you soon.' She was left holding the receiver and rebuking the disconnected tone.

'Who's Jay?' asks Alice quickly.

'Jay Robertson.'

Oh, shit. Secretly, I damn myself. J. Robertson on the team sheet wasn't a made-up or stolen name to avoid the authorities. He actually exists. I hadn't even bothered to look at the sheet myself, to see 'Jay', not 'J.', just assumed it.

Christ, I'm having a stinker on this job. First I miss out on pinching Packard when he was thirty yards away. Now this.

Why is it on some cases I work like the main character in a Jacko Jackson novel and, on others, like a bumbling plod?

143

Why is it that sports stars score a hat-trick one game and miss sitters the next, centuries in the first innings, ducks in the second?

It's more than just luck. Fitness, I suppose, that I don't have any more, but, more important, timing.

No, it's more than that, too. Technique. My technique's been all wrong. I didn't do the research, my homework.

Had I become a sportsman instead of a policeman, I'd be substituted now, benched, transfer-listed. That feeling from twenty-four hours ago floods back, an awful feeling that must at some time overwhelm every sportsman.

Maybe I'm past my best.

'Robertson, Jason,' says the duty woman in Records into an ear that's pressed lightly against my mobile phone.

Jason, I repeat to myself, mightily relieved. Even if I had looked at the team sheet, I'd never have tracked him down under the shortened first name of 'Jay' without his current whereabouts; not such a cock-up after all.

'Dispatched yesterday to Perry Road, yet again,' she goes on in a tinny tone. 'Want his form?'

In the driving seat of my Volvo, parked in a side street out of sight of the high-rise block, I shoulder the phone tighter to my ear and start making notes in my book rested on my knee.

'Age: thirty-two,' she begins. Same as Scott Packard, and, as it turns out, they went to the same inner-city comprehensive school. Classmates? I ask myself.

'Convictions for shoplifting, drug possession, joyriding, assault, burglary, drug supplying,' she continues.

The usual progression from juvenile tearaway to adult recidivist, so I'll not make a note of them.

'Released from Nottingham three months ago, two-thirds of the way through a four-year term for drug peddling.'

Perry Road, I think, where Scott was finishing his sentence before transfer to the hostel. Cellmates?

'Rearrested two days ago,' she reads on, 'for car theft that led to a lunchtime police chase and crash.'

The day Scott fled, and I wonder if Robertson was in on the escape as the getaway driver. Fellow conspirators? Lots of questions to ask, I purr contentedly.

'Appeared in court yesterday when, because of his record, he was remanded without bail. Legal aid granted.'

'Who's his solicitor?'

She gives a name that's not Lennie Gomaz. Ah, well. Only in Jacko's detective novels do you find nice, neat circles of suspects; not in real life.

'That's it, apart from UH from Criminal Intelligence.'

Heart sinking, I jot that down, ask for the prison's phone number, note it, too, thank her and switch off.

Alice, sitting at my side, peers at my book. 'What's that above the number?'

'Intelligence notation for "Unhelpful". It means he's a pro, coughs to nothing, shops no one, never asks for other offences to be taken into consideration. You can't cut a deal with him. You can ask all the questions you like. You'll get no answers.'

'Oh, dear,' she says, sounding old-fashioned. We sit side by side, discussing and agreeing tactics. It's beginning to get hot in here. As the weather forecast predicted, the sun came out at midday and it's going to be a lovely afternoon again – an afternoon for the park, not a prison.

'Let's get on with it then,' she orders.

I suggest we budget an hour for a late lunch at a pub I know with a garden. She cuts down the lunch allowance to thirty minutes.

Can't blame the humps and hollows of Hucknall Road or a bolted beefburger for this queaziness. Jails always have this effect on me; I don't know why.

We've stopped at traffic lights. The road ahead cuts through yellow rock with green railings on top of it and what promises to be a park behind them.

Instead, what you see beyond the railings when you turn right into Perry Road is the governor's old house that's a ringer for the

145

place where the late, lamented Mrs Bates lived, died and was preserved in *Psycho*.

Then comes a wire compound and a concrete-clad wall, both twenty feet high or so, both with semicircular topping that's sensitive to touch and that even the SAS couldn't scale.

Between wire and wall is the Victorian gatehouse, and when I park close to it where a notice says I shouldn't I can sense the cameras homing in.

We walk up to something that's like a post office counter with thick glass and the narrowest of gaps to slide things through.

Into it we post our cards and I speak into a black box fitted in the glass, repeating what I said on the phone, 'You will make sure he's told it's the lady who wants to talk to him.' The white-shirted guard nods and notes the details in a huge logbook.

Then we go through two stout blue doors, the second refusing to open for Alice until I've closed the first.

A uniformed guard waits on the other side in a courtyard that traps the sun as well as us. At the centre of the yard is a flower bed with marigolds and dahlias still in full bloom, a spreading cherry tree in full leaf and a grey pole that's sprouting a camera.

Ahead is a towering block, dark red brick, Victorian again, the remand wing where Jay Robertson will be. On its slate roof are turrets and a clock, gold figures on a black face that have just turned three. There are glimpses of a much more modern block where Packard would have been among the lifers.

From windows high up in B Block, the remand wing, comes shouting, loud, repetitive and occasionally obscene. Alice looks up, startled. 'Prison conversations, they're called,' I tell her – just parted pals chatting.

From an unseen kitchen floats the smell of hot cheese and I can't speak now, want to gag.

We're led into a single-storey building, its flat roof edged with razor wire. From a closed door to our right comes the hubbub of scores of quieter conversations, children crying, not much laughter on these family visits.

We are ushered left and into what could be a classroom with a dozen or so small desks with moulded grey chairs around them. Glass in the triangular roof lets in the sun. Among the hanging

146

strip lights is something that looks like an upside-down wok; another hidden camera, I suspect.

Our guide locks the steel door behind him, shutting in a strong smell of pine disinfectant. 'Sit where you like,' he says, heading for a desk on a raised platform next to the door. 'He'll be a minute or two.'

Alice wanders through the desks to the furthest away in the far corner. She places a Jiffy bag she's carried from the car on it, a prop of some kind.

I wander on and gaze out of thick glass with black bars on the outside.

Hot cheese. Got it now. Scores of times I've visited jails and only now have I worked it out. I can always smell hot cheese. It may not have been served up at any meal for months, but I can always smell it.

Cold cheese, the riper the better. Hot cheese on pizzas or toast, in burgers or potatoes, never. Can't stomach it.

It takes me back, must do, to my first day at college, away from home and gran for the first time. Hot cheese was being served in the cafeteria. Ever since I've associated its smell with gut-wrenching feelings of homesickness and strangeness and sadness and despair.

I couldn't hack it in here. Imagine the cameras and security checks, not once like we've just been through, but several times a day. And the noise of those shouted conversations and jangling keys and doors being bolted behind, the lack of space and privacy, or freedom to go to a football match or down to the pub or walk in the park with your wife and child.

And this is the visitors' end. So imagine a cellblock, the endless days, the sleepless nights, the smells, the sounds, year upon never-ending year of them.

Imagine all of this and hot cheese and being innocent. I can feel myself shudder.

More and more, over these last three days, I'm being driven, against my will to start with, to the conclusion that is what Scott Packard is and was through sixteen years in places like this – innocent of murder.

Imagine his anger when that finally dawns.

147

The next few minutes, I sense, could be the key. Sitting in the car, eating that cheeseless burger, we've rehearsed an opening aimed at getting Robertson on our side, win his trust.

A key rattles on the other side of the black door.

Don't let us cock this up, I pray.

15

Alice rises when the heavy black door squeaks open. I lean back against the sill of the barred window.

Another guard locks up behind him, gestures at us and peels away to join his colleague sitting at the raised desk.

Jay Robertson ambles our way, all the time in the world. Woven dreadlocks flow from the top of his head down short back and sides, nowhere near shoulder length. Funky, at an educated guess, not rasta.

Tall, broad and loose-limbed, he wears blue denim trousers and shirt and dirty white trainers.

He reaches us and stops. Alice smiles. 'Thanks for seeing us.'

He glares over her shoulder at me. Not the best start, I chafe.

Alice gives her full name and adds, 'From the Criminal Cases Review Commission.' She places her visiting card on the table and slips it in front of a chair opposite, nodding to both.

Jay stares down at the card. Alice motions at me. 'And this is a colleague, Phillip Todd.' The fact that I'm a police officer is deliberately omitted.

He looks up and across the table at her, ignoring me completely.

'We're reinvestigating the conviction of Scott Packard,' she goes on, still smiling, still standing.

Uttering something I don't pick up, he sits. So does she. I remain standing.

She launches into a well-practised preamble about Scott's application for a case review following the sighting in the magistrates court of the policeman he was supposed to have killed.

He queries nothing, but nods knowledgeably here and there. Scott, I'm sure, has confided in him.

'We're making some progress,' Alice continues, waving a hand at the Jiffy bag between them. 'Seen various police officers present at the events, Scott's mother, his MP, his former solicitor and so on. We'd like to speak to you.'

He looks across the desk, playing with finger and thumb with one lock by his ear, still says nothing.

She puts on a pleading expression. 'You may have information helpful to Scott.'

Finally he says something I can make out. 'This all right with him?'

She doesn't answer immediately.

'You talked to him?' His look is very suspicious.

She taps her Jiffy bag. 'We have his full statement on his application form.'

He firms up his tone. 'But have you talked to him?'

I hold my breath. Lie now and she's blown it, if Jay knows Packard is on the run.

'No.' She sighs. 'We can't. Not until Monday.' Picking her words carefully, she explains that a formal interview with him has to wait until he's completed evidence in the mugger's trial. She steals my phrase. 'Judge's orders.'

I watch his face intently. A sly smile might hint that he knows of Scott's escape and may even have been a party to it.

'Otherwise, it might be seen as though some behind-the-scenes deal has been cooked up.' Alice pauses. 'That doesn't, of course, prevent us from seeing people in the meantime whose advice he might have sought.'

Jay's expression has remained hostile throughout. Now he relaxes and nods his understanding.

Alice takes the plunge. 'When did you last discuss developments with him?'

He is sitting with increasing languor, but stops twiddling his lock, thinks for what seems a long time. 'Wednesday.'

Christ, he's going to admit plotting the escape. It's all I can do not to interrupt, flash my card and caution him, giving the whole game away.

149

'He asked me to find an old neighbour of ours from the flats,' he says. 'Spoken to her, have you?'

Alice gambles. 'Mrs Evans?' She gestures at the brown bag. 'She's on our list. What should we ask her?'

A slow smile. 'About her eyesight.'

'Is she colour blind, you mean?'

His face lights up a little, impressed.

'Is she?'

'Well...' Silence. Then: 'Liam Harries reckons so. Seen him, too, have you?'

Slowly, I walk up to the table and sit down in the remaining vacant chair, feel as if I have to.

'He's on the list, too,' says Alice. 'Tell us about him.'

Harries walked into Jay's local, the Green, on Tuesday evening, he begins. 'Long time no see,' he said.

Jay recognised him by his accent rather than appearance because Liam had put on weight and wore a smart suit rather than the casuals of his law centre days in the early eighties.

Robbie Hill wasn't with him. Since Jay had read in the *Post* that both were back in town, he asked where he was. Stayed behind after the Forest match in the players' lounge chatting to some old chums, he was told.

Harries said he barely recognised the pub. No surprise, that. Pubs with a thriving drugs trade are always being shut down rather than risk losing their licence. 'For refurbishment,' say the brewers, hoping the dealers and their clients will go away and stay away. They tart the place up, often give it a new name and reopen. The old custom always returns.

Jay and Harries talked football and the old days, neither mentioning that the last time they'd met was at the post-final celebrations when they'd been on opposite sides in a punch-up.

Jay was drinking rum and Coke – 'Cola', he adds teasingly, stretching out his legs, beginning to enjoy himself. Harries was on whisky.

150

Harries introduced Scott Packard into the conversation. 'Is he still inside?' he wanted to know. 'In a hostel,' he was told. 'See much of him?' asked Harries. 'Sometimes,' said Jay.

He breaks off the account to explain that he and Scott had bumped into each other in various prisons over the years. 'Showed me the ropes, watched me back.'

When Jay was between stretches and after Scott had been transferred to the hostel, they'd bummed around a bit, though Scott had to be back early for the curfew. Jay became a regular customer at the barber's shop.

He knew all about Scott's help in the arrest of the mugger. Surprisingly, for someone who never co-operated with the law himself, he approves. 'An animal, Matthews.'

I guess that some kind of criminal code has been broken by Matthews, don't want to pry, private business, prison business.

Jay gets back to his chat in the pub on Tuesday. 'He's appealing, I gather,' said Harries.

'Yeah,' Jay replied, and he passed on what Scott had told him about the sighting of the policeman he was supposed to have killed.

I hear him out, then come in for the first time to make sure I've heard it right. 'Harries knew that Scott was seeking a new hearing?'

'Yeah.'

'Sure it wasn't the other way round?'

His jaw sets. 'What you mean?'

'You didn't tell Harries.'

'Told you. He already knew.'

In which case, I conclude privately, Harries knew before Radio Trent made it public. How? I can only think of one way.

I nod acceptance and Jay returns to reported speech.

'Always thought he was a bit unlucky,' said Harries. 'That old biddy who made a statement against him. She had defective eyesight; colour blind.'

Recognising another plank for Scott's appeal, Jay asked how he knew.

'She was bowled over on a street crossing,' Harries answered. 'Came to see me at the law centre to ask if she could sue. Since she couldn't tell red from green, I said: "Hardly."'

'Did he put a name to her, this old neighbour?' I ask.

'Neither of us could remember it.'

They chatted on about old neighbourhood acquaintances, a bit of a where-are-they-now, never once mentioning that night. Then Harries drank up and left.

On Wednesday morning, Jay went to see Scott at the barber's shop. He repeated what Harries had told him.

That evening, Jay got a phone call at the pub from Scott. 'That old biddy's name was Mrs Dorothy Evans. Ask around for me and see if you can locate her. It's urgent.'

'Yes,' says Alice, 'he's rightly very, very keen on that lead you gave him. He's been in touch with an optician and studied a brochure on the matter. Did you know that?'

A slow nod. 'Told me on the phone.'

'Did he say where he got the brochure from?'

'Health centre.'

Let's get this in sequence, I order myself. Jay passed on to Scott what Harries had told him in the pub the night before. When the optician came in later on Wednesday, Scott double-checked on colour blindness and went to the trouble of picking up the pamphlet from a health centre.

After work, he'd go back to the hostel. In the defence papers he'd obtained from Lennie Gomaz, he'd find the name of Mrs Evans and get her first name, but not, of course, her current address. He'd asked Jay to put out a trace on her.

Fits, I think, satisfied. It all fits. 'Did you trace Mrs Evans?'

To Wilford, he says immediately. He gives a road and number in an attractive riverside village on the south side of the Trent that's spread out into a sizeable suburb. 'No reply,' he adds.

'On the phone or a knock on the door?'

'Personal visit.'

'How did you trace her?'

'Asked me old lady who put me on to a woman who used to work with her at Raleigh and they still meet up once a year at pensioners' dos.'

'Did your mum's friend confirm that Mrs Evans is colour blind?'

'First she'd heard of it, she said.'

Jay shrugs. 'Trouble is that to pay that visit I, well, borrowed a car. Someone heard me knocking, saw me peering through the letterbox, thought I was casing it and took the car number. I got gonged on the way back, a bit of a chase, a pile-up and here I am again.' He spreads his hands and smiles, unconcerned.

It would never have occurred to him to catch a bus, like anyone else, but I'm not going to knock him. Everyone could use a friend like Jay.

Instead, I'm going to take him back to a subject that Harries didn't mention when they had their drink in the Green – his memories of that cup final night back in July 1981.

Having appeared in all the previous rounds, he recalls, he'd been selected to play on the right wing. As bad luck would have it, he'd been collared for shoplifting and was held at the police station until his mum came home from work.

He arrived with the match in progress. Campbell Robins had taken his place. He knew him only as Scott's brother, not personally. 'Everybody was there – Scott, his brother, Liam Harries, Robbie Hill –'

'Lennie Gomaz?' I put in.

He shakes his head, scattering his locks.

'Ran the line,' I go on. 'Worked with Harries in the law centre. Big solicitor now.'

'I know who he is.' He thinks, frowning deeply. 'Don't recall.'

Everybody got high at the celebrations in the pub afterwards. I won't ask on what.

Jay conned Cammy into having a close look at the winners' medal. Having got a hand on it, he wouldn't let it go. 'It was mine,' he tells us earnestly. 'I helped to get to the final. I was picked to play.'

'Yes,' says Alice, 'your name was on the teamsheet.'

I want to cringe.

Jay beams warmly. 'Yeah, it should have been mine.'

There was a bit of a tug o' war over it in which Harries intervened, he goes on. 'All three of us finished up on the floor. It wasn't much of a rumble.'

I complete it for him. 'And Cammy finished with the shirt off his back?'

'Hanging upside down off his back, it was, inside out. Got me bombed out the team. The guy who bought the gear, that bookie...'

He looks at me and waits for my nod.

'...he refused to replace them, reckoned they were originals.'

'So the original shirt, rightfully your shirt, was destroyed?'

'Anybody's old lady could have repaired it.' He shrugs. 'I got the blame for breaking up the team. Not that it mattered. No heart for it any more after Scott got banged up. Soon after I got Y.O.' – Young Offenders institution, he means.

'Who got the medal?' I ask.

'Me.' A triumphant grin. 'At home somewhere.'

'Did that upset Cammy?'

A pleasurable smile. 'What do you think? Harries dragged him away, said they'd get another. Said he'd put Father Salmon on to me. Giggled like girls, they did.'

'Father Salmon's who? The parish priest?'

He pulls a face. 'Don't know who they were on about.'

Alice pats her bag again. 'There's no statement from you in the '81 court papers.'

'Scarpered, didn't I? Got out of it till things died down. Was already on bail. An assault charge would have put me inside.'

I lean back in my chair, convinced we've got the truth. 'Did you discuss all of this with Scott?'

'Over and over again. All he thought about since seeing that cop in the court foyer. Always going through the papers, always asking questions.' He looks at me intently. 'Know what this means, don't you?'

I nod.

Jay spells it out anyway. 'Mrs Evans fingered the wrong guy.'

I nod again.

'Help him, won't you?'

'Yes.' My sincere tone.

154

'Give him my respects. When you see him on Monday…'

So he doesn't know he's fled then, I deduce.

'…tell him sorry I wasn't around to take his call.' Scott, he explains again, had planned to phone him at the Green for Mrs Evans' address last night. Being inside again he wasn't free to take it.

'Promise,' I say.

'You've worked it out, haven't you?'

'Think so,' I reply cautiously.

'Then don't let Scotty near Robbie Hill, Mister Policeman.'

My mouth must have dropped open or something because he laughs loudly with sheer pleasure at my obvious discomfort at being outwitted.

Just as quickly his expression goes grim. 'Or he'll be back in here again – next time for good.'

Back in the car, freed from the smell of hot cheese, only stale burger fumes to breathe in, I phone Surveillance. Hill's gone to a game in Sheffield, they report. Double up on his shadowers, I order.

'Shouldn't you take him into protective custody?' Alice frets.

'He's my bait for tomorrow,' I tell her coldly.

16

Sharp raps on the metal knocker, long presses on the bell, but the maroon side door with 7B above the letterbox stays shut.

I step back and crane up at the side of a mock Tudor house in a narrow but busy road linking the old village of Wilford to modern housing estates which have colonised the countryside that rolls on and out to the Wolds.

A window directly above is too small for a room for living or sleeping in; the bathroom, presumably, but no steam coats the glass inside.

I turn and walk down a concrete footpath. Each step takes me further into deeper shadows cast by a large copper beech in the unkempt front garden. A high wooden gate at the end of the path is locked.

Alice is crouching, holding up the flap of the letterbox, peering through, playing the detective. 'Dark red carpet. No key on a string. No newspaper I can see,' she reports.

'Last person who did that got nicked,' I say out of the corner of my mouth, walking back and behind her. The flap slaps shut. She follows me round a corner where the path bows in front of a bay window.

A lined curtain was completely closed against the low sun when we headed up the footpath. Now it is being held open, just a few inches, and a small man with an old face is peering out at me. The alert neighbour who did for Jay, perhaps? Let's hope so.

Mouthing 'Sorry to bother you,' I point ahead to the front door. The curtain drops back into place.

I stop in front of a half-glazed door, delving into a pocket for my warrant card, and listen to a lock clicking, a bolt being drawn back and a chain rattling.

The door opens no wider than the curtains and the same unwelcoming face appears in the gap.

'Sorry to bother you,' I repeat out loud, holding up my card, momentarily blocking him from view while I make the introductions. 'We're looking for Mrs Evans.'

My hand drops to give an unobscured sight of a face that's not only ancient, but stunned. 'Don't you know?' Fingers on his mottled hands flutter, agitated. 'She died, I'm afraid.'

Always accepted there was a chance of that, I lament. No wonder Jay got no reply.

'When?' asks Alice at my side.

'Yesterday, very sudden.'

She rocks back and forth as if she's standing at the Wailing Wall. 'Yesterday,' she echoes. She sounds as if she's at the Wailing Wall.

I'm too stunned to get out a word.

He'd demanded I hand my card through the gap, kept the door on its chain and left us standing outside. We could hear, but not see, him reading over the details from the card. 'This is all very strange,' he'd said. 'You were here half the morning.'

After a longish wait, the door comes off its chain and is opened wide. We are let into a hall with a set of stairs chopped off in mid-flight by a low cream ceiling. Beneath it is a yellow phone on a tall stained stand.

He locks up behind us. We turn to face him. He's approaching eighty, I'd say.

His slightly stooping frame is clad in a buttoned-up cardigan and a thick shirt opened at a wrinkled neck. What remains of his hair is steel grey. His blue eyes are pale and watery. His nose has a pronounced hook. With a nightcap on – and he looks past his bedtime – he could double for Mr Punch.

He sniffs. 'Surprised you didn't know.' His hand trembles slightly when he returns the card.

'Sorry,' I apologise. 'I'm from HQ.' 'And I'm from out of town,' adds Alice, hurriedly. Between us we explain Mrs Evans had been a witness in a case we're reinvestigating.

Now he gestures to the phone on its stand. 'Wants you to call him back.' Tetchily, he adds, 'Straight away.'

I start to reach for the mobile phone in my pocket, about to say, 'I'll save you the expense,' realise I don't know the local nick's number and don't want to unnerve him further by asking for it.

'Thanks.' I pick up the phone, press the redial button, give my name and add, 'HQ Complaints and Discipline Department,' because I do want to unnerve the officer who answers, get some immediate action.

'Sir,' he says, coming mentally to attention.

I request a quick rundown and hear that police had been called to 7B yesterday morning by Mr Christopher Barsby from the flat below.

Mrs Evans had promised to do some shopping for him, but hadn't called round. He thought she might be ill, so he knocked on her door, called through the letterbox, got no reply, the constable continues.

Both have keys to each other's place, so he used his. He couldn't open it fully, but far enough to see that she was lying behind it.

'Paramedics certified her dead at the scene. Er...' He is clearly reading from a log, editing as he goes. '...CID called in because the same 999 caller had earlier reported a suspicious person outside her premises. Next of kin, a son, informed.'

I won't ask for his name and address yet. 'What did the pathologist say?'

'Dead about twelve hours. Death due to cerebral haematoma following a fracture at the back of the skull, consistent with a fall down the stairs. No suspicious circumstances.' Then, covering himself and to confirm that he's reading over someone else's report, he adds, 'It says here.'

No suspicious circumstances? I want to yell. Still, I calm myself, no one at the local cop shop knows what I know. They soon will. 'Call the CID officer in charge into your station, will you, right away?'

'Yes, sir,' he says immediately. 'No problem, is there?'

'No, no,' I say. Then, as much for the benefit of Mr Barsby's ears as his, I go on, 'She was a witness in one of my old cases, that's all.'

Mumbling under his breath, presumably about one hand not knowing what the other's doing, Mr Barsby leads us into a long lounge with comfortable-looking furniture, but uncomfortably hot. A gas fire is on. Heavy curtains at the far end of the room are tightly drawn in their bay.

'What case?' he asks very bluntly, as he sits slow and stiffly in a low armchair beside the fire and facing a TV set with *Grandstand* on mute.

He fumbles for and finds a pair of horn-rimmed spectacles on top of a high pile of tabloid papers and magazines on the floral carpet. 'What case was Dot a witness in?'

'It was some time ago,' I answer, motioning to a deep settee facing the fire and at right angles to him. 'Mind if we sit down?'

He doesn't say yes or no. 'Made no mention of it to me and she would have.'

We sit anyway. 'It was a very long time ago,' says Alice.

He's like an old dog with a bone. 'She would have told me.'

'It was an incident at her previous abode,' I add.

His nose twitches. 'That policeman's death in them riots?'

She had mentioned it to him after all. And why not? How many people are witnesses in a murder case?

'My.' He blinks rapidly. 'That was a long time ago.'

'I'm afraid we're going to have to ask you a few questions,' I say, taking out my notebook.

His eyes go up to the cream ceiling. 'She's been here...' He stops, thinks. '...since...' Another pause for thought and he gives up. '...since she left there.'

Mid-eighties, I think, but I don't prompt him. This is going to take long enough without me interrupting. He's already complained twice that he made two separate statements yesterday and can't understand why I haven't read them.

'Hated her old place, she did,' he goes on. 'No garden, see.'

Mr Barsby goes into considerable detail explaining how he had converted this house into two flats, up and down, and divided the garden into front and back after his wife died and he retired. 'Ekes out the pension.'

Dot was his first and only tenant. 'A good neighbour, the best.' He lifts his pointed chin. 'Never knew she was up there.'

He gives me a long look that defies me to read any more into it than the sort of mutual aid companionship my gran enjoyed with a widower neighbour when she was left alone. They watered each other's plants during holidays, fed each other's pets, collected the mail, watched each other's back; that's all. I nod solemnly.

She had talked occasionally, mainly grumbles, of life in the flats and had mentioned the riots more than once.

She'd told him she made a statement, but had not been called as a witness at the subsequent trial. She'd gone into some detail over what she'd seen.

Alice takes him through what she said. It doesn't deviate from her statement in the files.

Mrs Evans, he recounts, never expressed any fears about being the subject of reprisals. Nor had she ever given any indication of having second thoughts about what she had told the police. 'Doubt if she'd have changed or added anything.'

He wants to know why we're re-examining a case that's so old and Alice briefs him, not naming names.

'You don't think her...' He stops, doesn't want to say 'death' or even 'passing' so he starts again. 'You don't think this has anything to do with it, do you?'

Lots of fears and thoughts are crawling over my mind like a column of black ants, but I don't know for sure. I don't answer, just shrug.

'Impossible.' He answers himself firmly. 'Everyone says it was an accident.' His tone wavers. 'Surely?'

'To keep things in order,' Alice suggests, 'tell us about the stranger calling.'

'That's got nothing to do with it, surely?' He firms up again. 'Can't have.'

I smile. 'Tell us anyway.'

Dot had gone out for her usual Thursday lunch and league match at the indoor bowls club. A grey car pulled up outside the house. He noticed it because it was parked badly in the narrow road, reducing traffic to a single line. A black man got out and walked up the path to the side door.

Mr Barsby heard him knocking and ringing and trying the back gate. 'Like you two did.' To emphasise he's no Nosy Parker, he adds, 'I'm not double-glazed.'

He gets back on track. 'He was hanging around for a while. Became very worried, I did. We've had a few break-ins round here in broad daylight and you don't see many of them around.'

Black strangers, he means.

He went out of the front door as the man came round the corner. 'Can I help you?' he inquired.

The caller seemed surprised to see Mr Barsby and kept on walking. 'I'll call back,' he said over his shoulder, hurrying to the front gate.

The man ignored an offer to leave a message and climbed in the car which he hadn't locked. 'He fiddled with the ignition for an age...'

Jay Robertson was hot-wiring it, I'll wager.

'Took so long that I had time to memorise the number.' He looks pleased with himself. When the car sped away, he went back inside, wrote the number on the top of the *Daily Mail* and, after mulling it over, dialled 999.

'But he can't have anything to do with it,' he says adamantly.

Dot came home mid-afternoon and he told her what had happened in her absence, he answers. That evening, about eight, she came to his front door. Standing behind her was a police officer in uniform. She gestured to him. 'They've caught him.'

He invited them in. The number he'd phoned through belonged to a car stolen close to the city centre, the policeman informed him.

They'd chased and arrested the driver, name of Jason Robertson. He wasn't denying he was in unlawful possession of the car, but disputed he had been 'casing' the upstairs flat.

Under questioning, he'd claimed to be a friend of a former workmate of Mrs Evans at Raleigh, the cycle makers. He had called on her behalf to discuss arrangements for a pensioners' party.

Dot didn't believe the story because the social secretary always phoned or wrote with details of parties and outings. The policeman said he'd report it all. He had already charged and held Robertson for car theft, but didn't know if his superiors would proceed on attempted burglary.

A copybook answer from the cop, I accept privately, and an unbreakable alibi for Jay Robertson.

Mrs Evans was still alive while he was in police custody. The business about calling on behalf of his mum's friend was to cover his real purpose – checking on Mrs Evans' eyesight for his pal Scott Packard's appeal.

The policeman departed with fulsome thanks after taking their statements. Mr Barsby and Mrs Evans chatted for a while over a pot of tea and a plate of biscuits, bemoaning what the world was coming to, then she left, too.

161

'See you about eleven,' she'd said. 'Have your Co-op list ready.'

'Last thing she said to me, the last time I saw her.' With a very mournful face, Mr Barsby adds, 'Alive.'

Eleven came yesterday morning, but no Dot. He gave her half an hour, then went out of his door to hers. It was locked. He knocked and rang the bell; no answer.

'I thought she might be ill. You know, from the excitement of the night before. I mean, she does have, did have diabetes, a bit of blood pressure and the odd dizzy spell. Sometimes she'd have to sit out a bowls game or rest up while gardening.'

He motions towards a net curtain drawn across the back window. 'Loved her garden. Flower beds, hanging baskets all summer long.'

I wonder if someone who's colour blind would appreciate their real beauty, guess they would, some flowers anyway.

Mr Barsby returned to his kitchen, collected her keys from his corkboard and went back. He could only open the door an inch or two, just enough to see her green slippers. He came back here and dialled 999.

I yank my head towards the hall and front door. 'She didn't have a safety chain then?'

He shakes his head. 'A Yale and a mortise.'

'Did you use both to open it?'

'Well...' He fidgets, uncomfortable. '...some sergeant asked that and I said yes but now, thinking about it, I'm not that sure to be honest. I was in a bit of a panic, you know.'

My understanding smile. 'Did you go in with the paramedics and police?'

'Stood outside while they lifted her up and rested her against the stairs and examined her. There was quite a bit of blood about.' He feels the back of his head. 'Turned the carpet black.' He shudders. 'Can't have been a pleasant sight for Dave.'

Dave, he explains, is Mrs Evans' son. 'Very dutiful. Calls every week without fail, phones regular.'

Mr Barsby had called Dave at his office at the request of the detective in charge. He came round straight away, saw the

162

police and had returned again today to start the task of making funeral arrangements and sorting out her affairs.

I'll go through all of this with Dave personally, I decide. Meantime those ants eating away at my mind have turned red. Don't charge in, I order myself. 'In her dressing-gown, was she?'

'Why do you say that?' A sharp response, accusing me of misunderstanding their relationship after all.

'Only that you mentioned she was in green slippers and I was wondering if she was dressed for bed.'

'Her bowling slippers. She always wore them about the flat.'

'Was she wearing them when she came round here with the policeman?'

'Yes – and the same clothes she was found in.'

She could have died soon after leaving here at after eight on Thursday, never got to bed, I calculate; matches the time of death. She could have climbed the stairs, had a dizzy spell and fallen down them again.

Face up to it, Sweeney. Maybe there was no dizzy spell. 'After you'd said goodnight, did you hear her opening the side door?'

He points with a bony finger at the TV set. 'Put that on.'

'I suppose she could have missed her step,' I muse more or less to myself.

'But the staircase is well lit. And the light was still on. And the carpet's new.'

'And red,' Alice puts in, catching on.

'She picked it herself,' he says defensively.

I wonder who is legally responsible for the staircase, suspect him of thinking more like a landlord than a good neighbour now, worried about a writ from Dave, her son.

I'm still thinking colours – green slippers and red carpet. Again I won't rush it. 'Was her eyesight good?'

He touches his spectacles. 'Short-sighted, but she had a new-ish pair.'

Alice comes out into the open. 'Wasn't she colour blind?'

He works his bloodless bottom lip. 'Why do you say that?'

'Because that's what we've been told.'

'You've been misinformed. Dave is. Her late husband was, I gather. But not Dot.'

17

There are times in this dirty job for dirty tricks, though I prefer them to be called tactical ploys. There are times for total truth. Time for the latter, I decide, driving beneath gathering, ever-darkening clouds that seem to match my mood.

We'd looked in at divisional headquarters, a modern station tucked behind the main shopping centre at West Bridgford, an agreeable town separated from the city by the river. The file on Mrs Evans was so thin that we didn't stay long.

She hadn't even had time to digest her biscuits, the pathologist had established, pointing up the time of her death at soon after eight o'clock on Thursday evening.

'Must be a locked room mystery then,' muttered the detective sergeant, a burly, hard-nosed veteran of twenty-five years' service, who'd been in charge at the scene, ''cos the landlord claimed he used both keys to open her door.'

'He was in such a flap he's not so sure now,' I'd briefed him.

'But the doc said it was consistent with falling with the back of her head against a step.'

'Maybe it was meant to appear that way,' I'd said, 'so we're having a fresh look.'

'Oh, shit,' he'd sighed.

It wasn't, I knew, concern over the slog that comes with such a major inquiry. He feared he may have missed a murder and his pride was hurt. 'Plenty of time to redeem it,' I'd assured him.

We'd left him organising an incident room and rounding up a team of detectives to operate from it.

Now we've reached our latest destination – a neat, newish bungalow in a hilly village in the Wolds.

In orange light from a street lamp, the lawn in front looks immaculate, the chrysanthemums neatly staked and the summer herbaceous plants already trimmed, mulched and tucked up for the coming winter.

In the glass porch, I go through the usual – proffered card, names and 'Very sorry to bother you at a time like this.'

Dave Evans is early forties, I'd read in his short statement in the file. He looks way past fifty, too drained to say much other than 'Come in' and then 'Sit down' in the dimly lit lounge.

I lower myself into one of two matching rust-coloured sofas across an empty stone fireplace. Alice sits by my side. He joins his wife.

'It's right that you should know,' I come clean, 'that I have ordered fresh and thorough inquiries into the death of your mother.'

Anguish flows over a face that's already washed-out with grief and tiredness. His wife stiffens.

'You see...' I flick my head towards Alice. '...we were planning to reinterview her about a murder that occurred sixteen years ago...'

He swallows hard. 'That policeman's?'

I nod.'...in which, we now believe, there may have been a miscarriage of justice. In such circumstances, we are not prepared to accept her fall was accidental without further investigations.'

His wife takes and holds his hand to her lap. He turns his head towards her for a second, then looks back at me. 'What do you intend to do?'

I virtually tell him what I told the case officer – post a man outside the house in Wilford through the night. Then, in the morning, forensic scientists – I'm careful not to use 'scenes of crime officers' because I'm not sure that there is a crime scene yet – will go through the flat, staircase, path and garden. A squad of detectives will canvas the neighbourhood.

'And, I'm afraid, there'll have to be...' I avoid post-mortem and select '...a second medical examination.'

He sees what I mean and shuts his eyes tightly. No one likes to think of a loved one being cut up once, never mind twice.

'Will this hold things up?' he asks. Equally understandably, no one likes that empty void between death and funeral service to last longer than necessary.

'Only by twenty-four hours,' I assure him. Then, more truthfully, I add, 'Hopefully.' If the pathologist finds anything suspicious, the coroner may not release her body, but I won't tell him that yet.

165

'Do you think she was deliberately killed?' he asks, avoiding the word 'murder'.

'That's what we aim to discover.'

His wife speaks for the first time. 'Will this all be in the papers?'

'Not if we can help it. The inquest will have to be opened in public early next week. Mention of an apparent fall only will be made. If the press see or hear about our activities and approach you, refer them to me.'

Her husband gives the briefest of nods. 'And it's all got something to do with that policeman's murder, has it?' He has no qualms this time about the word, distanced from that death, at least.

'Let's see if we can work that out,' says Alice.

Dave Evans had never lived in the flats, he begins. He'd been born and raised on an outlying council estate, married young himself and found a small cottage. He'd moved twice since with advancements in his career in local government.

After he'd left the family home, his parents agreed to transfer to the flats because they wanted a smaller place and to live nearer the cycle factory where both worked. 'A mistake,' he grumbles mildly. 'It was noisy; rough at times.'

He visited weekly, eventually taking his own children, never stayed too long. 'Nowhere for them to play.' He got to know few neighbours, and had never heard of the Packard family until the 1981 case.

Before that happened, his father had a heart attack and died in hospital three months later, aged fifty. 'Afterwards, mum was even more anxious to get away.'

She had repeated to him more than once what she told the police about the events she saw and heard on the night of the riot – the commotion outside, turning down the TV, going out on the walkway, looking over the wall, seeing the black boy with a red shirt with number 4 on it hitting a man in grey on the head while he was lying on the floor.

'You're not saying...' He stops, expression agonised. 'You mentioned miscarriage of justice. That boy didn't go to jail because of a mistake, did he? Her mistake?'

166

I can't think of a comforting reply. Alice can. 'Any error, I promise you, was down to the lawyers.'

A shadow of relief passes over his pained face. 'I was desperately worried about it, thought she might be petrol-bombed to keep her quiet or something, but nobody bothered her. It was a relief all round, mind, when she didn't have to give evidence and her name wasn't in the papers.'

Mrs Evans didn't wait until the block of flats was pulled down to be rehoused. She could afford to move in above Mr Barsby on the compensation she received following her husband's death.

Compensation for a heart attack? I query myself; odd.

'She gave up work and these last – what?...' Dave stops to work something out. '...fourteen, fifteen years she's been very contented what with her bowls and her garden.' He's holding back his tears; just.

'Can you help us?' Alice leans forward and speaks very softly. 'We're getting conflicting information about your mother's eyesight. Was she colour blind?'

'Me.' He taps his chest twice. 'Not her. Inherited from dad, I expect.'

'She did wear spectacles?'

'Latterly. She became increasingly short-sighted, resulting from her diabetes, the doctor said.'

'So...' Alice cross-checks. '...though short-sighted, she wasn't colour blind, but you are and your father was.'

A slow nod. 'That's why there was no insurance pay-out until after he died.'

Alice speaks on behalf of both of us. 'I don't follow.'

Mr Evans Senior had been knocked down and seriously injured in the city centre. 'On a pedestrian crossing,' he adds.

Liam Harries, I realise now, had misformed Jay Robertson over their drink in the pub on Tuesday night. It was Mr, not Mrs, Evans who was bowled over.

He'd sued for damages, his son goes on. The motorist's insurance company stonewalled when they discovered he was colour blind, blaming him for his own accident because he misread the lights.

167

'First off, they offered nothing, then a paltry amount. Fortunately, his legal adviser stood firm and even upped the claim when he had a heart attack, arguing the driver's negligence had brought it on.'

The usual poker game, I think.

'Sadly, it wasn't settled until after he died. Along with their pensions, it's been enough to keep mum comfortable. He did a good job.'

'Who was that?' asks Alice.

'Mr Gomaz from the local law centre.'

I come back, 'Not a colleague of his from the same centre, a Mr Liam Harries?'

He shakes his head again. 'Not a name, that, which means anything...' He glances at his wife for confirmation and she shakes hers.'...to us.'

Alice is asking technical follow-up questions about the accident case, so I ponder on.

Evans Senior had been a client of Lennie Gomaz, not Harries. Yet Harries claimed to Jay Robertson in the Green that he'd been involved.

Why? A lapse of memory after sixteen years? Doubt it. You remember your cases, successful ones, at least.

Why then? Maybe he recalled the compensation claim, read the papers or something or Gomaz had gossiped about it at the time. So he introduced the case, if not the name, into the conversation. Why? To find out if Jay knew where Mrs Evans had moved to. Why?

Don't answer that yet, I instruct myself as the conversation dries up. Get an answer to this first. 'You know that your mother had an unexpected caller on Thursday lunchtime when she was out bowling.'

'Mr Barsby told me yesterday after he found her.'

'Not your mother?' Badly phrased that. Try again. 'I mean, your mother never mentioned the stranger to you?'

No, he replies. He'd phoned her on Wednesday evening for a chat. 'She was her bright, cheerful self. It was the last time I heard her voice.'

Tears finally well in his eyes and I go silent, using the time for more thoughts. They didn't speak on Thursday evening. Now

168

had my widowed old gran been at the centre of something like that – a mystery caller, police visiting with a tale of a car chase – she'd have been on the phone to me straight away, whether we'd spoken twenty-four hours earlier or not; wonderful gossip.

Confirmation that she died soon after leaving Mr Barsby on the ground floor. She never got into her flat to phone her son.

'Sorry,' he says, gathering himself.

'It's OK.' I smile my understanding. 'The caller turned out to be the son of a friend of an old workmate.'

'Do you think he's involved in...' He works his mouth to find the phrase. '...whatever's happened?'

'No. No. We can rule him out completely because he's been in custody since Thursday lunchtime. He's called Jay Robertson.'

He makes a puzzled face at another name that means nothing to him.

'He claims he called with a message from his mother's friend.'

Dave nods, but only to tell me that he is following.

'Mr Barsby says your mother didn't believe this, but the message was supposed to be about some old employees' party...'

Now he's frowning deeply.

'...but, as she was out, there was naturally no reply at the door.'

'Strange,' he says. 'There's supposed to be some invite coming to a reunion of former flats residents, but I know nothing about any works pensioners' do.'

'Where's that invitation coming from?'

An uncertain shrug. 'All I know is that on...' He looks down, seeking to get things right, then up again to give me the facts.

On Wednesday evening, he says, fully focused now, after he'd talked to his mother, he had a phone call, someone wanting to know if he was in any way connected with the Evans family who used to live in the flats.

'Why?' he asked.

'Because we're organising a reunion.'

'I wasn't, but my mother was.'

'Where shall we send the invitation card?' the caller asked.

169

He gave her address, didn't add that he doubted she would accept because she'd been glad to see the back of the place and lots of people who lived in it.

I ask to see his phone book. His wife drops his hand and gets up wearily.

Dave tells Alice the caller was a man who didn't give his name or number.

'Any accent?' she wants to know.

His wife hands a thickish blue phone book over my shoulder and I turn to 'Residential' to find E, then Evans, then the third of the column or so that begin with D.

This address is around midway. My eyes drop still further down. There are no Evans, D., with his mother's address alongside.

He senses what I'm looking for. 'She's not in. Went ex-directory. Got fed up with all those calls from double-glazing firms when she was trying to have a nap.'

I close the book and rest it on my knee.

'Local?' resumes Alice. 'The caller's accent?'

Dave lapses into thought again. 'I'd say not. Light, I'd say.'

She keeps trying. 'Singalong, you know, musical.'

He shakes his head absently.

'Caribbean?' A voice that sounds like it might belong to a black man, she really means.

He shakes his head more firmly. 'Nothing like that, no. But, well, light certainly, articulate, nice voice really, a bit put-on, come to think of it.

Stage Irish, I'm coming to think.

'What do you think then?' asks Alice.

With a mouthful of battered haddock, brought in from a chip shop because the station canteen is closed at this time on a Saturday night, I can't answer for a moment or two.

But I can think.

Between us, we've rung all the D. Evanses above Dave's number in the phone book. Five that answered had calls on Wednesday night from a man wanting to know if anyone in

170

their family used to live in the flats and qualified for an invitation to the mythical reunion. Of the other six who weren't in, two had answering machines.

We made random checks on D. Evanses below Dave's address. None had received a similar call. So, I'm thinking, he'd worked his way down the list until he got the information he wanted – and went no further.

That doesn't seem like an idea that would have occurred to Scott Packard. He hadn't the nous to look up Radio Trent's number, let alone old news photos of Craig and Benson. In any case, why was Scott vainly chasing Jay and the address on Friday night? It sounds more like research by a law graduate, Liam Harries, for example.

'You never share your thoughts,' she says, reprimandingly.

'I'm eating, for chrissake, woman,' I manage to protest.

But it's true, I have to admit to myself, on this job anyway. I'd distanced myself from her because I didn't like her pushy style. She's abrupt, but only because she's young and keen. She reminds me of me fifteen years ago, I suppose.

Alice can hold fire no longer. 'I know what you're thinking.'

'Go on then.'

She takes a small bite out of a golden chip in two fingers rather seductively, as if nibbling at a grape. She spoils the illusion by pointing what remains in her fingers across a desk in the incident room. 'You think Cammy killed your policeman.'

Level with her, I urge myself. This isn't one of Jacko Jackson's novels, the answer saved till last. He'll have to turn it into a 'how are they going to prove it and catch him?' for a change. I finally empty my mouth. 'Correct.' Three chips are scooped in *en bloc*.

She takes another delicate bite, chews. 'That's going to be a devastating blow to poor Mrs Packard.'

If she hasn't worked it out already, I muse, and done nothing.

'Maybe we shouldn't judge him – or any man – by the worst act he's committed in his life.'

Easy for her to say, I object privately. She's not the late Joey Craig's mother or lover. She's thinking as a defence lawyer, mitigating his offence. I'm a prosecutor and I'm not going to let Alice get away with that.

171

I swallow. 'I might have bought that if he'd come clean and pleaded panic, instead of pissing off out of it, leaving Scott in a lifetime of shit.'

Now I'm going to get the little shit, I privately vow.

She doesn't argue. 'And Harries covered for him out of love or future business or both.'

'That sums him up,' I concur. 'Young men and money are his weaknesses.'

'And,' she goes on, 'they would have got away with it for ever had Scott not seen that other ex-PC by chance all these years later.'

I'm munching again, just nod.

'So what are you going to do?'

I make her wait a few seconds for the reply. 'Pull Harries in tomorrow and ask him where he was around nine o'clock on Wednesday...' I flick my head at the green phone on the desk. '...when those calls were made and around eight on Thursday night when Mrs Evans died. Then grill him about '81.'

She picks up another chip, studies it but doesn't start on it. 'Is that wise? I mean, what if he has good alibis?'

A moment's digestion. 'Then I'll pursue the line that he hired someone. There are lots of hungry kids out there...' An airy wave in no particular direction. '...rent boys who want out, wannabe soccer starlets who'd kill for a good agent.'

'Yes, but...' She hesitates. 'Wouldn't it be better if you made gentle inquiries, find out from the hotel if he made loads of calls on Wednesday? Get the bill for his mobile?'

I try to say something, but she talks on, motioning at the phone. 'Wait to see if any Evanses can identify the caller's voice. No rush, is there?'

'He flies out on Monday,' I finally get to point out.

'He's bound to come back. His clients are over here.' Pensively, she picks some flaky white flesh away from its blue-black skin. 'What are your priorities here?'

Again I can't get in an answer.

'Bring Cammy to book for the 1981 murder and convict Harries for Mrs Evans,' she suggests. 'Mine are different. My task is to convince my Commissioners that there's sufficient doubt about Scott's conviction to go to appeal again.'

'And you've achieved that,' I say, a statement, not a question, no lingering doubts.

She nods firmly. 'It can be shown – at least strongly argued – that Mrs Evans' statement was flawed. The killer in the red shirt wasn't necessarily wearing number 4. It could have been red number 7 upside down and inside out, as Jay Robertson described – i.e. Cammy.'

She's eating again at last and I'm going to get out a sentence. 'It was only a quick glance and, with her poor eyesight, she got that little dash the French stick on their 7s... What you call 'em?'

'Crossbars,' she says.

Very appropriate on a soccer shirt, I think, then: '...in the wrong place. Call her optician and a few more specialists and Scott's cleared.'

Jay's warning in jail begins to nag. 'Unless he does something stupid in the meantime.'

On that, she doesn't bite. Instead, 'Why, then, did Harries tell Jay that Mrs Evans was colour blind?'

Dunno is the honest answer to that, so I speculate, 'To confuse things, buy time? In the hope that Jay would tell Scott and he'd check her out and suspect Robbie Hill?'

'Harries never actually mentioned her by name in the pub,' she reminds me.

'Maybe he was boxing clever, just sussing out Jay's memory.'

'If not, how did he get the name?'

'His old chum Gomaz? Or maybe Robbie Hill remembers her?' Pointless, this, I decide. 'I'll ask him tomorrow.'

Alice won't give up. 'Why did he kill or have Mrs Evans killed?'

I'm more certain about this. 'Because, if her eyesight was put to the test, he's implicated in the original cover-up, accessory after a cop's murder. He's looking at life. The evidence is building all the time.'

'Try it on me,' she volunteers enticingly.

'He knew before Radio Trent made it public that Scott was going for a rehearing.'

173

'How?'

'From Cammy in Cyprus who'd been told by Mrs Packard. Harries was asking Jay questions about Mrs Evans two nights before she died.'

'But without mentioning her name.'

'Come on,' I say dismissively. 'It's an old interrogator's trick. You hold back what you know to find out what he does.'

She is shaking her head sadly. 'The only witness to that conversation is Jay Robertson. All Harries would have to say is that Jay told him about the rehearing and he raised her evidence in that chat. Who'll be believed? A recidivist or a law graduate?'

Good point, but I'll not grant it.

'That's what I mean, you see,' she continues. 'Maybe you should wait until you get the result of the second post-mortem, establish where he was at those vital times, get a recording of his voice to play to all those Evanses, hope that he left a message on one of those answering machines for comparison.'

She's right, of course, but I don't tell her so.

'You see, Phillip...' For the first time in three days she uses my first name.'...if you arrest him tomorrow, unless you shake out a confession – and you're dealing with a professional smoothie here – you'll have to let him go.'

She looks across at me with a troubled face. 'And what's the first thing he'll do? Tip off Cammy to stay in Northern Cyprus from where he can't be extradited and go there himself.'

True, too, I fear.

'Why not let him fly off on Monday, totally unaware how close you are? Finish building your case in his absence. Make it so watertight that it doesn't matter if he confesses or not. Arrest him at your leisure whenever he's back here. That's my advice.'

My turn to shake my head. 'You forgot one priority; the first priority. And that's to save life. We may know that Cammy killed the cop. Scott doesn't.'

Gloomily, I look out of the window. 'He's out there somewhere thinking Robbie Hill did, because Jay was conned into hinting that Mrs Evans got mixed up between red and green shirts.'

174

My eyes go back to hers. 'He's already made one move on him outside the radio station. We frightened him off. He doesn't know where Hill's staying or what airport he'll fly from. But he knows from the radio where he'll be tomorrow.'

'There must be a way of protecting Hill that doesn't reveal your hand to Harries yet.'

'But they are always together,' I grumble.

She fingers up a scoop of fish and eats silently for a long time. Then a mischievous smile spreads across her greasy lips. 'I could make Harries an offer he can't refuse.'

18

An untroubled night's sleep, the plan in place. A full, leisurely breakfast with no mystery death story on the radio news about Mrs Evans to upset my appetite. A sunny day is forecast. A slow drive from home to headquarters for a latish start.

No rush, I've decided.

Alice is already here, as usual, sorting her papers into two neat piles on my desk.

I'm dressed for a sporty Sunday in tan-coloured slacks, green crew-neck and light brown jacket; she for business, her jet black suit reappearing.

Robbie Hill and Liam Harries are at their hotel after clubbing until the early hours, the surveillance duty man reports over the phone.

No point in asking where they were on Wednesday night about nine when those calls were made to the Evanses or Thursday evening when the mystery death occurred. They weren't under observation then, curse it. Instead: 'Any calls from Scott?'

'Not to his home or the pub where his old lady works,' he replies.

I call Mrs Packard anyway with two questions I already know the answers to. No, she confirms, she's not heard from her son since he phoned the pub asking for Jay. No, she says they aren't

Catholic, backing up what's on his prison file which gives his religion as Baptist.

'Hoping to find him goin' to church?' she chides me in a slightly amused tone. 'Forget it.'

I laugh briefly, forming a question I don't know the answer to, a loose end from that chat with Jay in jail. 'Do you, by any chance, know a Father Salmon?'

'No.' An immediate response.

'He may not be Catholic, could be Anglican or maybe a prison or university chaplain. Has either of your boys ever mentioned him?'

'No.' Flat, final. 'Why?'

I pass it off with, 'His name cropped up in conversation.' We chat for a while, me promising to get in touch with any developments.

The phone directory is hunted through; no Revs Salmon or Salmons. I consider phoning a few churches, decide against because they'll be busy today. Tomorrow will do; no rush.

I ask Alice for the inventory of the goods stolen from the looted sports emporium on the night of the riots. She finds it within seconds and slips it across the desk.

A long list to go through – cricket and fishing equipment, racquets, bowls, snooker balls and cues by the dozen, as well as camping gear, including the eighteen inch metal clamp Scott admitted taking. They must have gone through the window like locusts. Almost any item could have been the murder weapon.

I slide it back. 'Ready?'

'Just about.' Alice places a hand on one pile of paperwork. 'This is the sensitive stuff with Mrs Evans' statement in it. To be locked away.' Her hand moves to the second pile. 'These are inconsequentials, statements from the players and so on, gives nothing away.'

I wonder if it will work, wonder what I'll do if it doesn't. Borrow something from the Drugs Squad and plant it in Harries' hotel room, anything to hold him, sweat him?

Guilt jolts me to my senses. God in heaven, you can't even think about correcting one miscarriage of justice by committing another. You spend most of your time on the trail of policemen

who have gone down that mined road. And here you are thinking of following them. You should be ashamed of yourself.

I am. Truly, I am, but I understand now the feeling, the fear of
seeing a killer slip through your fingers.

Liam Harries is on a twin, untidy bed on his side, an elbow
crooked, his head cupped in the palm of one hand.

His eyes have already left the paper he was reading and meet,
but hardly greet, ours as we enter his hotel room after his 'Come
in.'

Alice leads, face deadpan. 'We'd like your help in our inquiries.' She pauses. 'At headquarters.'

Good job his head is supported, I think, imagining the shock
waves running all the way up to it from his stockinged feet.
'About what?' There's a frog in his throat.

'Scott Packard.'

He pushes himself up, a heavy load. His head hangs without
its prop, eyes no longer on us. 'What about?' Same question,
words transposed, not thinking clearly, I note with delight.

'To go through everything again.'

He swings his cord-clad legs off the bed. 'When?'

'Now.'

His eyes go back to the paper, anywhere but on us. 'Why?'

A door across the corridor opens. So does Liam's without
a tap. In strolls Rob Hill wearing only the briefest of under-
pants, sparkling white, setting off the smooth blackness of his
sculptured body. His legs don't look value for money at five
million, marred here and there by gristly knots and ancient
scars.

Piss off, I fume inwardly. This is something we didn't bargain
for in rehearsals when she drove me here.

There's no retreat by Hill at the sight of Alice, no 'Oh, sorry.'
Like most sportsmen, he's used to wandering around semi-
naked. He smiles easily. 'Hi.'

Hill ambles beyond us to the foot of Harries' bed. 'Anything
in?'

'Not that I've come across so far,' Harries mumbles.

177

Hill sits on the twin bed and picks another paper off a big heap of them, turning to the back page. 'What's up?'

Alice looks at him. 'I've just asked Liam here to give me a hand.'

Hill turns noisily to an inside page, searching for something. Harries is frowning at her change of tactics. I just hope I'm not, too.

'Checking statements from '81,' she plods on.

Relief pours through Harries' face. Shit, I think, we've lost him. 'Can't,' he says very crisply. 'Not today.'

'But you'll be gone tomorrow,' say Alice, a touch too pleadingly.

Weak, I think, angrily. That's weak, woman.

'Busy.' He pats the breast pocket of his thick check shirt. 'Got a match. Got tickets.'

'It's important.' She puts on a tantalising smile. 'The whole file's there, the full works, from '81, plus what's been dug up since. I want you to go through everything with me, looking for discrepancies.'

Harries appears more interested now at the prospect on offer – viewing through legal-trained eyes exactly what we've got, what line of inquiry we're working on, discovering what other witnesses may have to be bought off or bumped off.

He says nothing, mulling.

Hill drops the paper on the carpet, opens up another from the back and stretches out on the spare bed.

Alice continues, 'I'd like you to cross-check what everyone says against your own memory of events, see if everything adds up. You were there, after all. I wasn't. I need a second informed opinion and you are a lawyer.'

Better, I think.

'Not criminal,' Harries says.

'You know what to look for.'

'Why not tonight? Harries asks another question we haven't foreseen and I hold my breath for her reaction.

'Because,' she ad libs slowly, 'I've got to fax my recommendations to my Commissioners overnight.'

Brilliant. She's even presenting him with the opportunity to influence her decision.

Faced with the choice between going to yet another match and access to files worth killing for, Harries still bides his time. 'What do you think, Rob?'

Hill tosses aside another paper. 'A waste of time.'

Oh, Lord, he's vetoing it, I think, panic rising.

'Maybe it's in the Irish editions,' says Harries in an apologetic tone. 'I'll get the cuttings agency to check.'

'Who needs publicity in Limerick?' sneers Hill.

The room goes silent.

Harries tries again. 'What do you think about me skipping the game?'

Hill shrugs his broad, bare shoulders, doesn't look up. 'Will it help Scotty Packard?'

'Might,' I say.

'What about the game?' Harries persists.

Head still down, Hill says, 'It's not as if we'll be talking money.' A bored yawn. 'It's just an afternoon out.'

'Sure?'

Now Hill does look up and across to the TV set. 'Watch it on Sky. What's the harm in helping?'

Harries repeats, 'Sure' – no question mark after it this time.

Hill remains stretched out on his borrowed bed after Harries has departed, leaving the complimentary match tickets, car-park pass and keys to a hired car behind on the dresser top.

Neither did he take his brown trench coat, accepting Alice's assurance that it's a nice day, her car was right outside and she'd run him to HQ and back.

Hill isn't so much studying the papers as rummaging through them, tearing most apart and dropping them on the carpet in pieces.

I'm sitting on a chair in front of the dresser, pretending to read a tabloid, thinking: Must be hard for Harries, given his sexual preference, to travel around with this Adonis. Maybe he only has eyes for little Cammy back at Cyprus. Why should a gay be more promiscuous than I am? Let's face it, if Michelle Pfeiffer

179

walked in here now, dressed like him, I'd like to think I'd carry on reading – or pretending to.

Hill discards the last paper.

I look up from behind mine: 'No joy?'

He pulls himself up and swings his sturdy, scarred legs off the bed. 'On what?'

'That article you were working on when I was here on Friday; not in?'

He remembers I was in on some of the telephone negotiations. 'No, not a word.' A cross expression. 'Another three grand down the drain. Prat.'

I sense friction between star and agent. I'm going to play this like a fisherman, letting out plenty of line first. 'When did you get here?'

'Tuesday. Be glad to get away. Bloody boring. I'm bored out my wits.' He looks it.

'Not working out?'

'Doubt there's anything for me round here.'

I begin to wonder if Harries has merely used him as a clever excuse for the real reason for being here.

He stirs the scattered papers with surprisingly small feet. 'That's why I've got to keep my name in. People forget when you've been abroad.'

A bit of buttering now. 'Liam's done pretty well for you publicity-wise over the years.'

'Now's when I need a big write-up.'

'I mean, those five million dollar legs.'

'Yeah.' A fond smile.

'Great gimmick.'

'Genuine.' He slaps both hardened thighs simultaneously. 'Had to pay a big premium to get a policy so it could be photographed for the papers. He renews it every year. Mind, he gets a big cut if it's ever cashed, the greedy bastard.' He smiles rather affectionately.

I ask what he means and hear that the policy pays out for a career-ending injury before his thirty-fourth birthday. 'The legs business . . .' He massages them roughly. '. . . was just a stunt for the Italian press. The small print covers every injury.'

180

Behind my fixed smile my mind is racing away. Being hit over the head by Scott Packard might qualify as a career-ending injury, life-ending even.

Jesus, Harries has plotted this cunningly. He'd had a dual purpose in seeking out and chatting up Jay Robertson in the pub. Not only did he want to find out where Mrs Evans lived, he wanted to hint that Hill was the cop killer.

It wasn't careless talk, a false memory about her colour blindness. He was planting the suspicion in Jay's head that Mrs Evans had mistaken red number 4 for green number 4.

He'd already know that Jay was still big buddies with Scott and that he'd pass the false lead on.

The clever sod. Even I'm shocked. Alice is right. I'll get no admissions from him.

He's not going to confess he was setting up his unsuspecting client. There's not much mileage left in those battered legs. If Packard reacts in the way he hopes, Harries will get his cut from the insurance pay-off for loss of future earnings.

Two birds with one blunt weapon.

The evil, evil bastard.

'Listen.' I'm going to start to tug in some line. 'You know how Scott tried to approach you on Friday. He knew you'd both be at the studios because it was advertised on the radio. Remember?'

He nods.

'I have to work out who he wanted to see – you or Liam.'

'Me,' he says immediately. 'He hardly knows Liam. Cammy's his big buddy.' He grins salaciously.

'Yes, but he may have wanted to talk to Liam about his brother.' It's not very convincing and I hurry on, 'If I know where you two have been since Tuesday, where other approaches could, but haven't, been made, I can eliminate some places to look for him. Can you tell me your programme?'

Understandably, he looks extremely suspicious because it wasn't a good pitch. 'What's Scotty done? It's more than just AWOL or busting parole to go to all this trouble, must be.'

'I'll level with you later, if you'll level with me now.'

'OK.' His features are totally frank.

'Start with Tuesday,' I urge.

He gives time of arrival at the airport where the hired car was waiting, and at this hotel where the rooms were pre-booked.

'Did you go out that night?' I ask.

'Nar. Knackered, me. Liam did. Saw a few old faces in our old local.'

Confirmation of the meeting with Jay Robertson, I realise.

He runs through Wednesday to dinner here at the hotel with a former international team mate and his wife talking over old times. 'Liam went off on his own again.'

To the nearest phone box with a load of loose change to call all those Evanses, I'd wager.

He reaches Thursday evening. 'Benefit do down at Meadow Lane.'

I nod to tell him I know the city's other soccer stadium across the river from Forest's ground.

'On the panel for one of them celeb sporting questions nights,' he goes on. 'Packed out.'

'Was Liam there?' I repeat.

'In the audience somewhere.' Harries had driven him there in the hired car.

He could have sneaked out of a packed house unseen, I conjecture, and transport would be on tap to get the mile or so to Mrs Evans' place at Wilford.

Elated, I think: I've got the double up – motive and opportunity.

Hill doesn't start on Friday. He's looking more than puzzled now, deeply disturbed. 'You checking up on him?'

I was going to slip in a question to establish if Harries had dropped the name of Mrs Evans or her whereabouts, daren't now. I've clearly asked 'Was Liam there?' once too often and have already alerted him.

Time to get the catch on board, I decide. 'On the basis of what you've just told me and what I already know, I think Scott is after you...'

'Told you that.'

182

'...I mean, after you for a confrontation.'

Slightly startled, he points out, 'But he's an old pal.'

'Because he thinks you clobbered that cop to death back in 1981.'

'Eh?' So deeply shocked is he that he can only stammer, 'But...not...I know nowt about it.'

'I know that, believe me. He doesn't. He's got hold of some bum info. I think he'll try to tackle you again today because he knows from the radio where you're going.'

A twisted expression, as if an unjust penalty had just been awarded against him.

'Now I can get a stand-in for you...' Some hope, I fret, with his well-known features. '...or you could travel to the game with me...' I gesture to the wardrobe. '...with me dressed in the trench coat Scott saw Liam carrying on Friday lunchtime.'

He gives me a dead-eyed look.

'So he won't smell a rat,' I go on.

He swallows. 'Has he gone on the run to kill me?'

'Confront you, certainly, if he gets the chance.'

He begins to protest, 'But I know nob all about any copper –'

'I know that,' I break in. 'I know, believe me.' I put on my soothing face and voice. 'I'll tell him. I'll put it right. We don't want him to get himself into more trouble, do we?'

He purses his lips. 'So he didn't do it then?'

I shake my head.

'Poor sod. All this time.' A thoughtful pause. 'Who did?'

I shake my head, smile thinly.

An aggressive look. 'Not Liam?'

'Oh, no,' I'm able to say easily and with complete honesty,

Another longish silence. 'Will it help Scotty?'

'Could save his life.'

'What do you want me to do?'

19

Robbie Hill has big match nerves. He declined lunchtime sandwiches. 'Don't know how you can,' he'd chuntered, watching
me eat rare beef on brown from room service which we put on
Liam's bill.

'Got to have your beef on a Sunday,' I jested, trying to cheer
him up.

At my suggestion, he's dressed in the high-buttoned black suit
he wore on Friday. 'To make it easy for Scotty,' I'd explained.

Going down in the lift, he said apropos of nothing, 'I've got a
wife and kids back in Milan, you know.'

'We won't be alone,' I promised, going on to reveal that he'd
been under observation since Friday in case Scott had been
stalking him. Instead of settling him, it made him all the more
twitchy.

His alert eyes kept ranging the sparsely filled multi-storey car-
park seeking our minders or Scott. I took the keys and got
behind the wheel of the hired red Rover, top of the range.

To tempt Scott to effect the sort of quick entry he pulled on
that woman's car in his juvenile days, I've kept all the doors
unlocked. Hill was too busy looking around to notice.

Now we're on the A52 passing the university with its neat
rows of halls of residence, a place where his crooked agent
learned his law and I didn't learn much at all.

Sun filters through the majestic trees on either side of the road,
more of an afternoon for cricket than football.

Yet again, he swivels awkwardly in the passenger seat to
glance out of the rear window.

'They'll be there,' I assure him.

I instruct him to unlock his safety belt to give more freedom
of movement. 'Highly illegal but I'll take the rap if Traffic
stops us.'

He doesn't smile, let alone laugh.

'Don't forget,' I re-emphasise. 'First sign and you dive head
first into my lap and I'll drop over you.'

'Undo your belt, too, then,' he says, thinking practically.

I free one hand from the wheel to do as I'm told and pull slightly over the centre white lines, earning a hoot from a motorist coming towards us.

'Good job I'm insured,' he quips, grimly.

Almost half-way there now, no alarms and – what the hell's this?

A Ford Capri, silver, flashes by on the outer lane, one occupant; black. He cuts sharply across my path. I grip my wheel and touch the footbrake. My heart misses several beats.

Relax, I tell myself. Scott went inside at sixteen, won't have a licence to drive or money to hire transport. Could have nicked one though, an inner voice argues back, like his cellmate Jay.

The car ahead increases the distance between us and indicates a left to drop down a slip road on to the M1.

Pride Park is in sight now, an astonishing sight, more like a vast space station than a soccer stadium, all gunmetal panels and cream breeze blocks; not much colour, appropriate, really, for a side that plays in white and black.

Gigantic robotic arms, hinged at the elbows, seem to grab at its roofs to stop it drifting off into weightlessness from the moonscape of the flattened, desolate acres all around; alien territory.

Hill is moved to say, 'Bloody hell. It's different.'

Different? It's a world away from the homely old Baseball Ground in the back streets where I used to watch him play. I'm not sure I'm going to like it.

The traffic has built up all the way on new roads from the A52 and, approaching a roundabout, is moving so slowly that pedestrians are weaving in and out of it.

Sodding jaywalkers, I silently curse, eyes fixed to the front.

The shout, the pounding comes from the left. Hill goes rigid beside me. I look across him. He is staring blankly ahead.

Two pimply white youths in black and white woolly hats and scarves are tapping on his window. 'Reject,' they taunt. 'Reject.'

'Only fans,' I say across my shoulder. 'Give 'em a wave.'

185

He turns away from the windscreen and half raises a hand. They jig and applaud. They'd have been small children when Hill left the club, will only have read of his exploits and seen him on TV or his photos in newspapers, but they still regarded his departure all those years ago as desertion. Now he's acknowledged them they are welcoming him back into their yobbish tribe.

'False alarm,' he mutters. 'Pathetic, aren't they?'

'Agreed, but that's not the point. It could have been the real thing. You were supposed to dive into my lap.'

'Sorry. I froze.'

The crowds and the grandstands cast shadows over the road and I'm inching forward, surrounded, lost.

A steward in a gleaming yellow waistcoat spots the car-park pass inside the windscreen and points towards two squat, dirty green gas holders and three flag-poles on a traffic island.

With extreme caution, I drive between two brick pillars and on to black asphalt with numbered slots and find a space close to dark grey double doors with 'Players' written above them.

No sooner have I stopped and switched off than the rear nearside door is wrenched open by someone in grey or blue or both, can't tell at first backward glance. There's a programme where the face should be.

This...my brain seems sluggish.

'Bastard' is hissed from behind the programme; a male voice. The hand holding the programme is black.

...could be...My brain sends out a confused message.

Hill turns round towards the sound.

'Dive,' I command.

His head keeps going away from me. The programme drops. Scott Packard's face appears in its place. His other hand holds something silver.

This is it. *This is it.*

I rise out of my seat, hook Hill round his neck and yank him down into my groin and fall forward over him as far as I can.

A thwarted growl from outside. 'Your fucking legs then.'

A flash of silver.

Clank.

I cradle Hill in my lap.

Clank. Metal on metal. Clank.

Another figure is at Scott's back, pressed up so close as to seem obscene. Scott's face, hands and arms I can no longer see; just grey trousers below blue denim.

Behind the two writhing male bodies a knot of spectators gather, but hang back, observing.

I push up Hill into a sitting position, shoulder open my door and jump out. Across the roof is the top of a black head of hair, neatly trimmed. Just an inch or two away is the grimly purposeful face of a thick-set white man.

He is gripping both arms at the wrists, pressing them down on the roof. A short reach from their hands is a spanner.

'Let him go, pigs,' shouts a scruffy man among the onlookers.

'Give him an autograph, Irish git,' calls a tubby woman.

I pull the spanner off the roof, bend inside and across the empty driver's seat to put it in the glove compartment. 'Smile and wave,' I whisper.

Hill obeys.

Scott Packard is in the back of the car, handcuffed to a sergeant from Surveillance who is barely out of breath, let alone sweating. I get behind the wheel and start up to a chorus of boos and jeers. I drive out of the car-park against heavy incoming traffic.

'Bastard!' Scott is shouting repeatedly, close to my left ear. 'You stitched me, you bastard.'

Hill is half turned, expression gravely wounded. 'Didn't, mate. Didn't.'

'Shut up,' snaps the sergeant.

Scott ignores him. 'Sixteen fuckin' years.'

'I didn't,' gabbles Hill. 'Didn't. Honest.'

Can't be doing with this for fifteen miles back to Nottingham, I decide.

I drive on, a slow battle, some distance against the constant flow of cars and people to the roundabout and on towards the new road and pull into a car-park that serves a brand new supermarket.

All the way Scott is rocking in the back, cursing, shouting. 'I'll get you if I have to wait another sixteen, you shithead.'

In the face of a never-ending wave of obscenities and threats, Hill has given up protesting his innocence.

I stop, turn off the engine, lean sideways and turn. 'Now listen to me, you gobby bugger.' I yank my head sideways towards Hill. 'Rob here didn't kill that cop.'

There's hate in Scott's face and voice. 'Because he's fuckin' famous now?'

I begin again, louder, a prison conversation to get through to him. 'He didn't do it.'

'Tell it to the judge,' he says scornfully.

'Shut up and listen. I know you didn't kill him. I can prove it. He didn't either. Are you listening?'

He's beginning to.

'Neither of you did. Got that?'

Not fully, it seems, because he nods urgently at Hill and snarls, 'That old lady –'

I don't want Mrs Evans' name dropped out in front of Hill, so I talk louder still over Scott. 'I know what you were told.'

He looks at me, hard.

'Your school and cellmate got it wrong,' I go on. 'Not his fault. He was misinformed.'

'But he got it from –'

Don't want the next name mentioned either, have to raise my voice again. 'Shut up and listen. I know where he got it from. He got it wrong, too. Now . . .' Pause. '. . . are you listening?'

Head hanging, he hears me out. 'That form your MP filled in,' I start, staccato. 'The case review. It's been granted.'

I force a smile. 'If you'd have stuck around in court on Thursday afternoon instead of going off to play that black detective in *Homicide – Life on the Streets*, we'd have told you.'

He doesn't lift his head.

'That woman I was with outside Radio Trent on Friday lunch-time...'

There's no way of knowing if he's following.

'...she's from the Commission your MP appealed to. We've been working on your case ever since, going through all the papers, tracked down the cop you saw in court, lots of witnesses. We know now you're not guilty.'

Slowly his head begins to rise.

'There's no question here of getting mixed up between his green number 4 shirt...' I flick my head at Hill. '...and your red number 4. It's nothing to do with anybody being colour blind. Got that? That's a bum lead, not the issue. We've checked and double-checked.'

His face is full up now, engrossed. 'What is then?'

'The issue is that it wasn't Rob and it wasn't you.'

'Who then?'

I breathe deeply. 'You'll get bail pending a rehearing. You'll be cleared publicly, get compensation.'

His shoulders shake and tears form in his eyes. 'What bastard did it? Who? Tell me. Who?'

There'll be more, I fear, many more tears, when he lies on his bunk tonight, goes through everything Jay Robertson and I have told him and he works it out for himself.

'Not you. That's the big thing. Now, are you still listening?'

A heavy nod.

'I'm going to have to hold you overnight. The judge is upset about you pissing off like that.'

He sighs deeply and shakes his head. 'More trouble.'

'Not really. As long as you turn up to give evidence tomorrow, you'll be fine. Have a good sleep tonight, go to court and we'll have a long chat afterwards. OK?'

His face is mournful, glistening and tearstained.

The sergeant next to him speaks up. 'We may have a problem with that incident in the car-park. Lots of witnesses there.'

We may, indeed, I accept. I picture it, recalling what those two hooligans shouted. 'If it gets out to the media,' I propose, 'let's say it was a drunken fan who made a nuisance of himself trying to get Rob's autograph.'

189

'What about the spanner?' asks the sergeant.

'Let's say it was a novelty pen.' I look at Hill. 'OK with you?'

'What spanner?' he asks, entering into the spirit of the conspiracy.

My eyes stay on Hill while I tackle what could be an even bigger problem. 'Look, you could make ten times the amount you missed out on this morning from the papers by selling this and I can't stop you.'

I give him my pleading look. 'But if you do, it could harm Scotty here. There's a hell of a lot of work left, people to question. The surprise element will be gone. It could bugger it completely for us all.'

He's not responding.

'In a few months' time, fine, but now means disaster all round.'

He doesn't offer any hope.

'You've helped so much so far –'

Scott butts in from the back, 'What you mean – helped? He's stitched me.'

I turn back to him. 'Only by helping to flush you out, so we could save you from yourself. You've a lot to thank him for.' I return to Hill, 'All I can do is appeal to you.'

He smiles brightly. 'Can I use it in my autobiography when I hang up my boots?'

I volunteer Jacko Jackson as his ghost writer – 'Ex-detective, writer, soccer fan, just the man for the job.'

He laughs. 'OK, then.'

I turn back to Scott. 'I'm dropping Rob and his car off at the ground. We three are going back.'

On the short journey, Scott says, 'Thanks' to the sergeant. 'Wasn't going to whack you, just threaten the truth out of you,' he tells Hill. 'Sorry.'

'Any time, me old mucker,' says Hill.

I don't believe either of them.

Back at Pride Park, only a few stragglers cross the car-park to join the crowd that's alternately roaring and groaning in unison.

Near the grey doors marked 'Players', Scott safely out of ear-shot in the back of an unmarked blue car from the police pool, I note down Hill's contact numbers. Pocketing my pen, I look him straight in the eye. 'What are you going to tell Harries?'

He holds my gaze very steadily. 'You suspect him, don't you?'

Time for truth, I decide. 'Not of the murder, no, but certainly on the cover-up.'

He rubs his bottom teeth along his top lip.

I press on, 'If you tackle him about it or bin his services immediately, he'll rumble something happened here.'

He runs his tongue along his bottom lip, still contemplating.

'How are you going to play it?' I ask outright.

'Down. Stick to the drunken autograph hunter, shall I?' He polishes it. 'Missed the first bit of the match, didn't want to press charges, don't want publicity of that sort at this time. How's that?'

I hold out my hand with the car keys. 'You've played a blinder.'

He takes the keys, then my hand. 'My reactions have slowed.'

'Whenever I'm in trouble, yours will be the first name on my team sheet.'

He drops my hand, grinning. 'I'd sooner play in Limerick.'

At the Central basement lock-up, I sign over Scott Packard. 'Protective custody only,' I instruct the sergeant. I look at Scott. 'Want me to let your mum know where you are? Bring in some fresh clothes?'

He nods quickly.

'Let his mother visit with a change,' I tell the sergeant. 'Feed him up, give him a paper and get him to the crown court in the morning.' I add a line unused for a couple of days. 'Judge's orders.'

'Thanks,' says Scott, calm now.

Back at HQ, I call Mrs Packard and tell her where and how her son is. 'You can visit him, if you like.'

No 'Thank God' or gushed thanks, just 'Might.'

Nothing of note yet from the house-to-house, reports the officer in charge of the Mrs Evans inquiry. The second PM has been fixed for tomorrow.

I phone home to book an extra place for dinner. Beef and two veg, Em informs me. Have something veggie on standby, I advise her.

Soon Alice walks in. 'How did you get on?'

'You first,' I say, wanting to keep the best till last.

Harries, she recounts, not sitting down, went through the filleted papers. 'In his legal view, the only new evidence is Packard's sighting of the policeman he was convicted of killing. Since both the victim and the injured policeman were dressed alike and after this length of time, faded memories and all that, he's of the opinion there's insufficient evidence for a new hearing without further corroboration.'

She chuckles. 'I didn't let on that we've already got plenty of that.' She pauses. 'You?'

I tell her.

She stands there, eyes sparkling behind her spectacles, and claps her hands long and loud, as if we'd just won the FA Cup.

20

The one advantage in working through a weekend is that you avoid that Monday morning feeling. There's a bounce in my step as I mount the stairway at the crown court, Alice at my side.

No mention of Packard's arrest on the radio news, another nice day is predicted with only an outside chance of rain later; a good start.

The stride slows and the spring goes as I pass the witnesses' room – door wide open, no one inside. 'Where the devil is he?' asks a startled Alice, taking the question out of my mouth.

I push open the swing doors to court number 1. The lawyers and the clerk are in their places, the prisoner in the dock, the jury in their box, the usual groupies in the public seats, apart from Frenchie Lebois's pony-tailed look-out. Only the judge's bench and the witness box are empty.

Alice heads for the woman prosecutor and I for Inspector Mann. Before we can reach them, the judge emerges from his chambers. Everyone stands. He sits. We back away to the first row of the public gallery.

The judge waits for us to tip down our seats, then peers over the ledge of his bench at the defence counsel. 'I gather your client wishes to have the indictment put to him again.'

'M'Lud,' comes the reply, which the black-gowned clerk takes to be 'Yes.' He rises and begins to reread the charge.

I don't listen, already know what's happening. The mugger is changing his plea to guilty.

My Lord, I think, smiling sickly. All this chasing around operating without the help of publicity, the hours we've put in, the money spent, the chances taken – and Scott Packard's evidence isn't going to be required after all.

I know who's behind it, of course – Frenchie. He's got a message to the mugger in the remand wing over the weekend: Admit it and there's a job in it for you when you come out, broken legs if you don't.

This way Packard stays out of the witness box and doesn't get to repeat in public the mugger's admission, 'I did it for the Patron.' More importantly, from Lebois's point of view, Mrs Lebois doesn't get to read it in the *Post* or hear it on the radio and ask her hubby: 'What have you got to do with this ex-beauty queen?'

Explains why the pony-tailed heavy's not here. Lebois already knows what's happening. You've got to hand it to him, I grudgingly concede.

Inspector Mann goes into the witness box to give the mugger's long record of violence. Defence counsel rises to his feet to plead for his belated acceptance of responsibility to be taken into account in sentencing.

The judge apologises to the jury for two wasted days, rebukes the mugger for unnecessarily putting his victim through the mill of cross-examination, sees his change of heart as the first sign of redemption, enabling the seven-year term he had in mind to be reduced to five.

Everybody rises and the judge exits without questioning the whereabouts of his missing witness or expressing a word of thanks for finding him.

I like a little pat on the head now and then, and had put on my Sunday best, midnight blue lightweight, to receive it. Flat-footed, I go back down the staircase, thinking: Not the best start to the day.

'Perry Road have reclaimed him,' says Alice coming off the green phone in our bunker.

'He's seeing his social worker and a psychologist.' She'd booked a two o'clock appointment.

I nod, accepting that he had broken curfew and they'd want to reassess him before releasing him back to the hostel and the barber's shop... which reminds me.

'He won't be making it for a few days,' I tell the bossman at the hairdresser's. To protect Scott, I go on, 'He's done nothing wrong himself, but he is a vital witness in another inquiry. We don't want him pestered at work.'

I put down the phone feeling good with myself.

The green phone rings as soon as I put down the receiver after speaking to the fifth and final Father Salmon on a list that took all morning to draw up with the help of clerical directories and diocesan offices. None had worked in the city, prisons or colleges, or knew the Packard boys.

'Sorry, sir.' The divisional sergeant has no need to introduce himself. 'Not a locked room mystery after all.'

They'd found specks of blood on the footpath in front of the side door. They'd also located two neighbours who'd seen a big red Rover parked round the corner between seven thirty and eight thirty on the night Mrs Evans died.

The pathologist had confirmed the cause of death but was of the opinion that the blow had been inflicted with something rounded rather than straight like the leading edge of a step.

I visualise the scene, Harries sneaking away from the sportsmen's charity quiz, driving the rented Rover to Mrs Evans' house, parking round the corner.

He creeps up the garden path and listens at the ground-floor window to her and her landlord chatting over tea and biscuits.

He hides in the dark shadows by the gate to the rear garden. He clubs her on the back of the head as she opens the door. He bundles her inside. He drives back to the benefit do without ever having been missed.

'Widen the search for the weapon,' I order. 'Check on guests at that benefit night.'

I put down the phone, feeling bad, sick, seeing Harries sitting in first class, Madrid-bound, sipping whisky, smirking to himself as he jets further and further away.

Should never have let Alice talk me out of pulling him in, I rebuke myself, dialling the coroner's number. He can only fit me in at two.

'Put back our jail date,' I tell Alice, picking up the phone again to offer Mrs Evans' son a lift.

'Let's stroll and lunch out,' I suggest.

We emerge from our artificially lit bunker and through the security doors, expecting to step out into sunshine. Instead, huge spots of rain are falling, splattering the pavement, spreading, but not yet joining together.

She has no coat to wear over her grey suit. My mac, unused for days, is in the back of the car. We retreat back inside and up the two flights of stairs to Rumpole's Food Court for tea and sandwiches.

No tactical ploys at this meeting in the coroner's book-lined study, nothing held back from my briefing. The whole background is given, the events of the last four and half days detailed. Liam Harries is named, his motive and opportunity disclosed.

'Right now, he doesn't know we have made the connection and are after him,' I go on. 'My worry is that publicity from tomorrow's inquest could force him to lie low abroad.'

The coroner, a small, bespectacled, tubby man, sees straight away that reports of the inquest could make the national newspapers which are available in Spain. 'Couldn't you have him arrested and extradited from there?'

'There's still a lot of work to do to get a fire-proof case,' I counter. 'If he cottons on while we're working on it, he could move on to somewhere like Northern Cyprus where he has...' I put it no higher than, '...personal connections.'

'And from where there is no extradition,' adds the coroner musingly. 'Do they get British papers there?' He dismisses his own question. 'If not, he could still hear about it on the phone from a friend or relative back here.'

Even as he's speaking, a fresh idea is forming which I won't share.

He addresses Mr Evans with a solemn face. 'In these unfortunate circumstances, I'm afraid, I couldn't release your mother for cremation.'

'She wanted to be buried with my father,' says Dave.

The coroner mulls for a moment, makes up his mind. 'I would agree to interment.' Humanely, he doesn't add that when we finally arrest Harries his lawyers may demand a third postmortem to check the medical findings and ask for her to be dug up again.

He looks at me fiercely. 'You're not suggesting that evidence be suppressed, are you?'

I'd like to, daren't, so I shake my head.

'But, I suppose...' He thinks again, looking down on the thickening file on his littered desk. '...I could say that the blood spots outside the door could have resulted from an earlier fall due to a dizzy spell, then, having opened the door, she collapsed again, fatally.'

He's sounding as if he is trying to convince himself. 'I could, I suppose, place greater emphasis on the first autopsy and ignore

196

the sighting of the car. An accident verdict is out of the question, but an open verdict, perhaps?'

Which will be interpreted in the press as a mystery death with no hint of the evidence against Harries. It also covers the coroner, won't make him look a dunderhead when the truth eventually comes out. All in all, the best I can hope for, so I nod.

He looks from me to Dave Evans. 'If that's all right with you?'

'If it helps to bring my mother's killer to justice,' Dave says in a firm tone I've not heard before.

'It will,' I say, equally positively.

'Good,' Alice pronounces after I'd reported all back at the bunker.

'And I've been thinking about how to get Cammy home to face the music,' she continues with an evil smile.

When all the loose ends are tied up, she begins, why not go to see Frenchie Lebois, tell him only as much of the truth as necessary, ask him to put his name to a letter to all ex-members of Racing Club of Radford, the soccer team he once sponsored?

Enclosed with the letter would be a nicely designed invitation card saying something like: 'A reunion to celebrate the freedom of your team mate, Scott Packard, and the restoration of his good name.'

She'd clearly been doing much thinking during my absence because she insists we would have to track down all players so that, if Cammy is still in contact with any of them, he'd be convinced the event is genuine.

Jay Robertson would have to send his regrets, otherwise detained, I think.

The covering letter, she suggests, might have to offer financial assistance with fares and accommodation for those ex-players now living some distance away.

'They'd all realise Frenchie's rich enough to foot the bill, though he wouldn't pay. You would.'

By 'me', she means Eastmids police, I hope.

'Still cheaper than long-range inquiries and costly extradition proceedings that go on for months and which might fail anyway,' she concludes.

'A superb sting,' I enthuse. 'Cammy could hardly decline a party to celebrate his brother being cleared.'

'If we make the invitation "and guest", Cammy might even bring along Harries,' she adds.

'Gets better all the time,' I beam.

Her face clouds. 'Do you think Frenchie will agree?'

'Sure he will,' I reply, confidently, thinking of the undeveloped roll of film locked in my office safe.

Alice picks up the ringing phone, listens for a moment, says, 'Speaking,' then listens for a lot longer, her face growing more and more agitated. 'Just a minute.'

She holds the phone down. 'Perry Road. Cancelling our appointment to see Scott. Lawyer's instructions, they say.'

Impatiently and rather rudely, I flick my fingers to ask for the receiver to be handed over. 'What's this about?'

An admin man goes through it again. Packard had seen his social worker and shrink this morning. This afternoon a solicitor had turned up.

'Who?' I demand.

'Mr Gomaz,' comes the reply.

Alarm bells clamour in my head. 'Who hired him?'

'The mother, and when Mr Gomaz left he gave strict instructions that Packard should not see you without him being present. Doesn't stop you coming, of course, but Packard might not see you or speak to you.'

'These are my instructions,' I say starchily. 'Get back to Mr Gomaz and tell him we'll be there in half an hour.'

'He's already said that he won't be available for the rest of the day.'

I replace the receiver in such mental turmoil that I can't begin to unravel what's going on.

Alice tries to help. 'Either Scott has worked out who killed your policeman in the riot or his mother has.'

198

Should never have let her visit him last night, I chide myself. Mistake after mistake I'm making on this bloody job.

'She might want to prevent the prison gates shutting on her big boy after they've just opened up for her little boy,' I agree.

She wasn't overkeen on Scott's application for a case review in the first place, I reflect; understandably so, if she knew the truth all along.

'Or Gomaz has got to Scott via his mother,' Alice speculates on, 'to talk him into finishing what little time he's got left and save his brother from doing life.'

'And his own reputation,' I add bitterly.

'It's got to be sorted out,' says Alice, gesturing at the phone.

I look up the directory and call Gomaz's office. 'Out of town,' his secretary informs me.

'Tell him this. I shall be at the prison tomorrow at 10 a.m. I shall be arresting and questioning his client.'

'About what?' she queries.

Don't want to tip Gomaz about the progress we're making on Mrs Evans' murder. I'm not really sure yet if he's still close to Harries or not. 'Possession of an offensive weapon – to wit, one spanner – with intent to endanger life.'

'He'll be there,' she says tartly.

I slam down the phone, overwhelmed by overdue Monday blues; late by a shift.

Driving out of the city, Alice declines an invitation to come home with me to Em and Laura for a quiet evening. 'I'm bushed,' she apologises. 'Just drop me off. All I want is sleep.'

It's prematurely dark and the rain is steady and heavy, forming puddles on the road.

The Indian summer is over.

21

Unusually, Alice isn't waiting on the top step of the Fairways Hotel.

I switch off the engine, but not the radio, and listen to the nine o'clock news summary. The mugger gets about three sentences. More showers than sunshine are forecast. Mrs Evans isn't rating a single word.

A glance at the pillared entrance, still empty, then I get out, not locking up for the minute or two it will take to walk up a path, darkened by overnight rain, and collect her.

Her tiny back to me, Alice is at the reception desk, signing something. Hooked to the teak counter is one of those canvas holdalls in which her power suits must be hanging because she's in her check jacket and long black skirt. At her feet is a suitcase, RAF blue, matching the holdall.

'What's up?' I ask, walking up behind her, fearing a crisis within her family.

'Pulling out,' she mumbles, head down.

'An emergency?'

She doesn't answer, thanking the receptionist instead, collecting her receipted bill and stowing it and a credit card in a black shoulder bag. She unhooks the holdall from the counter. I pick up the suitcase.

Approaching the double doors, she nods to a small table with two soft chairs in front of a rubber plant in a black pot. We put the bags down. She sits, as if weary already. 'I've been recalled.'

'Why?' I lower myself into a chair, in the general direction of my sinking heart.

She glances around the almost empty foyer, judges it safe to answer. Overnight, her office in Birmingham had received a fax from Lennie Gomaz's firm officially withdrawing Scott Packard's application for a case review. 'Apologies for any inconvenience caused and all that, but no explanation.'

'He's been talked out of it,' I react immediately and angrily.

'I know.' She sighs deeply, defeated. 'But no application, no review.'

'But we still have to tie up the ends on Mrs Evans.'

'Police work, not our department.' She'd argued passionately to stay, but had been given a fresh assignment. 'Sorry.'

I feel betrayed, almost bereft. 'Someone somewhere is pulling strings.'

'My thoughts, too.'

We sit awhile, trying to work out what's happening, fail. Finally, she taps her wrist-watch and says, 'You'd best be off.' She places a cool, dainty hand on mine. 'You will stick with it, won't you, Phil?'

Squeezing it gently, I say, grimly, 'Leave it to me.'

The usual rigmarole at the gatehouse, booking in, IDs, doors automatically locking and unlocking. At least, the divisional sergeant and I are spared what solicitors routinely have to go through – the proffered tray into which pockets have to be emptied, airport style X-ray on briefcases, body check. Privately, I hope they strip-searched Gomaz.

Crossing the courtyard, our escort seeks some shelter from the steady rain by walking between the high wall and a yellow line a yard away – pathways barred to prisoners.

Every twenty or so yards a large black number is painted on the creamy yellow walls, so that cameras, which will be on us, can pinpoint every move.

The marigolds and dahlias look forlorn in their bed, not much life left in them now, like me. Damp always brings an ache to my gammy leg.

The single-storey building with razor-wired gutters is opened from the inside.

Scott Packard, back in prison blue, sits next to a dark-suited Lennie Gomaz at a small desk in the same room where Jay Robertson was interviewed. The globe-type camera revolves. The low-slung tube lights are on. Rain from a grey sky drums on the glass apex roof.

No subterfuge today, no withholding of identities. I lead the way up to them and formally introduce myself and the sergeant who sits first. He sets down a mobile interview box, a double tape cassette recorder. He places a mike on a black stand at the centre of the desk.

More mind-numbing procedure follows as he reads the statutory notice to prisoners and goes through the caution while I gaze absently at a 'Crimestoppers' notice on the grey wall.

I'm not smelling hot cheese today. I feel no less depressed. Alice's departure is a shattering blow.

The sergeant switches on the tape and gives the date and time. I come out of my dark reverie, look across the table at Packard, blanking Gomaz. 'I am investigating your possession of an offensive weapon, namely a spanner, at Derby on Sunday.'

Packard peeps sideways, nervously, like a child with a teacher, at Gomaz who says, 'With intent to endanger life, you told my office yesterday.'

Did I? I ask myself. I was so worked up I can't really remember what I blurted out.

Gomaz gives me a pedantic smile. 'Whose life?'

I nod curtly at Packard. 'He knows.'

'He's entitled to have it on the record.' There's icy politeness in Gomaz's voice. 'Who, please?'

'One Robbie Hill.'

'Has he made a complaint?'

I ignore Gomaz again, addressing Packard. 'You said to Hill in my presence, and I quote, "I was going to threaten the truth out of you." What truth?'

Gomaz doesn't let him answer. 'My understanding is that Mr Hill himself said: "What spanner?" That hardly sounds like confirmation of your allegation, let alone a complaint.'

He's well briefed this time, I acknowledge, looking down on a pile of scribbled notes in front of him.

Having seized the initiative, he holds it. 'Have you anything in writing, notes made at the time that we can examine?'

He is quite good, I have to concede, must have grown in the job. I've let Hill jet away without taking a written statement. The notes I've made in my pocketbook aren't contemporaneous, having been entered up when I collected the sergeant from his station. I resisted the temptation to fit them into date order; a sure way to exposure in the witness box. He's got me.

Gomaz senses it, leans forward, exuding confidence, speaking sonorously, as if addressing a court. 'Let's put our cards on the table, shall we? You are not here to speak to my client about Sunday, but about his withdrawn application for a review of his 1981 conviction. Let's talk about that, shall we?'

Not yet, I decide, turning my head to signal the sergeant. He talks directly at Packard. 'Where were you on Thursday evening?'

Packard is clearly bemused by the sudden switch. Gomaz groans impatiently. 'Why?'

'I am investigating an offence –'

Gomaz butts in. 'What offence?'

'I'm not prepared to reveal that for operational reasons at this moment. Now...' The sergeant repeats his original question.

Scott looks sideways again. Gomaz nods approval for an answer.

'Watching TV,' says Scott in a rather timid tone.

'Where?'

He names a boarding house where he'd spent three nights close to the Forest ground, an embarrassingly short walk away from the station at West Bridgford.

'How did you pay?'

'Drew out the Co-op.'

Banked tips from working the barber's shop and I didn't check it, I groan to myself; gets worse all the time.

He stayed in at night, watching TV, fearing every news bulletin in case his face popped up on screen over a caption: 'Wanted'. He gives the first names of two fellow lodgers who watched *The Bill* with him.

The sergeant sits back.

Gomaz smiles thinly. 'Get to the point, please, Mr Todd.'

I do, rapid fire, no holds barred. 'Who talked you into withdrawing your application for a case review?'

'Nobody,' Packard mutters, eyes down.

'Was it your mother?'

Eyes up, defiant. 'She doesn't know.'

'Was it Mr Gomaz here?'

Gomaz breaks in. 'He asked to see me.'

203

I glare at him, raise my voice. 'I'm asking him, not you.' Then, softer to Packard. 'Well?'

'It's all gone far enough.'

'What's gone far enough?'

No response.

'You've worked it out, haven't you, Scotty?'

No response still.

I motion at the solicitor. 'What Mr Gomaz here should have discovered in '81 if he'd been up to the job.'

Gomaz sets his face. Packard's eyes are still avoiding mine.

'Your half-brother Cammy killed our policeman.' I pause for effect. 'Not you.'

A longer pause waiting for something, anything in reply. Nothing comes.

'Don't misunderstand me,' I have to continue. 'I have no great regard for you. You severely injured another one of my colleagues, ended his career.'

Packard swallows hard, stays silent.

'You deserved time. But you didn't kill anyone. You didn't deserve sixteen years.'

Nothing still, blood out of stone.

I'm going to have to drive a wedge between them. 'You've served sixteen years for a cop-killing you didn't do, because of an incompetent defence.' I flick my head at Gomaz. 'And yet you still listen to him.'

'My decision.' Packard stirs in his chair. 'I want to do what's right.'

I come back swiftly. 'And it's right for you, is it, to have murder on your record, never completely free when you're out on licence, subject to recall for anything at any time to this bloody place with all its smells and sounds – and all to save your brother who ran out on you?'

He's gone quiet again.

'Is it right that this terrible cock-up isn't corrected and made public...' I lean forward towards the mike to indicate that I'm happy to go on record. '...merely to save your sloppy solicitor's reputation?'

Gomaz makes no attempt to defend himself, sits there taking it.

I move Packard back through everything he did at Pride Park on Sunday, everything he said. 'Why did you want to talk...' I smirk. '...to put it no higher, to Robbie Hill?'

'Check something out,' Packard talks to his chest. 'But, like you said, it was duff info; a mistake.'

In some detail, I disclose we've reinterviewed the policeman he saw in the magistrates court. Picking my words carefully, I reveal we've seen the family of an eyewitness and have worked out how the mistake over identity was made.

'Thanks for trying,' says Packard throatily.

'Don't thank me.' My pleading tone. 'Help me. Help me to help you.'

He shakes his head dumbly.

'You know now it wasn't Robbie Hill. I know it wasn't you. We both know who...'

Packard is finally provoked. 'The time's been done. Almost anyway.'

'But by the wrong person,' I persist.

He holds my eyes for the first time. 'Does it matter?'

'Of course it matters.'

'To the general public, I mean, the man in the street, the dead cop's family.'

'They'll be horrified, I'd imagine, but...'

He interrupts, eyes wandering again. 'Don't tell 'em then.'

'...but comforted when they know we got it right second time round,' I go on.

His eyes come back. 'Look. A life was lost. A life sentence's been served. Leave it like that. I want to leave it there. Do what bit's left, try to forget. Just leave it. Let sleeping dogs lie.'

'Never,' I say firmly.

Frustration fills his face. 'I've had enough.' He stands suddenly, pushing back the chair, almost tipping it over. 'Leave it.' He glares down at Gomaz. 'I want to go.'

I lean back. 'You can leave it. I can't.' I look up, hard at him. 'And I won't.'

Gomaz returns to the table after walking Packard to two guards at their desk on its platform. One rose and escorted his prisoner out of the room, not locking the door behind him.

He is standing over us, wearing an appeasing smile. 'Now, perhaps, you'll appreciate how difficult he can be when he's made up his mind.'

He's preparing the grounds for an excuse for his mishandling of the case, but I'm not going to listen. 'Seen Liam Harries on his trip?'

'No.'

'Sure?'

Now he's wiping away his smile. 'I've just said so. No. Why?'

'Because I want to speak to him again. And why not? He was there in '81, wasn't he?'

A trace of his smile returns. 'You're not going to give up, are you?'

No, and, to prove it, I'd like to throw in Mrs Evans, see his reaction, ask if Harries raised her name with him, sought her address, but I'm not sure I'd believe his answers anyway. All I say, very menacingly, is, 'It will all come out. Trust me.'

Back at HQ, I phone Mrs Packard. 'Don't ask me what's happenin'. I get no sense out of him, never did.'

'Me neither,' I sympathise, not believing her either, but needing to keep her on my side.

I contact Giles Johnson at the Commons. 'Very awkward.' He's dreading follow-up inquiries for progress reports from the media. 'I'm just going to have to hope it dies the death.'

Not me, I determine.

I call Milan, speak to Hill's wife who gives me his hotel number in Madrid. He's pleased to hear from me, even more pleased with a two-year contract he's been offered by a top club, jokes he won't be writing his blockbuster of a book for some time yet.

'How's Harries?' I ask casually.

'Gone.'

'Where?' Not so casual now.

He'd flown on to Ankara to see another client, a Turkish international, whose contract was about up, he tells me.

And from there, I suspect with near certainty, he'll fly on to Northern Cyprus to see Cammy, tell all, and I'll lose them both.

I close my eyes for a second, grit my teeth and get to the point, the idea that came to me talking to the coroner. I remind Hill of my last visit to their hotel on Sunday, the exclusive that didn't make the papers and Harries' undertaking to put a cuttings agency on to the Irish editions.

'Every big agent has 'em.' Hill names the agency Harries uses.

'How does it work?' I ask.

Cuttings agencies take every edition of every newspaper, national and local, he explains. They scour them for names from lists provided by clients who retain their services, photocopy any references to them and post them on.

'I've got scrapbooks full.' He laughs. 'Only keep the nice write-ups, mind.'

'Same with your ghost-writer and his book reviews,' I say, not altogether joking.

Right, I gird myself, about to step before the chief constable in response to an urgent summons from his secretary.

Walking here from my office through weak sunshine and sodden leaves, thick on the ground after a heavy fall, I'd made up my mind.

Any criticism about the way I verbally roughed up Lennie Gomaz and I'm going to do what I told myself to do when I failed to catch up with Scott Packard – quit.

He's going to have me on the mat, no doubt about it. Frenchie Lebois can't have shopped me, not with those photos in my safe. It has to be Gomaz, must be, or Whitehall acting on his behalf.

Bollocks to all of them. I'm not having it. I knock.

'Come in, Phil' is called heartily from behind his half-open door. He smiles from behind his desk and waves a hand at an easy chair. 'Sit down.'

Not on the mat then, I think, feeling slightly deflated as I pad across the blue carpet.

He motions to one of his three phones. He'd had the Criminal Cases Review Commission on with grateful thanks for our first-rate co-operation, he begins.

I relax, thinking: No wonder he's happy. He likes thanks. They make a change from whinges.

'I gather the job's over,' he adds.

For Alice maybe, I reply; not me. I brief him fully, the Packard family, Mrs Evans, Hill, Harries, the lot, even a sanitised version on Lebois. If a complaint does come, I can honestly say, 'Told you so.'

He doesn't dwell on it long, asks a few questions, smiles now and then at my replies. He's a sporting nut, a groupie almost, loves dressing-room chat more than bedroom gossip, so it's no surprise that he homes in on Robbie Hill, asking the question all fans do. 'What's he really like?'

'Nice bloke,' I reply truthfully, and I tell him of the help Hill's just given me about the cuttings agency and why I need it. 'Looks like he'll be playing in Spain,' I add.

'Pity,' the chief laments. 'We could have done with him.'

'We' is a first division club in London which he claims to have followed man and boy. With soccer all the rage, every chair-borne executive boasts such lifelong allegiances these days; middle-class trendies.

He gets back to the case. 'You seem to have it well under control.' He reaches left to his in-tray, takes out an internal memo and rises briefly to hand it over the corner of his desk. 'Have a look at this, will you?'

A formal complaint against an inspector alleging drug-planting gets the quick once-over. While I'm speed-reading, shuddering slightly, he adds, 'Give it your best.'

My eyes come away from the memo. 'I want to stay on Mrs Evans.'

He shakes his head.

I'm tensing up. 'But it's the only way of getting to the bottom of the whole business.'

'Murder isn't your business.' He flicks his head at the memo. 'Complaints are.'

Christ, he's reassigning me. A surge of anger bubbles through me. Don't boil over, I order myself. Count to ten.

One: I plead that we're on the verge of cracking it.

Two: He argues that all that's left is routine case building, mainly the search for the murder weapon.

Three: I counter with loose ends – Father Salmon and the cuttings agency.

Four: Leave them to the divisional sergeant and his team, he comes back.

Five: But it's my case, I protest.

Six: He gestures at the memo in my hand. 'That's your case.'

Seven: I inch myself forward to the edge of the chair, about to spring, have it out.

Eight: He goes on the defensive. 'Keep a supervisory eye on it, if you like.'

Nine: A sop. It's a sodding sop. He's been got at by either Gomaz or his powerful political friends, the weak-kneed bastard. Go for him.

'An idea for you,' he says, sitting back. 'Tackling the cuttings agency head on might lead to them alerting Harries. Last thing you want.'

Several soccer agents had been getting a bad press of late, he goes on, with hints of kickbacks. 'I'll phone the chairman of my club, an old pal, if you like, and get a list of about half a dozen of the shadier characters in the business.'

A sly smile. 'Give them to Fraud along with Harries' name, get them to go to the cuttings agency with a court order asking for complete lists of all their clients. That way...' An easy-going shrug. '...we cover our tracks.'

Ten: 'Thanks, chief,' I say, rising, smiling, creeping.

22

THIRTEEN WEEKS LATER

New Year's Eve, my last day in this cosy, isolated office.

Outside, the weather is sunny and unseasonally mild. I'm spending a reflective afternoon throwing forward loose ends and anniversary dates I can never remember from the old to the new Letts desk diary, a Christmas present from Laura.

Four days off from tomorrow, then I start my new job as assistant chief constable. Should be looking forward to being back in the mainstream with joyful anticipation. I'm not.

At the Home Office's request, the chief has put me in charge of a series of armed sexual assaults that have escalated into murder. 'You wanted real crime,' he'd said, 'You've got it.'

All were committed on or close to motorways. 'The M-Way monster', the media call him.

CID chiefs held a conference and formed a task force. They couldn't agree if they were seeking a serial or spree offender, or both, or what pyschological profiler to call in. It ended in the usual clash of egos.

The story leaked. Every force with an unsolved sex crime within a day's march of a motorway dumped it on the task force who then fell out among themselves over who should head it.

That leaked, too. One paper totted up the total to twenty-two outstanding crimes. With MPs demanding action, the Home Office panicked and ordered that one supremo should run the inquiry. 'Operation Catch 22', the press are labelling it.

No Alice to rely on, I've had to do the reading myself – file after file, on screen and in hard copy. Both eyes and mind are boggled. These evenings I tell the tale of Thomas the Tank Engine by rote.

Catch 22? I'll be lucky to catch one. There'll be no room for other cases in this new diary, that's for sure; or any future diaries for the rest of my career; a depressing outlook.

I flick the old diary on to its final three months and my depression deepens.

The drugs job took six weeks. The inspector had been set up by a big dealer who wanted him off the inquiry. I gave him a rocket for being naïve enough to walk into a trap and not keeping his notebook up to date.

Soon afterwards, Frenchie Lebois phoned, inviting me and wife and/or bit on the side to a charity race meeting in his private box at which, he suggested, we might swap packets – money for the photos, he meant. The box would have been bugged, of course.

I filed a report on my visit to the flat above his betting shop, explained the photos were taken before realising he was not the bound victim of a stick-up and got Exhibits to post back the undeveloped film with a formal letter of explanation and refusal of his kind invitation.

I've not spent eighteen months in this department without learning something.

Lennie Gomaz was appointed to a government think-tank on reducing the numbers of miscarriage of justice cases, spoke up for tighter regulations on the police, never mentioned duff defences.

Such had been my desperation that I'd even considered approaching Gomaz, cap in hand, with a variation of Alice's sting – a reunion of old law centre workers with Harries invited to bring a guest.

I slept so badly one night, tossing and scratching and sighing, that Em kicked me out of the matrimonial bed.

Gomaz's confident 'We'll see' when Alice threatened him with full disclosure kept bouncing around my head. Couldn't rid it of the suspicion that the chief had somehow been conned from high up in Whitehall to jock me off the case.

Against that, the chief's idea paid off. The name of Mrs Dorothy Evans stood out among the list of sports stars the cuttings agency is monitoring for Harries. The reports of the inquest won't have told him much. Mystery death is about all. The promise I made to her son weighs heavily sometimes.

The divisional sergeant more than redeemed himself. He tracked down a former Racing Club player, a successful businessman these days, who'd had a call out of the blue from

Harries during his stay in the city. He'd chatted about old times, casually mentioned Scott Packard and then asked: 'What was the name again of that old biddy who did for him?' 'Dot Evans' came the reply.

Even without the murder weapon, Crown Prosecution reckon we have an unassailable case. Alice drove across for dinner and an overnight stay, read the file, and declared, 'Rumpole couldn't get him off.'

The only trouble is that we haven't got Harries.

Jacko Jackson is far keener on 'Operation Catch 22' for his next book, though he admits he'll have to find a new title. He's given up pestering me about what he calls 'the-back-from-the-dead cop'. 'No confrontation, no climax, no happy ending, no good,' he pronounced at a get-together last week.

Harries and Hill have parted company. 'He binned me, not the other way around,' said Robbie when we last spoke on the phone. 'I told him nowt. Said he wanted out of the rat race. He's spending his time sea-fishing in Kyrenia.'

Intelligence reports came too late to act on another quick trip Harries made to Ankara. He flew back with that out-of-contract Turkish soccer star, spends more time with him than Cammy, the sergeant's heard on the Interpol grapevine.

Scott Packard returned to his hostel after three weeks inside. He's on course for full parole. He's no longer in denial over the policeman's death, has reclaimed full responsibility. His wobbly was variously attributed by the experts to 'false memory syndrome' and 'pre-release stress arising from institutionalisation'.

I haven't been to my regular barber for two months. In November Scott trimmed it, a neat job. We talked sport. As he pulled away the sheet, he came close to my left ear. 'Sorry, but thanks, mate,' he whispered. I didn't leave a tip.

I went back for a pre-Christmas cut. He wasn't there. 'Got permission to take out a passport,' the bossman told me. 'Gone with his mum to see the grandfolks in Trinidad.'

You never know, I mused, Cammy might turn up for a family reunion. I put police in Port of Spain on to it. They've not come back.

The phone rings.

Might be them now, I think, because you never know in this job.

The divisional sergeant identifies himself. 'Fax from Cyprus, sir, Turkish side,' he begins, so clipped he sounds almost breathless. 'Two Brits on a boat. One dead. One in hospital. Both with head injuries. Identified by their mother as Cammy Robins and Scott Packard.'

I close my eyes. 'Who's dead?'

'Cammy, sir. They think there might have been some sort of fight. Scott's in hospital under guard. Mum's obviously talked 'cos they're requesting full background.'

'We'd better give it to them.' It takes only a moment to make up my mind. 'Personally.'

'Welcome.' The superintendent rises from a desk bigger than the chief's back home with twice as many phones on it, one of them red.

A short, portly man with a complexion made all the darker by a black moustache, he offers a hand with manicured fingernails. His grip is strong.

'Thank you,' I say.

He asks about my trip first – seeing in the New Year sitting alone in the departure lounge, a delayed flight through the night, a hairy trip from the airport, ferried in a dusty black Daimler by a grumpy Greek driver laid on by the High Commission who pointed out the Turkish gun positions in distant brown hills. 'Fine, thanks,' I lie.

'The cross-over, no problems?' At the checkpoint, he means, an old sandstone hotel with lots of washing hanging from balconies.

Zig-zagging between two walls, having my papers checked twice at Portakabins and emerging through barbed wire and beyond bombed-out homes took less time than getting into Perry Road. 'Fine,' I say truthfully.

My eyes go to a wide-open window-cum-door with a railed balcony outside.

213

The sun is out and the temperature is already approaching 60°F. A breeze brings to life a red flag with white crescent moon hanging over his headquarters, another sandstone building.

'Forgive me, please.' Beaming, he gestures expansively to a deep armchair beneath a picture of Ataturk. Before I sit, I drop my briefcase on his desk, open it, take out a thick file and place it before his chair. 'The background you requested.'

Politely, he waits until I sit, then sits himself, not looking down on the file. 'A bad happening, would you not be in agreement?'

His shiny brown eyes are on me, his thick eyebrows knitted together.

Gravely, I nod. 'Yes.'

Campbell Robins was well liked throughout much of Northern Cyprus, he goes on in a heavy accent. 'A valued son of the island by adoption.'

His fame as a footballer had preceded him when he arrived to work in the marine academy six years ago. He lived quietly in a small villa overlooking Kyrenia. 'No girlfriends, people are telling us.'

It was known, he continues, that a strange fisherman with both English and Irish passports called Harries visited often and stayed with him. An expressive shrug to tell me: So what?

His men had been called to a large motor boat owned by Cammy's academy. They had found him dead in a cabin below deck, his brother injured at the foot of the stairs leading from it. The door at the head of the stairs was locked.

Been here before, I realise.

Scott Packard and his mother had arrived via Izmir ten days ago for the holidays, he goes on. They had stayed with Cammy. Harries was in a rented villa with an even more famous footballer.

Mrs Packard had identified her sons – Cammy in the morgue, Scott in hospital. Afterwards she'd sobbed and said to one of his officers, 'Oh, why ever did they let my sick son go?'

I flinch, feeling my guts wrench while recalling her words on the radio, 'Free my innocent son.'

214

Naturally, the super says, they asked the poor woman what she meant and the story came out of Scott's conviction for murder and his restricted release, hence the faxed request for background. 'I am very grateful for you to come all this long way.'

He spreads his hands. 'We are bound to be thinking here of the possibility of yet another fatal moment of madness.'

'What's Scott saying in hospital?' I ask tentatively.

With a clenched fist, he bangs on his desk and shouts something that sounds like oaths, startling me into thinking that my very first question has upset him.

He continues as if it hadn't happened. 'He has no memory of the events, says that he went into the village to buy beer for a short sea trip. He opened the door at the top of the steps and crashed down them. Against his story comes the fact that the cabin door was locked behind him.'

The old locked room again, I sigh to myself.

The current theory, he postulates, is that Scott smashed Cammy on the back of the head, then fell backwards, hitting his own head, as he hurried up the steps from the scene of the crime.

'Did you find any keys?' I ask.

'On both brothers, yes.'

And Harries, if they'd bothered to look, I'd wager.

A dark young man appears through the opened door. Like the super, he is dressed in what could be the summer outfit of a British bobby – light blue short-sleeved shirt, dark blue trousers, polished black shoes.

He is carrying a golden tray, which he rests on the desk. He pours thick black coffee in cups that just might take a boiled egg, and serves them to us with glasses of water.

The super ignores him and talks on. 'The Packard boy's fractured skull is genuine. We thought that he may have been already drunk, but the doctors and witnesses at the beer shop say not so.'

I sip my coffee. It's very sweet. And my water. It's warm.

No murder weapon had yet been discovered and the scientific evidence is inconclusive, I hear. The brothers were found after the owner of a boat on the same moorings heard groaning and raised the alarm.

'Where was Harries at the time?' I inquire.

'With his friend, the footballer. They swear to it.'

Suddenly he stops and smiles. 'I now welcome your views.'

The days of senior British policemen with knees not yet brown acting the know-all colonial chief in foreign climes are over, I decide. I'm going to tell him the truth. 'Scott Packard didn't kill our policeman. Cammy Robins did.'

His swarthy face is filled with disbelief. 'But his mother says it was her younger boy, the hurt boy, the survivor.'

Scott had spoken the truth when he told me his mother didn't know, I now accept. He still hasn't shared the secret with her. 'His mother doesn't know.'

Straight away he spots the opening I've given him. 'That is a good reason for revenge, serving for so long in prison for someone else.'

Now that Cammy's dead, I tell him, the only murderer I know on this island is Liam Harries.

Between sips of coffee and water, I brief him fully on the '81 riots, the cover-up by Harries for Cammy, the unchallenged mistake in Mrs Evans' eyewitness evidence and how and why it cost her her life almost three months ago.

He hears me out, fingering his moustache, his face growing increasingly grim.

'We have a great case against Harries,' I conclude, 'but, of course, we have...er...difficulties.'

'Diplomatic, because of non-recognition of our independent state,' he says, a touch aggressively.

Don't want to get into this; it's the dialogue of death, as bad as Irish politics. 'So what shall we do?'

Buying thinking time, he asks if I wish to see Harries and the mother. Harries would rumble how close we are and vanish for good, I fear. Mrs Packard would tell him of my presence here and the result would be the same. 'Neither.' I explain why in some detail. 'But I'd like to see Scott.'

He looks at a heavy gold wrist-watch, picks up a phone, talks urgently, then replaces it. 'It is done.'

216

He smiles again, coming to a decision. 'You have worked very hard and your case is much stronger than ours.'

He would have to hold on to Scott until his investigation is complete. 'If you can arrange for Harries to return to your jursidiction...' He eyes me sternly. '...legally and with respect and regard for our constitution, I will not stand in your way.'

We rise and shake hands on it.

'You again.' Scott grins weakly, pleased at last to see me. 'A long way to come for a short back and sides.'

His own hair is totally hidden behind a thick white bandage which highlights the matt blackness of his face.

His smile fades and he closes his heavy eyes. 'They think I killed Cammy. I'm in big trouble again, aren't I?'

'Not any more.' I pull up a chair to his bedside, sit down and tell him of the conviction I've just shared with the local police chief that Harries killed Cammy. 'You know why, don't you?'

He nods. Pain passes over his face.

In the early hours, after a night of much Christmas booze, he recounts, Cammy confessed all – how he'd hit the policeman just the once, how Harries had alibied him and had talked him out of coming forward with the truth when Scott was arrested because it would have meant life and the end of their promising careers, the almost suicidal torment he'd felt over all these years.

Crap, I think, angrily.

'When I worked it out...' He points to his temple with an index finger, not quite touching the bandage. '...after you caught me, I thought, well, what the hell? Why put him through it, too, all those years? He'd look after me, see me right with a home and a job out here where no one knows me. That's the real reason I came, to talk about it.'

'Telling the bossman at the barber's shop that you'd gone to Trinidad.'

He fiddles with the crisp white top sheet. 'Knew you'd be coming back for a trim.'

Tears gather in his eyes when he talks about his mother. She didn't know the truth about '81 – 'thinks I killed not just that policeman but also Cammy.'

Such is her grief that she hasn't visited him here at the state hospital, a rather battered building on the outside, concrete crumbling, clean and quiet inside. No flowers, fruit or books are on his bedside cabinet.

He believes she is staying with Harries who's taken charge of her and is fixing up the funeral.

That last word implants in my mind for later use. 'Has Harries visited?'

No, he replies. He'd seen little of him during his stay. Cammy had been avoiding him. 'A drunk and a bully,' he'd called him. 'He was scared of him.'

He knew, because Cammy had told him, that they had once had a relationship. Made no difference to him. He'd seen many such affairs in his time in prison.

Harries, I guess, has found a new love who is alibiing him – a reversal of roles from '81.

What happened on this island was more than an ex-lovers' tiff. Cammy knew the truth and, in drink, had revealed it to Scott. Harries decided he had to go.

But what happened here is not my problem. My problem is to get Harries back to stand trial for Mrs Evans.

'If your mum does eventually visit,' I instruct, 'don't tell her I was here. Harries mustn't know. Not a word. Got that?'

'Yes.' No nod this time.

I tell him of the deal I've struck with the local police. 'Now you don't have to protect Cammy any more, you'll give evidence for me, won't you?'

'Yes,' he says simply and thrillingly.

I'm purring with delight. His co-operation will bring his mate Jay Robertson into the witness box to tell of his chat with Harries in the pub.

Gomaz, he assures me, wasn't protecting his professional reputation. Scott was protecting his brother. Ah, well, I think, you can't get everything right.

218

I ask about the funeral arrangements and get the unexpected, unwelcome news that Cammy will be buried over here.

Harries' idea, I decide, deeply dismayed. He'll have talked his mother into it. He won't he flying back with her and the body. Shit. A drowning feeling. Shit, shit.

My dejection must be showing because he asks, 'Anything wrong?'

I shake my head and smile confidently, another idea appearing like a boat on the horizon, back on top form today.

In lieu of the tip I didn't leave when he cut my hair, I'm going to give him one now. 'Keep pleading blinding headaches and stay here as long as you can.'

He gets the message. 'To keep out of prison, you mean, while it's sorted.'

I rise. 'Tell me, how did you work it out?'

He doesn't answer immediately.

'Was it what Jay Robertson said about the torn red number 4 shirt?' I prompt.

Sensibly, he doesn't shake his head. 'What mum said in the police cell after you caught me.'

'About what?'

'You phoning and asking after Father Salmon.'

I sit down again, puzzled.

Harries, he explains, is a fly fisherman. Cammy had to catch and kill fish to cut up in his marine biology studies at university. Harries bought him a lead-filled little cosh to deliver a sharp blow on the back of a fish's head.

I wonder if Cammy was carrying it on the night of the riot or stole another in among the fishing tackle taken from the looted sports shop.

'They joked about it, gave it the pet name of Father Salmon,' Scott goes on.

The name they'd used when they made those veiled threats to Jay Robertson after the fight that tore the number off Cammy's back, I recall. It was the murder weapon, I'm sure of it. And Harries used similiar instruments on Mrs Evans and Cammy. Got it. Finally, I've got everything but Harries.

'Never knew why,' says Scott, softly.

I do. I used one many times trout fishing with grandad up the Peaks. Priests, they call them. Because they deliver the last rites.

23

TWO WEEKS LATER

Another night without sleep, too excited, and I'm dozing, or pretending to, not looking at those illuminated blue boards on the M1 which will tell you that London is getting ever closer.

I'm taking time off from the M-Way Monster, not out to catch 22. One will do today.

Not yet dawn, cold, but dry, and we are making good progress in fairly light traffic.

Last time I made this journey the chief was at my side. We were heading for a West End restaurant where, at some expense to the taxpayer, we lunched the chief's chum, his football club chairman. Don't know whether it was public duty, the old pals' act or the thought of mounting bills for policing on match days, but it didn't take much persuasion.

As instructed, the chairman phoned the club in Ankara and not only got permission to speak to their out-of-contract star but his temporary phone number in Kyrenia.

He called it, introduced himself, but couldn't make much sense of what was being said until a voice with a faint Irish accent took over. 'I'm his agent, Liam Harries.'

'Thank goodness,' said the chairman. His club was looking for a striker to spearhead their promotion push in the second half of the season. Scouts had recommended his client and he had seen several videos of him in impressive action. The club which held his registration had consented to this approach.

Harries talked money. 'On a par with the Premiership,' the chairman assured him.

The sort of signing-on fee it takes me a year to earn was floated down the echoing line. 'Agreed,' said the chairman, 'subject to a medical by our own club doctor, of course.'

Promotion bonuses and living and moving allowances were raised. 'Can't we go into details when he's seen our set-up, our medic and met the staff?' the chairman replied. 'We'll fund all expenses for both of you to come to negotiate.'

With the surveillance sergeant driving and the divisional sergeant by his side, I'm sitting in the back seat, as befits an assistant chief, eyes shut, amusing myself with thoughts on just how to greet him. 'The game's up' perhaps, or 'It's a no-win situation.'

But I know I'll play it very formally and politely, so that, in sixteen years' time, no Alice of the next generation will be able to probe for holes in a case that's watertight, tighter even than the security at Perry Road jail he's about to experience.

'Ah.' He stops and points to his name pencilled in thick black capitals on a stiff white sheet of paper held up by the divisional sergeant. 'I'm Mr Harries,' he exclaims.

His other hand comes away from a luggage trolley and he throws his arm around a tall man with handsome, youthful Mediterranean features, pulling him closer; a gesture that's both excited and affectionate. 'The chairman's sent his limo.'

Ah, I purr inwardly, the trappings of financial success, the showing off for his young men, the weaknesses that have lured him back. 'A police car, actually,' I say.

He spots me standing behind the two sergeants in the busy arrivals hall.

His face fills with fear and fury and every adjective begins with F when the protests start as the sergeants take an arm each.

He struggles, elbows flapping, shouting, 'Set up' and 'Entrapment' and 'Illegal'.

I take no part in it, no job for an ACC. Besides, they don't need any help. He's buckled at his knees now, lathered in sweat and trembling violently, wild eyes not seeing the streams of passengers sneaking looks at us as they hurry by.

Embarrassing, I think, but that's the trouble with these money men cashing in on sport. They're such poor losers. No Corinthian spirit, see.